MW01036988

# The Redemption

Dear Rosa,
Until then...

S. L. SCOTT

Rock on,
S. L. Scott

***The Redemption***
First Edition



ISBN 13: 978-1-940071-26-8

Interior design: Angela McLaurin, Fictional Formats
https://www.facebook.com/FictionalFormats

Cover design: Sarah Hansen of Okay Creations
http://www.okaycreations.com/

Cover photographer: Kari Branch

Cover model: John Humphrey

# The Redemption

# Prologue

Sadness surrounds me and I feel bad for not feeling worse.

I stand at the back, near a tree, separate from the families and friends that have gathered. I stay back here, away from the crowd, and watch her. She tries to hide her devastation and tears behind big sunglasses that she slipped down over her eyes minutes before.

Her hair is down, hanging over her shoulders and longer than I remember from the last time I saw her. It's been too long since then. But even in the middle of a sea of black, she still stands out, strikingly beautiful and I'm drawn to her, wanting to be with her in ways I can't.

With all of these people around, I'm finding it hard to swallow despite being outdoors. A lump formed in my throat earlier this week, making me wonder what caused it. *Maybe guilt*. Squeezing my hand tightly around the coin, I realize a tragedy has given me hope where none existed before. And despite one of my closest friends dying, an uncertain future, and the realization that with his death, my life has been forever changed, I can't stop thinking about the woman he left behind.

# 1

# Rochelle Floros

The funeral was... it was what it was. Johnny and Holli drove me and the kids home. There were too many people staring at me, waiting for my breakdown. I needed the silence of the ride to be able to face the waiting mourners at my house, and they gave that to me. Just after we park, Johnny turns to me and says, "The Resistance is a family. We take care of one another. I'll always be here for you, Rochelle."

I nod, not sure I can speak under the weight of my emotions. I want today to become a distant memory sooner than I should. I don't want to remember Cory's death. I want to remember his life, his life with me, his life with our four-year-old. It's a life that our newborn will never get to experience and the significance of that drags me under. I rush out of the car right before the first tear slips down, but I wipe it away before anybody can see.

*But he sees.*

Antonio Dexter Caggiano sees right through the facade I put on for everyone else, but doesn't move from Neil's side. He knows where he's needed without me saying. They sit on the tire swing together, spinning slowly, talking, bonding in a way that seems almost abnormal for the man I've always known Dex to be. A magic trick reveals a pair of drumsticks and Dex hands them to Neil. My oldest son starts banging on the tire and up the chains, happily distracted from the sadness of the day.

Staring across the lawn—faded black jeans, long, shaggy hair, bandana back in place after we left the cemetery—I find the most unlikely ally on such a depressing day. He's just here, silently supportive without asking anything of me.

Dex is kind to spend time with the boys. He has a playful smile on his face, and assuming from Neil's laughter, which I hear echoing across the yard, Dex is also funny. He left his ego at home, an anomaly from every other day. He's fascinating to watch. Kids are genuine in their emotions and Neil seems to like Dex.

Neil deserves laughter and fun, but he also deserves his father. I get up and move to the side of the yard where I plant my small garden each year. My tears water the lettuce that is just starting to grow. Cory planted that. I wanted strawberries.

I stomp on it. With both feet, I jump up and land down on the plant because he didn't live to see it grow. "Damn you!" Picking it up, I rip it from the ground and throw it against the fence. "Damn you, Cory!"

A burning regret coats my insides as I panic and rush to pick it up. Through watery-vision, I drop to my knees and take it in hand, holding it to my chest. Suddenly strong arms wrap around me from behind, pulling me into his lap. Dex's body against mine feels so foreign and yet, like the only place safe for me to grieve.

The sobs break free, the ones that I've been holding back all day, and my body is wracked with every emotion that I don't want anyone else to see. My breakdown feels like a failure. I should be the one to comfort others today. Pressing my head against his shoulder, the light hum in his chest is soothing. "He left me, Dex. He left me here all by myself to raise the boys on my own. I can't do it."

"You can. You will. I'll be here for you."

He's the least expected person to find comfort in, but he's the only one that feels right. I nod. My head is tucked under his chin while his fingers gently but firmly open my fisted hand. He takes the lettuce that is destroyed and sad, just like me, and says, "It's gonna be okay. Maybe not for the lettuce, but you're gonna be okay."

We sit there a few minutes, the slight breeze feeling good against my hot face. Maybe he's right. Maybe I will be okay. It's hard to tell right now. With a deep breath and even heavier exhale, I look up into his eyes and all that he said is repeated in his expression. I get up and start walking to the backyard again. He follows, but he stops and plants the lettuce back into the garden, and says, "It's worth a shot."

"Yeah, it's worth a shot."

We come from around the corner and Dex goes inside without another word and I join Neil on the swing. No one's the wiser that I almost fell apart, or that Dex held me together. My strength is back on display for everyone else. His bad boy reputation as the drummer for one of the biggest bands in the world is back intact.

*TR*

***Six months later...***

It's hot in here. I need fresh air; the crowded party is steamy from all the bodies crammed into the living room. Looking out at the pool area, it's not any better. "I'm gonna walk around," I say, leaving the safety of Johnny's side.

"I'll be here," he replies before taking a drink of his beer. Johnny Outlaw may be one of the most famous musicians in the world and the lead singer of The Resistance, but he's also been a shoulder for me to cry on. He's like the brother I never had. Along with that role, he's become very protective of me in public settings and these types of situations. Holli, his wife, is usually here to keep me company, but she had a business trip and is out of town. So I'm here with the guys from the band. That's a lot of testosterone to be around while drinking your sorrows away.

Remembering there's a small balcony off the master bedroom, I head for the stairs. The balcony has a great vantage point overlooking the pool. Dex is the master of throwing awesome parties and he's gone all out for his birthday. Everyone from Academy Award winning Directors to young starlets jumping at any casting couch opportunity that comes along is here. Current rock musicians are mingling with Pop Princesses, and I just spotted Tommy, the tour manager with some of our roadies at the bar. I used to be more of a free spirit, comfortable in social settings... when Cory was alive. But my happiness died when he did. I never imagined I would be expected to live in a world without my heart. I'd gotten good at hiding my sadness, but lately I've been struggling to put on a happy face for others.

Dex's party is a sea of beautiful people and definitely intimidating. The heat and drinks making my mind blur into a mixture of emotions. I start walking faster, hoping to stave off the panic attack I feel coming on.

I pass some familiar faces, saying hi as I walk by. Seeing other people, the ones I don't know, makes me want to lower my gaze to the floor and block out the stares. Sometimes the stares bother me. I was relatively unrecognizable before Cory's death, but I made headlines as the 'Poor Widow' and my photo was everywhere. So I see the looks, the sideways glances, and feel the sympathy lying heavy from their curiosity. Nights like this usually help me escape the sadness of losing the only man I ever loved. Alcohol also helps, so I down a shot and slowly make my way upstairs, trying not to let the liquor knock me off-balance.

The double doors of the master bedroom are closed along with the other bedroom doors down the hall. Taking the knob in hand, I turn slowly. It opens and I'm greeted with darkness. I'm hoping no one is in here doing something I don't want to see or hear, so I enter with caution. Although there is no light except for the moonlight coming in from the balcony doors, I walk in when I hear silence. Closing the door behind me, I don't bother looking around. I just go to the French doors and open them wide. The night is clearer up here, the miles of LA lights laid out before me with a stunning view of the city. The area around the pool below is more crowded than I realized when I was in the mix of it.

A heavy exhale of smoke draws my gaze to the left. Dex sits forward resting his elbows on his knees and eyes me.

He doesn't look bothered that I'm here, but I feel the need to explain anyway. "I wanted... I needed to get away."

"From what?" he asks while stubbing his cigarette into an ashtray on the Spanish tile.

I lean against the doorframe, my head resting back, my eyes lulled closed by the voices carrying up from below. Over the last six months, we haven't spent a lot of time together, but he's stopped by a few times to talk, reminisce, or just sit with someone who knows what he's going through, empathizing through moments of silent understanding. He makes it easy to just be, to be whatever I need to be. "Everything… from me."

"It's hard to escape yourself."

"I know. I've tried."

"Me too." The ice in his glass shifts, clanging against the walls of the double old-fashioned. I look just as he sets it down, and asks, "Drink?"

"Sure," I reply. "Why are you trying to escape?"

"Sometimes being the bad guy sucks."

"You're not a bad guy."

"Everyone else thinks I am."

"I like to think you just play one on TV… or in your case, on stage. The infamous bad boy drummer of The Resistance isn't all that bad, you know."

He hands me his glass and I hold it up to toast him. "Happy birthday, Dex." The straight bourbon feels thick as it slides down my throat.

His expression changes and he stands, moving behind me, his chest against my back. "Do I get a birthday wish?"

I feel his every breath coming in and out, each one hot against my neck. My heart starts beating faster, the air that felt freer moments before now ripe with innuendoes. This tension between us is new, but I like it. The hesitation I thought I would feel drowned with the last gulp of his drink. I take one last breath before turning, my gaze now meeting his. "Make a wish."

The warmth of his hand covers my cheek and his lips are pressed to mine and mine to his, connecting us like never before. I would have thought I'd get careful, gentle, tentative. I get pressure swarmed with confidence, a wanting that feels more lustful, caressed in need. My body reacts, moving closer, edging into the kiss, wanting it, needing it. I'm pulled inside, the doors shut behind and he whispers, "Too many people can see up here."

I nod, though I'm not sure he can see as I stand in the shadows of the curtain. He's seen clearly, the window panes reflecting an abstract design across his body. Taking a sip, his eyes find mine. There's nothing hurried about his movements as he takes me in. While setting his glass down on the table nearby, he says, "I've wanted to kiss you longer than you'll understand, longer than I had a right to."

Licking my lips, the action involuntary, I'm starting to think that maybe I've wanted to kiss him longer than I had the right to as well. But I see him. I've always seen the real him and not the showman or the manwhore he wants everyone else to see. I see the way the light reflects in his brown eyes, giving them more life than one would expect when labeled just "brown." The liquid tone of where sand meets the ocean at night might do them more justice. His eyes are lighter than mine, and hold a history completely different. But they draw me in, his body wagering me closer.

When I go, I lift up this time to kiss him. With a tilt of our heads, our mouths open and our tongues meet. I shouldn't want him like I do. It's wrong to feel this way, but every physical urge I have overrides my thoughts and deepens as our breaths become each others.

Immersed in a passion that alleviates other burdens I've carried for too long, I enjoy the loss of control, my tension slipping away as he maneuvers me back toward the bed. I go willingly in all ways, wanting to grab hold of this feeling of freedom and release it sexually. I sit as he stands in front of me. The expression on his face highlights his handsome structure—a cut jaw, strong when juxtaposed against his soft gaze. I realize he hides behind his sunglasses so much that I'd forgotten how truly striking he is. His hair is shorter than a year ago, but still hits just below his chin in a jagged-style, carefree and uncalculated.

He slips his shirt off, dropping it to his feet before leaning down and popping open the front of my jeans. I let him as I lean back on my elbows. My shoes come off and then my jeans, slowly, but with no doubt. Neither of us are naïve to what's happening or what's to come. I sit up and take my shirt off before lying back down and asking for the drink. When he hands it to me, I finish the amber liquid and take an ice cube into my mouth, finishing the remaining traces.

Standing up, I demand, "Take your jeans off and lay down." I set the glass back on the dresser across the room and when I return, his lean, muscular body, all six-foot-three of him is on the bed. Crawling up the large mattress, I sit down on his middle, his hardness feeling so good between my legs. I take the ice from my mouth and it drips on his abs, making them twitch. Another drip and another.

"You like to tease," he says, not a question, just an observation.

I lean down and run my tongue over each drop, my chest pressed to his erection.

Lifting my eyes up to watch him, I drag my tongue lower and slower before hearing him mutter, "Fuck."

His head falls back and his eyes close. I drag my fingers over the ups and downs of his defined muscles, appreciating every sit up he does for this exact reason. When I blow across his stomach, his reaction is felt everywhere. Sitting up, he pulls me by my arms and flips me under him in one smooth move. Desperate lips are pressed against mine as his hips flex down, his knees maneuvering my legs apart. Ten inches taller than me, but our bodies seem to fit in so many ways. He kisses my neck and I moan unexpectedly, well aware I just made the only sound in the room. Lifting up, he looks at my face as his hand gently squeezes my left breast. "You're beautiful. The most beautiful woman I've ever seen."

If I thought the moan was unexpected... that tops it.

Never knowing he thought this about me, I'm not sure what to say, so I lift up and kiss him instead. I let the bourbon take over for a bit and enjoy the other ten inches he has on me. His hips come down again, and my body tingles from the contact, my hips reacting by moving against him.

My chest presses against his as his body weighs down on top of mine. Another moan escapes me as our tongues caress. The slightly rough skin of his hand slides under my bra and he takes me firmly, massaging and peaking my nipples. Rolling onto our sides, our mouths part and our eyes meet again. With a soft whisper between us, he asks, "You sure?"

I reply with a kiss to his cheek before I roll onto my back and unfasten my bra. After dropping it to the floor, I lift my hips up, removing my thong. The moonlight streaks in, accentuating the want found in his eyes as he stares at my body. Boxer briefs are removed and he lies next to me. When I look over at him, the reality of the situation is clear even through the wavy goggles of alcohol. His penis is long, thickly attractive, smooth, but hard. He reaches for a packet from a drawer next to the bed and rolls a condom on before turning to me and staring at me without reservation. His gaze is heavy enough to feel as it envelops me in desire. The way his tongue slides over his bottom lip while looking at me makes me anxious for more. But I remain still, letting his lust linger between us, building, just like my yearning for him.

Patience has no concept of time, but cravings do, so I touch his arms, encouraging him closer... closer... until he's centered on top of me. He leans down resting on his elbows and kisses me. Pushing in, my body welcomes the stretch and burn, desiring the long lost sensation. Deep inside our bodies, our feelings emulate the intensity of the act. Our pace picks up in a frenzy of kisses and caresses. Heated bodies move together in sync, out of sync, and everything else that feels good and natural. A bite to my neck, a nibble to his earlobe. We cover each other in panting breaths over skin that becomes slick with passion.

Every thrust elicits sounds from our mouths we can't contain. Guttural. Sensual. Every thrust purposeful and rough, sexy, and caring. Our connection is not casual but filled with an unbridled passion I wasn't aware lay deep beneath the surface.

Pushing his hair back with my hands, I look up at him as a sheen of sweat starts dotting his forehead. His body moves fluidly, his experience showing. I push him over and readjust on top, slipping down slowly. His three gun tattoos wrap around the muscles of his arm and flex when he steadies me on top of him. Our pace slows. I don't want this to end too soon, but my insides urge for more. I close my eyes, willing the darkness behind my lids toward the imploding light I know is buried, longing to be seen.

Fingers rub assuredly, a confidence in the action. I feel. Feel. Feel. My head drops back as his touch drives me closer. I want. Want. Want. I move, rocking on top of him, increasingly selfish in pursuit of my own ecstasy. With a gasp, I catch that elusive sensation that makes me feel Heaven and Hell equally. "Oh God! Cory!"

Everything stops.

Just when I peak, I fall back into reality, well aware of the damage I just caused. I open my eyes, seeking his out. It's not a soft gaze I find but a glare cloaked in hurt and shock. I'm still, afraid to move at all, but the words come tripping out. "I'm sorry. I'm sorry. So sorry."

Then shame fills my racing heart. "Oh my God! What have I done?" I'm swift to my feet as disgust fills my soul. "What have I done?" I mumble again. Cory's face flashes in my head, memories of his laughter ringing in my ears as a torturous reminder. "Shit. Shit. Shit." Not sure what to do, I stand there mortified.

"You wanted this," Dex says, sitting up. His voice sounds as confused as I feel. "You fucking wanted this. You wanted me."

His words are messing with my head as guilt slithers in, drenching me on the inside. How could I betray Cory like this and with Dex, his friend? "Fuck. I've gotta go." I run for my jeans, pulling them on, then drop to my knees to feel for my shirt. I slip it over my head and stand, my thoughts are like broken nerves, the pain of what I've done covering the raw ends like pinpricks of shame. I feel Dex's gaze heavy on my backside as I put my shoes on and run out of the bedroom, slamming the door behind me.

Down the staircase and through the party-goers, I run for the front door, not bothering to shut it or look back this time.

Outside, I stand on the stairs that led me away from his bedroom and the disgrace, hoping I can escape the cramping in my chest. I hate Hollywood and their fucking valets and mansions. Humiliation like this needs a quick escape, but I have to wait for my car to be pulled around. When it is, I jump inside, relieved that I didn't run into anyone I know while waiting. I leave through the gates of the neighborhood and speed home. My hands are shaking, so I hold the wheel tighter.

*What would Cory say?* I've disrespected his memory. *What*

*will Johnny say? He barely tolerates him since his drug use almost destroyed the band. He would never support me and Dex being together*. Shame coats me. *And Holli? Will she be disgusted that I gave into a physical desire instead of using my head and mourning quietly like I've done for the last six months? Will I be able to face them if they find out? What if Dex tells them?* I'll become one of his many, but this time with a face, a name for them to judge. *Will I be able to face myself? Look in the mirror without feeling disgusted for a lapse in judgment?*

I flip the visor down and open the mirror. The lights are bright, making me squint. When my eyes adjust, mascara is smeared on the left corner. My cheeks are flushed, not from the night or the rash exit, but from sex and lust, desire, and dishonor—everything I had managed to avoid until tonight.

Flipping the mirror back up, my eyes fill with heavy tears. I hope to find physical safety in the distance from him before they fall. But no distance will protect me from betraying the memory of the man I loved so much.

# 2

***One month later...***

The phone call comes just as I return to my car after dropping Neil at preschool. I'm strapping CJ's carrier into the base when the ringer sounds. I double check the straps before answering and climbing into the driver's seat. "Hello?"

Tommy sounds panicked as he asks, "Rochelle, I need a favor. Can you meet me at your house in thirty minutes?"

"What's up? What's wrong?" I can't lie, my heart is thundering in my chest, knowing something is wrong.

"It's Dex. I need you to come with me."

There's no question I'll go because I'd do anything for the guys. I drop CJ off at his grandmother's. Luckily, I had already arranged the visit and I can run my errands tomorrow. I drive back home and spot Tommy's silver Mercedes G-Class parked at the curb. The gate closes behind me and I take my purse from the passenger's seat and walk toward him. I get in the SUV and buckle in. He says, "He's been missing for three days—"

"What? Why am I just hearing about this? Where is he? Is he okay?"

"He's fucked up, Rochelle. Johnny can't know. We just hired the new guys and are talking shows and tours for the first time..." He turns back to the road and I see his hands tighten around the wheel. "...since Cory's death. If Dex blows this, the tour will never happen and the band will be done."

"Damn it, Tommy. Why didn't you tell me before?"

We hit the highway and he's off, way over the speed limit. "I know what happened... between you two. He told me. His head's all messed up... I should have seen this coming."

I stare out the windshield, watching as we pass car after car after truck, staying quiet. I don't want to talk about that night or what happened.

"Rochelle?"

When I turn and look at Tommy, he says, "It's okay. I understand. And I won't tell anyone."

"Thank you," I whisper. Setting my elbow on the door, I tilt my head, resting it against the glass. "Where are we going?"

"Barstow."

I sit straight up. "Barstow? I can't go to Barstow today. I have a meeting in three hours."

"Dex needs us."

Closing my eyes, I exhale, knowing he would do it for me, just like I would do it for any of the guys if they needed me to. "I'll reschedule." I call my part-time assistant and ask her to move the meeting to tomorrow or Wednesday. Then I call Cory's mom to pick up Neil for me after school. When I hang up, I ask, "What's he doing in Barstow?"

"He wasn't clear on the phone when he called. I think he called me by accident."

I'm still in shock over hearing this news. I feel so bad for not knowing, for not noticing. "He's relapsed?"

Tommy hesitates to answer. I only know of two reasons why: one, because he doesn't know or two, because he doesn't want to tell me. I'm thinking it's more the latter. His large fingers turn the dial of the air conditioning up so it gets cooler inside the vehicle, then he replies, "By the way he sounded, my guess would be yes."

"And your gut?"

"Same answer."

"How can I help him?"

"I'm hoping he'll listen to you, so I need your help to either get him home or checked into rehab."

"Why me?" I ask, but I think I know the answer already. My hunch is confirmed when he remains silent. I sigh, letting the burden of the situation be heard. "What is he trying to do to himself? What is he trying to prove?" Tommy doesn't answer because he knows I'm not asking him.

The miles pass as I return emails and phone calls, set more appointments and touch base with Johnny. It's been our thing since Cory died. "So you doing okay?" Johnny asks.

"I'm okay." Fine and well aren't answers either of us can give these days. He sounds better since he and Holli moved to Ohai a few months ago. He's writing music, playing his guitar and moving forward with the band.

My sadness and guilt haven't left my side or my heart. My kids are daily reminders of their father's death. I don't know if I'll ever be enough for them, if I can fill the role of both parents the way they deserve. But I get out of bed and try my damndest every day despite my secret fears.

Johnny says, "I'll drive us to the cemetery tomorrow."

He goes with us sometimes. I like the company. "Okay. Pick us up at 4?"

"See you then."

"Bye." I see a mileage sign just as I look up from the phone. "Ten miles to Barstow."

Tommy says, "Ten miles. Johnny doing okay today?"

"Getting by."

"And you?"

I reply, "Getting by."

Tommy has never been one for forced conversation, which I've come to appreciate over the years. He may not have started with the band back in the day, but he's been with us for eight years, so he is one of us. He's also someone we all can rely on even when it's not band related.

A sand colored motel with blue doors is visible up on the right. When we pull into a parking space, I wonder if it's painted that way or if it used to be white and the surrounding desert colored it naturally. "Which room?" I ask.

"Twenty-two." He leans forward over the steering wheel and points to the top right.

"How do you know?"

"I don't. It's either the girl's age or the room number. We're about to find out."

A sick, sinking feeling fills my stomach and I push open the door and step out. "Great," I reply sarcastically.

Tommy follows me up the side stairs to the second floor. Room twenty-two's door is cracked open. The music is loud and I recognize it as Jane's Addiction's "Summertime Rolls." We glance at each other, take a deep breath, and then he moves in front of me before pushing the door open further. Our eyes struggle to adjust to the darkness of the room after being blinded by the brightness of the desert.

The curtains are drawn on the only window, which resides next to the door. A broken coffee table is in front of the loveseat that has some girl with long brown hair asleep on it. She's in what looks like Dex's T-shirts and by the way it rides up, I can tell nothing else. The bathroom light is on, the door to it closed, the sound of the shower coming from inside. Dex's shoes are on the ground and two empty bottles of Jack Daniels and Fireball are on the floor next to them. White powdery residue is on the nightstand. Dex is passed out on the bed next to it, lying on his back. He's wearing his leather jacket, revealing a shield tattoo on his chest, one that he's become known to show at concerts when he plays. His jeans on with the button fly are wide open. His hair covers his eyes, his signature bandana fallen and knotted tightly around his neck. My heart breaks seeing him broken like this. This is not the man I've know all these years. This is the shell of what remains when someone sells their soul to the devil.

I push down my emotions and rely on logic. Besides immediately wanting to check and see if he's even alive, my second thought is to look for needles. My third, for condoms. No needles are found, but I see three condoms near the trash bin. That relieves me for some reason.

Tommy looks at me and says, "Stay outside the door."

I see the concern in his eyes, so I step back without asking questions. Peeking inside, I watch as Tommy goes to the bed and shakes Dex. Dex doesn't respond, so he calls his name, grabbing his face to look at him. Dex shifts, but doesn't come to. Tommy grabs his phone and turns off the music right when the door to the bathroom opens. I lean back, not knowing who to expect. A female comes out with a towel wrapped around her body and stops when she sees Tommy. As if this is a normal situation, nonchalantly she says, "He's been out like that for a while. Is he okay?"

"How long?" Tommy asks, watching her.

"Two hours maybe. I think he had a seizure poor guy. Jenny and I didn't know what to do. It really freaked us out. I think he just wanted another shot, so we gave it to him. But we need to get back to campus. We have evening classes and a test to study for. Can you drive us back?"

Knowing they won't hurt me, I hurry to Dex's side. I hear the girl asking who I am, but neither of us bothers with her. "Dex? It's me. Can you hear me?" When he doesn't respond, I lean down, resting my cheek to his. He reeks of alcohol and sweat, but I don't care. His cheek is warm and he's alive. While rubbing my hand over his tattooed heart, I whisper into his ear, "Dex, it's Rochelle. Please wake up. Wake up for me, Dex. I'll take you home."

I feel his hand cover mine and his breath against my skin. "Rochelle, beautiful Rochelle." His other arm comes up and wraps around me.

"I'm here, Dex."

The words just murmurs, but I hear him say, "Stay with me."

"I'm here with you. Can you sit up?" I lean back to find his brown eyes dull and bloodshot, so unlike the roguish ones I'm used to. Running my hand over his cheek, I say, "I want to get you out of here. Okay?" He nods, and when I try to move him, I feel every pound of his muscular body. "Help me, Dex."

Tommy snakes an arm under him and says, "Hey man, it's Tommy. We're gonna help you."

Dex nods again, talking seeming like too much of a chore for him.

When he's standing, the girl on the couch wakes up. "Are you our ride?"

"No," I snap. "I'll call a car for you if you promise never to repeat what happened here again." We get Dex to his feet, an arm over each of our shoulders.

Tommy says, "He's able to walk. Get his stuff and let's move him to the car."

"A ride? That's it?" the one girl says, putting her hand on her hip.

Pissed, I glare at her. "You left him here on the bed to die and you expect what exactly?"

"We were just having a good time. He didn't seem that out of it," she protests.

I don't say anything else because I need to control my anger, which I'm struggling to do. With Dex's boots and wallet in hand, I walk out, leaving the girls for Tommy to come back to handle. Catching up to them on the stairs, I help by holding Dex's waist. Dex's arm comes around and he holds me tight. "I've missed you."

"I've missed you too," I say, meaning every word.

We get him into the back seat where he lays down. Tommy runs back upstairs and is gone a few minutes before heading to the motel office. I assume he's paying the bill and for the damage to the room.

As soon as Tommy pulls back onto the highway, Dex puts his forearm over his eyes. I gulp, hearing the pain in his voice, the strain of the death that has destroyed us winning the battle when he says, "Cory was my best friend and I slept with the woman he loved."

Tommy reaches over just as my tears begin to fall and squeezes my shoulder. I'm reminded that everyone grieves differently and Dex might kill himself in the process. Even though it's obvious to us he's hitting bottom, hitting his lowest, the worst stage in the grieving process, I look out over the flat desert and realize my turn is coming.

# 3

It was the harder decision to make, but Tommy and I made it while driving back to LA. Dex had passed out again and we refused to second guess ourselves. It will leak to the press by tomorrow, but we can't worry about that. Dex needs help. If he had died... we're not equipped to give him what he needs right now.

He's not talking to us anymore. Sitting in the backseat, he's staring blankly out the window, quiet for the last hour. Before that, he was talking a mile a minute trying to convince us that what we were about to do was wrong. Empty promises he can't guarantee were being made. Anything he could think of saying to change our minds, he tried. We're holding strong.

My heart starts racing after entering through the large wrought iron gates of the rehab in Santa Barbara. The cobblestone driveway is lined with short pristine grass and flowering bushes. It winds around a large fountain and there's a bench off to the right that overlooks a large ocean vista. With doubts and the possibility of regret seeping in, I glance back to Dex. When he finally turns and looks at me—his own pain and regrets are showing. I'm betraying him, but I can't help but think this is seated in the best of reasoning. I apologize anyway. "I'm sorry."

He looks away from me again and as soon as the car comes to a stop he gets out without hesitation, then slams the car door shut. Tommy sighs, glancing at me before he reluctantly gets out.

When I get out, I overhear Tommy say, "It's only two weeks, man. You need to clean up, clean out. You know the deal with the band. If you're using, you're out."

Dex pushes past him and spits, "Fuck off, Tommy."

He treats me worse. The glare he gives me comes without any words at all.

A woman walks out with a clipboard and a fake smile to greet him. He doesn't look back before the door is slammed shut. From this point on it's up to him.

*TR*

***One and a half years later...***

The curtains puff like sails of a ship as the wind slips in through the small crack of the open door. The weather is turning from cool to warm as spring settles in, reminding me that the grass needs to be mowed again. I should call the lawn service in the morning and get them back on a regular schedule.

My mind can't rest despite how much I wish to sleep, so I roll over and grab the journal I've come to rely too much on and begin writing.

***Dear Cory,***

***The night is always the hardest—nightmares plague my sleep. I go to bed hoping for the best, but the best has become the worst.***

Closing my eyes, I squeeze my lids tight, hoping to stop the inevitable. But when I release them, the tears I've become too acquainted with are there for their encore—night after night the memories come back.

***I see you in my dreams. I'm transported back to when we were seventeen and I taught you how to play guitar. The way you looked at me, the way you learned the notes by studying my fingers, and when I caught you stealing glances… this perfect moment in our lives has become a nightly haunting for me. In the last two years, my memories have stilted my ability to play guitar without you. My loneliness is most exposed at this dark hour.***

***I miss you so much. All the time.***

***XO***

Sitting up, I grab for his pillow beside me and hold it to my nose, inhaling. His scent is gone. It used to be strong and comforted me when he traveled. His smell has left me, just like he did. So I throw the pillow across the room.

The curtains blow again, so I get up and slam the door shut before stepping over the pillow and crawling back in bed. The tightening in my chest starts to ease; the heartache of losing my soulmate lessens as I begin to drift off.

TR

"I'm tired, Neil. Can you please have some cereal this morning instead?" I look over at my seven-year-old and my heart momentarily stops altogether. At least once a day this happens. Neil has my eye coloring and olive skin, but his hair and the way he smiles is just like Cory. I turn back to the counter quickly before I get lost, staring at him 'again' as he puts it. He doesn't even have to beg, these kids own me. "Fine, I'll make you scrambled eggs."

"Thanks, Mom," he replies, a drumstick beating against the top of his thigh.

A sleepy little guy leans his head against my leg, one of Cory's T-shirts in hand. It's become a security blanket for him. With my free hand, I rub the top of his light brown hair, and say, "Good morning, buddy."

My three-year-old looks up and says, "Morning." His blue eyes flash with an inner happiness.

"Are you hungry, CJ? I'm making eggs."

He nods as he makes his way to the table. I finish the morning routine and take them to their schools. After drop-off, I head back home and shower. Working for the band allows me flexibility in time management and attire, so I pull on jeans, a cream colored blouse, and flats before heading out with the contracts I printed off last night.

Twenty-minutes later, I knock on the door. Dex answers, no greeting. He just sways his arm in front of him allowing me entrance. With little eye contact, I walk past him, and say, "I see the month on the road hasn't sullied your sparkling personality."

"It's before noon," he replies with an annoyed sigh. "It better be fucking good."

We've never quite recovered from that night. He has no patience for me, but I deserve that. Looking back, I wish I could change things, so many things.

I walk to the kitchen and sit down on a barstool. This is what we do—we can be around each other, but we tend to pretend the other isn't there—parallel universes. When it's just the two of us, like it is now, that's impossible to do. The coffee machine is started and he stares at the mug. I'm sure to keep from looking at me. "What brings you by, Rochelle?" He glances my way briefly before returning his gaze to the brewing coffee again.

"I need you to sign off on these contracts. The other guys all signed them last week when you were in Toronto. Why didn't you? You don't like the deal?"

"I don't understand the deal—"

"Oh. No problem. I can explain. So the video game characters will be modeled—"

He turns suddenly, his glare burning into me. "I understand that part. What I don't get is when we became *that* band."

"What band?"

"The one that sells out. The one that does video games and deodorant ads."

Tilting my head, with a smirk I say, "You've never been offered a deodorant ad."

"Fuck that! You know what I mean." He walks to the large window that overlooks the patio and pool. "When did it stop being about the music?"

"It's still about the music, Dex. The band is changing, growing, evolving. There's a vision we all have that will set you guys up for life. So if one day you develop carpal tunnel and can't play or

Johnny has throat issues and can't sing, you'll not worry about money. This is about The Resistance, the brand."

"When you walked into that club on Sunset, you didn't ask me if I was interested in building a brand." With his back to me, he says, "You asked me if I would play drums for a band you put together that had a gig down on Ventura in some dive pizza parlor." He turns around with his arms crossed over his chest. "Did I go?"

I eye him, wondering where this is going. "You did."

"You're damn right I did. I took my sticks at intermission and left a paying gig to go meet your boys. Do you know why I did that?"

"No. Why?"

"Because I was better than a cover band drummer on a Tuesday night in Hollywood, even with the pay."

I nod. I'm following his train of thought as he drives his point home.

"So stop treating me like I am. We're The motherfucking Resistance and we're better than this year's video game simulation that followed some cheesy, hair-band from the 80's in last year's edition."

I gather my papers and slip off the stool. As I start to leave, he grabs my wrist as I pass, and I stop, my breath caught in my throat just from his touch. His grip loosens, and I try to steady my voice when I say, "I got the message. I'll talk to the guys, but majority rules. You agreed to that when you left that other band."

He releases my wrist and my skin is left bare, his touch feeling better than I remember.

I open the door, and step out, but stop. Looking over my shoulder, I add, "I like the shorter hair on you. You look good." Closing the door behind me, I don't wait for a response. The boy I convinced to leave a dead-end band on Sunset way back then has turned into a man and a force to be reckoned with—mentally and physically. Memories of our night together before I screwed up come flashing back, but the humiliation of my mistake overtakes the warmth I'm feeling.

I should have gone with my gut. I convinced myself that we were wrong before I even gave the alternative a chance. My instincts told me to stay with him despite my mistake of calling him Cory. My head said to run. My more logical side seems to always get in the way.

"Wait up, Rochelle." I hear him behind me.

When I look back, he's leaning against the door opening, his eyes set on me. Even at rest, his muscles are defined. His arms carved from strength and power. Despite being hidden under the cotton of his T-shirt, his abs tease me as I remember how I once licked them. "What's up?" I turn the focus back on business, trying to sound indifferent.

"It's been a long time, a couple months since I saw you." He pauses. "It's good to see you again."

"Thanks. It's good to be seen again," I joke, trying to cover my nervous excitement.

He nods, a small smile tugging at the corners of his mouth as he stands upright. "You should come to the show in New York. The band always has fun there."

I open my car door and step up on the running board, looking at him over the top of my SUV. "Yeah, I'll give it some thought."

"Yeah, okay."

With a small smile of my own, I give a little wave. "See ya around."

I start to step into the vehicle, but I stop when I hear him say, "See ya around. Oh, and Rochelle?"

Popping back up, I answer, "Yes?"

"You look good, too."

My smile isn't little anymore. It's full on ridiculous. "Thanks."

If I wasn't so aware of every nerve in my body and beat of my heart when I get inside the Escalade, I might have missed how my heart just leaped.

While pulling out of Dex's gated community, I call Johnny. It's only ten-thirty, so I'm not surprised he doesn't answer. I leave a message, warning him that Dex may not sign and I might just agree with him.

I call my nanny, Beth, and let her know that she'll need to pick up the boys today. With all the thoughts crowding my head, I need therapy. So I call one of my best friends, Lara, to meet me. I met her in yoga years before it became trendy. We quit after two weeks, preferring to cocktail together rather than work out. We've been great friends ever since. "Shopping?" I ask, when she answers.

"Beverly Center, Melrose, or the boutiques down near the beach."

Today is about shopping for me, so I reply, "Suru on Melrose?"

"Suru. For sure. They just got in their new collection."

"I'll see you there in twenty."

"It will take me thirty."

"Cool." We disconnect, and I smile, excited to see her. She's always up to go out and I like that.

Just over an hour later, I'm standing near the far wall of Suru in front of newly altered frocks, and I say, "I think I like Dex." I peek over at her.

Her head remains down, focused on finding her size in a stack of jeans. "I like him too. He's always been cool. Haven't seen him in a while."

"He got his hair cut."

She looks up, so I look down. "Really? I liked the medium

length on him. He could pull it off."

"It's shorter. Short now."

When I look up again, she's staring at me. "Why are we having a full-blown conversation about Dex's hair?"

I shrug it off. "No reason. I just saw him this morning about some contracts. Just making chitchat."

"Oookaay," she replies like I'm crazy before returning her attention to the clothes in front of her. "The boys are good?"

"They're great. Dating much?"

"Too much. It sucks. Be glad you've decided to stay single."

My hand stops on a blue dress. "I didn't decide to stay single."

"Oh no, I didn't mean it like that. I just meant that since... well, you know his death—"

"You can say his name. Cory."

There's an awkward pause that I would rather avoid. I'm glad she doesn't leave it to build. "Since Cory's death, you've remained unattached. You're strong like that."

"We're all tested in life. I just got tested in the worst of ways. Anyway, I haven't chosen to stay single. I just haven't dated."

"Do you think you're ready?"

"I'm not sure. How will I know?"

"Maybe if you start getting that feeling, the tingly one deep inside when you meet someone." She comes over and puts her hand on my shoulder. "If you are ready, I'll help anyway I can. If you're not, that's fine too. You know what's best for you."

"Thanks. I'm just..." I sigh. "I don't know what I want."

She nods toward the door. "Come on. Let's cut the shopping short and get a drink."

TR

While sitting at the café inside Fred Segal, I smile. "We should have just started here."

She laughs. "I thought you actually wanted to go shopping. Next time just say you want a drink."

We order salads and a bottle of white wine before sitting back and easing into talk of our lives. After taking two sips, her hands go into the air, and she continues the story she's been retelling, "So I told them, 'Honey, the 90's have to leave before they can make a comeback.' I got the job and she burned the valances that afternoon."

"Beverly Hills is a lot different from Hollywood style-wise."

Lara is an interior decorator and has a huge celebrity clientele. I've watched her grow from working out of her spare bedroom to buying a large house with an entire floor dedicated to her business and five employees. She's very animated when she talks, passionate about what she does. "Totally. In Hollywood, they like clean and modern. The celebrities I've worked for all give me carte blanche. They're adventurous. Not so much in Beverly Hills. This new project will be fun though, something different for me to tackle."

"Let's toast to that. To your new project."

Our glasses clink right as our salads are served.

She smothers the lettuce in dressing, very un-L.A. like, and asks, "I have a job in New York next week. Want to come with me. We can move our 'shopping' to the other coast."

Dex's words replay in my mind. "You're the second one to mention going to New York next week."

"Oh really? Who was the other?"

"Dex. They're playing there. He said I should come."

Dragging her fork through the vegetables on her plate, she lowers her gaze. "Interesting."

"What's interesting?"

"Oh nothing." Her eyebrows go up and her eyes go wide, her expression hopeful. "So is that a yes?"

"It might be fun. Maybe I can get Cory's mom, Janice, to watch the boys for a few days. They'd love that. She spoils them rotten."

"That's what Grandma's are supposed to do."

"Yeah, we're lucky to have her living so close by."

"So that settles it. They get Grammie and we paint the Big Apple red. Yay! It will be awesome," she adds with another tap of her glass against mine.

# 4

My thoughts wander to Dex a lot over the next few days, but why? It's Dex, after all. He sleeps with everyone he can and has a temper to rival the titans. He smokes too much and drinks heavily. He lives off junk food and is moody. He swears too much but has a wicked sense of humor. His new haircut emphasizes a strong jaw that sometimes looks a little too sexy when it has a day or two's growth on it. His eyes are the most unique color, so close to caramel, but more soulful. Wait...

*What? Why am I thinking of him? When did I start thinking of him? Or like the little sweet nothings we've been sharing? This is something that's crept up on me when I wasn't looking.*

I drop my head to the mattress and cover myself under the pillow. No. I refuse to think of him that way. But I can't help it. Somehow over the last week, things have changed, shifted into something different, something new, something exciting.

*And then the tingles began...*

I know what it is, recognizing the feeling that's sneaking in without my permission. And now I wonder if these small gestures and occurrences aren't so random. I felt safe in his arms. The warmth between us is new, but I felt safe and wanted. It's the *wanted* that scares me most. Liking the thought that Dex might want me leaves me restless and I roll over, hiding beneath the covers

***Dear Cory,***

***It never bothered me before, but now I hate flying. My therapist... I know. I know. Yes, I have a therapist. I think that officially makes me an Angeleno now. Anyway, she once told me that it was a natural fear since you died in a plane crash. But she also gave me the statistics of car crashes, death by mosquitoes, and lightning to help put it in perspective. Not sure if it worked since I shudder just thinking about mosquitoes and hide under my covers during storms. I'm in my car too much and have a false sense of safety there.***

***I have a flight to see the band in NYC tomorrow, so I should get some sleep. I miss you.***

***XO.***

My hands are sweating and my knee is bouncing, anxiety getting the best of me. I wish I had something to take to calm me, but for now, the shot of whiskey will have to do. Staring out the window, I try to think of happy things like my kids, the beautiful weather California has been having, and try not think about plane crashes, mosquitoes, or cars. Adjusting my neck pillow, I move to lean back in my chair and turn up my music. I close my eyes and lose myself in the music.

Once I arrive at the hotel, the same one where the guys are staying, I shut the door to my room and flop back on the bed. Not even five minutes later, a light knock on the door makes me sit up and go. Expecting the bellhop, I open the door wide, then walk back inside, signaling for him to come in. "Just put the suitcases there please."

"Sorry, no luggage. Just a shit ton of baggage."

Surprised, I turn back to find Dex standing in the middle of the doorway. I quirk a grin and reply, "Well, get your ass and all your baggage in here anyway."

As he walks by, he says, "I wanted to see how you're doing?" I'm sure my face is showing my confusion, his unexpected concern taking me by surprise. He laughs. "I know. I know. I have this tough exterior, but believe it or not, I have a heart buried deep down in here somewhere. I just haven't felt it in a while."

"Well, I hope you do soon because I'd hate to think of you going through life without a heartbeat."

"A lifeline."

I nod.

He asks, "So how are you?"

"I'm good."

His eyes lock with mine, holding me steady just through a look. "No, how are you really?"

Tilting my head, I remark, "I appreciate it, but I'm not sure where all the concern is coming from."

"Just a friend checking on a friend."

I sit in a chair by the window and start swiveling back and forth. "Are we friends?"

"Are we not?" With his eyebrows up, he seems genuinely surprised.

"Sometimes, I'm not sure."

"We're friends, Rochelle. I'm sorry if I gave the impression we weren't."

With all of this apologizing going on, I take a chance. "I'm sorry for the past stuff."

"You don't have to be."

"I am though." This is the most we've ever broached the topic and the whole conversation catches me off-guard. I used to have planned rebuttals, but today, with our defenses down, I don't worry about those and just go with it.

He looks around as if searching for an escape in case he needs one, but it's just us here in this hotel room with one door in and the same door out. No other escapes, not even the luxury of an interruption.

"I wanted to know if you wanted to go out after the show... with the band?"

"Yeah, that will be fun. My friend Lara will be with me tonight."

"Cool." He nervously shoves his hands in his pockets like a seventeen-year-old. The vulnerability on his face is quite charming. "I should go."

"I appreciate the welcome wagon."

"No problem," he says with a short chuckle. "I'll catch ya later."

"At the show. Break a leg."

"I'm not superstitious."

"I am," I reply.

"Good to know." He opens the door and the bellhop is standing there with his hand raised as if he was about to knock. Handing the kid some money as he passes, Dex says, “That’s for her.”

“Thank you, Sir.”

As the bellhop carries my case inside the room, I’m left standing there baffled by what just happened. Dex has always been hard to figure out, but this time, he’s near impossible.

TR

The night started off innocent enough. Lara and I had dinner and drinks, then headed to see The Resistance. In the past, New Yorkers have always been crazy and fun at their shows. I assume they won’t disappoint tonight.

Feeling sexy in my new black jeans and tank top, I decided my high-heeled knee boots, silver and black necklaces would complement. The outfit is a departure from my normal California style, which tends to be very laidback and more free-flowing with some Mom mixed in. Tonight’s theme is sex appeal and rock n’roll. Lara was influential in the ensemble.

She looks amazing—effortless, but always at the edge of fashion. Together, we are both beauty *and* brains. We learned a long time ago that we can be sexy without coming off like bimbos.

Clutching her purse under her arm, she glances my way. “So I’ve been thinking about our conversation last week. Maybe it’s time for you to start dating again.”

There’s a quiet between us as we both take that in. Finally, I say, “And why do you think that?”

“Seems like you might be more ready than you think.”

I shrug. “I dunno. I don’t think about it much.”

“Tonight seems like a good time to start.”

"Start what? Thinking about it or dating?"

She shrugs this time. "Maybe both."

With a laugh, I say, "I can tell you're gonna be trouble with a capital T tonight."

"Is there any other way to be?"

Shaking my head, I laugh again. I love her spirit and energy too much to deny her the possibility of the fun in store for us. I also feel my more adventurous side revealing itself. It feels good to let loose. It's been too long and the rush of adrenaline hypes me up after so many years. Taking her hand, I pull her into the massive crowd toward the doors.

When we enter, I realize it's also been forever since I've been on this side of a concert. The T-shirts, buttons, posters, and passion displayed for the band makes me smile. But I'm soon tugged to the left by Lara when she spots a bar. "Shot time."

While we wait in line, I ask, "You're gonna get me wasted, aren't you?"

"If my plan works."

"Fine. First round is on me." I bump her hip with mine. "If we're gonna do it, we're gonna go big."

After two shots and a Jack and Coke to-go, we make our way backstage, flashing our badges when necessary. I leave the guys alone, not wanting to interrupt their pre-performance routine. I lead her down to the VIP area off to the side of the crowd next to the media. "This is great," she says, squeezing in next to me.

The anticipation builds just like it always did when I used to come to their shows. I would watch Cory, my eyes fixed on him. Tonight I stare at the spot where he used to stand to start the show, but he's not there. I take the other shot, wanting to drown out the memories and live in the here and now. The music being piped in overhead stops and the arena goes black. My heart starts thundering in my chest from excitement. This is how The Resistance has started every show since the first tour, and for tradition, they still do. With one loud hit on the drums, the entire place goes quiet. Dex is at his kit, doing a countdown even though the arena lies trapped in darkness. I smile.

I can't see, but I know Kaz and Derrick should be in place. Dex kicks into the opening solo and we start screaming along with everyone else. Like I've seen so many times before, a spotlight hits Johnny center stage, his guitar hanging upside down on his back, his hands gripping the microphone in such a seductive way, the way that made him the star he is.

His voice carries over the screams. The girls next to me start to cry and the guys holler. Johnny's pitch is flawless, something that's always come so easily for him. Dex is in the background—sunglasses on, no headband anymore like he used to wear when his hair was long, ripped shirt where the sleeves used to be, and a rhythm that no other drummer on the music scene can rival. I close my eyes, the alcohol and song melding perfectly together. For a minute, I forget all that's happened in the last three years. For a moment in time, I feel, just like I used to feel when I played guitar and wrote songs with the guys. When I open my eyes, a wave of emotion takes hold and I finish the drink in my hands, dropping the plastic cup to the floor and throw my arms in the air, letting the melody wash through me, over me, taking me whole.

The only thing more powerful than music is love. The music will have to be enough for now.

Five songs in and the audience is much drunker and less aware of their bodies. Lara and I follow as the vibe of the night carries us. I spin, dancing my ass off, and embracing the freedom. Before the band breaks for the encore, we sneak backstage again and make a cocktail. The guys have a full bar setup back here. They don't drink before or during the shows anymore, but after, I know they like to have the option. With fresh drinks in hand, we go to the dressing room and plop down on the couch together. It only takes one look in each other's direction and we start giggling. "You're a mess," I tease.

Poking me in the arm, she says, "Look who's talking."

The door swings open and the guys come in one-by-one. Dex smiles when he sees me—cocky and annoyingly sexy. The rest of them greet us before retreating to different parts of the room. Johnny makes a call. Kaz goes into the bathroom, and Derrick hops up on the counter, his back against the mirror, and starts playing on his phone.

Dex sits next to me, a bottle of soda in his hands. He takes a long swig, his eyes steady on me and asks, "Are you drunk?"

Leaning my head back, I reply, "A little."

"Don't get wasted... yet. We're going out later." He stands up and heads for the door. But he stops to look in the mirror and run his hands through his hair first. He puts his sunglasses back on and leaves with a bodyguard in tow.

I'm left there with my mouth hanging open and very much looking forward to later.

Derrick gets up, looking annoyed. "Damn Kaz, hogging the toilet." He walks out. I guess in search of another bathroom.

Johnny hangs up, then grabs a water from the fridge. "It's a good crowd tonight. Holliday says hi."

"New York," I reply as if that's the only answer needed. "Tell her hi."

"I'm glad you flew out, Ro. It's good to have you back on the road again."

"Thanks."

When he leaves, I turn to Lara. "You still up for going out?"

"Umm. Have you met me?"

"Silly question. What was I thinking?" I laugh, then ask, "Where exactly are we going out tonight? Any idea?"

"Hopefully not to jail."

"So that's our goal? Just to stay out of trouble?"

"No one said anything about trouble. Trouble is definitely still on the agenda."

TR

It's been a long time since I've hung out with the band in public. My mind has blocked the chaos that came along with it. But I'm quickly reminded when we get out of the SUV and have to walk one block up to a private restaurant and bar. Derrick and Kaz went to party across town with some friends of theirs. Johnny went to the hotel. Tommy and Lara lead the way inside while Dex walks next to me. Our hands accidentally touch a couple of times and I notice each one, wanting more. My desire is fulfilled in a different way when we go inside the bar. His hand presses lightly against my lower back, guiding me in, and making me wonder if he's ever done that to me in the past. I don't think he has because that one caring gesture is felt throughout my entire body. I think I would remember this sensation. Once inside, the crowd is subdued, calm is being restored as the adrenaline starts wearing off. So does the booze, so I tell Dex, "I'm ready for a drink."

With a smile that reaches his eyes, he says, "I'm ready for a few myself. Our table's over here."

The music is exotic—seductive, the lights dim, and the crowd stylish. I recognize a few celebrities, some I've met before—one is an actor, Chad Spears, who hit it big in the last year and hit on me at an after-party of an awards show a couple years back. He was young and cute then. He's more man and more handsome these days. Sitting on a white leather couch, he has his arm draped over a woman who is either a model or a wannabe actress. Chad's gaze meets mine and a wry grin appears. With a nod, we acknowledge each other just as Dex's hand slips to my side, redirecting me to the corner where our booth is located.

We settle in and order drinks. Tommy jokes about a screw up backstage while Dex eyes me. "You look good tonight."

"Good?" I tease with a nudge to his side, liking the fact that he's looking at me.

"Better than good. Hot."

I tap my head lightly to his shoulder. "Aww, thank you. You look go—"

A smooth voice interrupts us, "Hey, Rochelle." I know it's Chad before I even look up. Glancing past him to the VIP table he was recently occupying, I notice the girl is gone. "Good to see you."

"Hi," I reply just as our drinks are delivered.

"Chad," Dex says with a harsh emphasis on the name.

"Interesting to see you here... in a bar, Dexter. How's post-rehab working out for you?" Chad eyes Dex's drink insinuating everything.

Dex is calm considering the insult, and says, "I don't do drugs anymore, so it's working out just peachy." Dex is about to say something else, but bites his bottom lip as he looks away. Picking up his glass, he drinks like he's got a point to prove.

Chad bumps his leg against mine, making me look back up. He straightens his suit jacket and puts a smile on for me. "We should catch up. Can I buy you a drink?" I start to say no, but he cuts me off. "Just one. Please."

He holds his hand out for me. Feeling it would be rude not to, I take it. Dex grabs me by the belt loop and stops me. "Stay."

"Just one drink," Chad interjects. "Relax, I'm not gonna steal your date."

"Stay." There's a plea in Dex's eyes that makes me start to pull my hand back from Chad, but Chad tightens his grip and pulls me to my feet.

"Just one drink," he says. I can tell he's trying to charm me. "He'll be okay without you. He gets plenty of company. I want a little time with you."

"I made plans with my friends tonight. It would be rude if I left."

"Maybe later then."

"Yeah, maybe later," I reply and sit back down.

As he walks away, Dex's hand covers my knee. "Stay away from him. He's an asshole."

"That was uncomfortable. What's the history between you two?"

Dex sits back and looks over his shoulder at Chad across the room. "We went to high school together."

"You did?"

"Yeah. He was an asshole then, too."

"Let me guess. Star quarterback, dated all the hot girls, Class President?"

He chuckles. "Something like that."

"Tell me about you," I say. "Give me all the dirty details of when you were younger."

"The past doesn't matter, Rochelle. Only tonight."

His words and his eyes, the way they've latched onto mine, possession taking hold, I'm shocked I'm still upright. My body is flooded with want for him and I quickly reach for my drink to cool myself down. I close my eyes and sip. When I open them, I find myself gravitating even closer to him, pressed to his side. I whisper, "You can't say things like that to me, Dex."

His hand warms my leg and he leans in until I feel his words cover my skin. "Why not?"

Just as I'm about to answer with that there is no reason or maybe with a kiss, we're interrupted by a group of women. "You're with The Resistance. Can we have your autograph and a picture?"

She shoves a napkin and a pen in front of him. As he scribbles his name, my gaze meets Lara's across the table and our silent conversation begins. Her lips purse and her eyebrows are raised. She signals toward Dex with a nod, questioning.

He's hot and I don't know, I guess I like his attention. I like him. I say all that through a guilty smile and a playful shrug.

Looking at Tommy, she leans in and tells him something. He jumps and sits on top of the booth. "You need another?" He asks me from across the table.

"Yes. Thanks."

Slipping out of the booth, he leans in when he passes and says, "You guys be careful. Okay? You know what happened last time."

I'm not sure if he's giving me advice or warning me. I know he cares about both of us and his concern is showing tonight. Understandable worry since he's had to watch Dex and I flirt so much tonight.

Suddenly I have a bare midriff with a temporary tattoo of gold hearts circling her belly button pressing against my shoulder as one of the girls pushes in. She's trying to get closer to Dex... as if I'm not even here. When I turn, my head jerks back. I get more than an eyeful of breasts because of her low cut shirt. I lean closer to Dex to get away from her, but she presses in even more.

Jealousy wells up inside and I shake my head, trying to rid myself of it. It's ridiculous I feel anything remotely close to that emotion when it comes to him. This is Dex. He's a free man. Our flirtations were harmless, just hanging out like we have for years. Then I realize we haven't really hung out like this before. Sure, we've partied many times in the same group of friends and I've gone out a million times with the band, but this is different. This is me hanging out with Dex specifically... and Lara and Tommy, of course, but I know deep down I wanted to spend time with Dex.

Lara taps my shoulder. "Let's go to the bathroom."

We slip out of the booth and with the girl vying for Dex's attention, I'm not even sure he notices we're leaving, which bothers me. *Ugh.* I follow Lara to the restroom where girls line the hallway, waiting impatiently.

"What's going on?" she asks. "You seem upset."

I lie. "I'm not upset."

She looks at me and then bursts out laughing. "So that girl hanging on Dex's every breath doesn't bother you at all?"

Tweaking my lips to the side, I say, "Nope."

We move up a few spots in line. "Okay, keep telling yourself that. Maybe you'll start to believe it."

"I'm not lying to myself. Dex is Dex. I've known him for years and he's definitely not someone I should get involved with."

She stands on her tiptoes and looks ahead. Only two more people until we're at the front of the line. When she spins around, she says, "Look, you mention him all faux-casual while shopping the other day. Now we're here with him tonight. I saw how you watched him during the show and how he looked at you backstage. If you guys aren't attracted to each other, then I have no idea what's going on. But if you ask me, you have feelings for him. I know you feel guilty for having them, but your heart doesn't feel guilt. That's all in your head. You aren't doing anything wrong. If anything, you're doing what's right."

"So follow my heart?"

Shrugging, she says, "Beats letting the guilt win."

The line moves and my boldness peaks. "You're right. I may regret this in the morning, but I'm ready to see if there's more between us."

"He's also damn sexy. You were right. That haircut is making him even more irresistible."

When we walk out of the bathroom, I'm feeling determined. The only thing that holds me back, stopping me in my tracks is the girl who has slid into the booth next to him taking my spot. She's so close with her arm around the back of him, and I detour, letting Lara return without me. I stop behind a column and peek back, not spying, just checking to see if it's safe to return. Lara's looking for me and Dex downs his drink.

"Couldn't hide his stripes for long." Chad is next to me, both of us watching Dex from afar. "Dex may not be snorting his fortune anymore, but he's still the same guy, Rochelle."

"Not now, Chad," I say, starting to walk away.

He stops me, by taking my hand in his. "Hey, I know you've had a hard time the last few years, but Dex isn't the answer. He's the problem. You deserve better—"

Rolling my eyes, I retort, "You mean someone like you?"

He laughs. "I'm not perfect, but at least you know what you're getting with me."

His arrogance is getting on my nerves, but his cockiness still fascinates me equally. "And what is that exactly?"

Rubbing his chest with pride, he says, "The rumors are true."

"The rumors? And which rumors would those be?"

"I'm the best fuck in Hollywood—"

"What did you just say, Spears?" Dex startles us, his body hard against my back, his breathing jagged.

Chad stands, his ego making him brave. "Fuck off, Caggiano. Go back to your whores and hookers. The grown-ups are trying to have a conversation here."

"You've always been such a fucking prick, but now you're just a sad asshole too."

"This sad asshole gets more pussy than you can dream of."

Dex looks at me and if I'm not mistaken, I see disappointment residing there. "C'mon, Rochelle. I'm ready to leave."

Taking my own stance on the matter, I say, "Maybe I'm not."

His eyes narrow on me, puzzled. "You want to stay here with him?"

"Beats being the third wheel over there."

My words shake him, taking him aback like a slap across the face. He leans down, eye-to-eye with me. "You could never be a third wheel. Not to me." My breath catches from his intensity and he adds, "Do you understand me?"

"Yes," I reply, believing the truth I see in his eyes.

"I will always treat you how you deserve." With promises swirling around us, Chad and the other girl are forgotten and our own world seems to form. "I want you to come with me," Dex says, sincerity on his face and heard in his words.

I take his hand and we leave together not knowing where this will lead to, but knowing that right now, tonight, this is right.

# 5

Dex puts two fingers in his mouth and blows, hailing a cab.

"You sure are good at that considering you're a Cali kid," I say, giving him a smile. The way his hand is possessively around mine suddenly feels like we're more than friends. And I like it.

"I've spent enough time in the city, enough to learn how to get a cab when I need one," he says.

The cab pulls up, the door opens, and we climb inside. "The Bowery," he tells the driver as he sits back. Our hands drop to the space between us.

"Why did you want to leave, Dex?"

He looks at me with all the confidence in the world backing him. "Because I want to be alone with you." He nods as if that's all the response needed, and suddenly it is. It's good enough.

When we arrive, we don't talk or hold hands. I'm sure we don't even seem like we're together as we walk through the lobby of the hotel and take the elevator up. Trying to appear normal to the outside world, like things aren't about to get heated in a sexual way is harder than it seems. I try to avoid eye contact but we catch each other's in the trim of the door. "Where are we going?" I ask, whispering though we're alone.

"My room."

"Why?" I ask to be clear.

"I already told you. I want to be alone with you."

"Why?"

A smirk appears. "Good question."

The elevator doors open and he walks out without further explanation. Reaching back in, he takes my hand again and pulls me out of the vestibule. "Come with me."

It's not like I'm going to say no or anything, but still... *Why?* He holds the hotel room door wide, letting me enter. Looking around, it looks very similar to my room, but larger. The door slams shut and I'm spun around. My face is taken between his hands as his lips meet mine. Two beats pass before I close my eyes, relaxing under his touch, and return the kiss.

"I want you," he whispers. "All of you this time."

"I'm yours. With you, Dex," I reply between kisses and caught breaths.

His hips press against me as my body finds purchase against the wall. Hands move with speed and diligence, finding the backside of my bra as warm breath covers my skin and his lips cover my neck. I slide my fingers up his back and into his hair, holding him there as my body squirms from his touch.

Just when I think we might have sex against this wall, a female voice scares us in the dark. "I wanted to surprise you... guess I'm the one who's surprised."

"What the fuck?" Dex is in front of me, his hand on my hip, holding me protectively behind him.

The lamp on the nightstand is turned on and a woman I recognize not only as one of Dex's ex-girlfriends, but also as a popular lingerie model, stands next to the bed. I've never met her before, but saw the tabloid stories. She's dressed in a red lace bra and matching g-string, and her hair rivals Bridgette Bardot's sex kitten do. I try to swallow down the fact that she makes me look like I just got rescued after being stranded on an island for six months with my mismatched underwear and my messy hair.

With her hands on her hips, she looks offended by our intrusion. "Dex? Who is she?" Her accent is thick—Eastern European, I think.

"How'd you get in here, Alexia?" he asks. His tone firm but tinged with an authority that makes me take a step back, closer to the door.

She points at me while looking over his shoulder, making me feel short and unattractive compared to the supermodel standing before me. I'm usually in jeans and my hair is messy most days. She wears skin-tight dresses and her locks always look professionally styled. "I'm here," she says with a stamp of her high heel. "She can go now."

I take another step toward the door. "I'm gonna leave."

"No," he says with authority, turning to face me. "She's leaving." His expression is stern, leaving no room to argue.

I need to escape this fiasco though. "I want to," I add with a little less strength.

"I don't want you to." He lowers his voice and says, "Stay, Rochelle. I want you to stay with me." He reaches for my hand, but when we hear *her* demand his attention, he looks back and I reach for the door.

"Dex!" We turn to see her arms crossed over her chest and a

look of determination on her face. "You told me to come here, so I'm here."

"That was when we were together. We've been broken up for months. So I want you out, Alexia. I want you to get the fuck out right now." When he turns back to me, his tone softens again. "I'll come to your room after I settle this."

With three quick nods, I leave the room. The heavy door shuts behind me and I remain leaning against it for support while I right my senses. Dropping my head back, I close my eyes. "Damn. Damn. Damn. Damn. Damn." Then I push off the wood and head down the hall to my room.

Once inside, I lock the bolt and flip the safety slider over. Now I'm pissed. I can't compete with a supermodel. These are the women he's dated... dates. Not a five-foot-three mom of two young sons who eats salad for lunch six days a week to keep most of the cellulite at bay. I flip on the bathroom light and lean forward. My brown hair is in disarray, the colors of summer not yet affecting it. My skin is more pale than olive these days and my eyeliner is smeared from the gropes in the dark. The alcohol sloshes around in my stomach, rattling my thoughts and self-esteem, or maybe it was the glamazon lying across his bed in nothing but lingerie like a gift being presented to Dex that has me shaken.

There's a soft knock on the door and I look down, trying to collect my thoughts back together. With a deep breath, I turn and go to open it. I unlock the bolt but leave the slider in place. Three inches of visual is all I'm allowing in the state I'm in. The offense is caught in his expression. The subtle message that he knows this is going nowhere is now obvious.

"Hey, what's going on?" he asks, keeping his voice low.

"I'm gonna go to bed."

"What about we try this again?"

I shake my head, looking away from him. "I'm tired." My heart pounds but I know what's best for me.

"Roch—"

"No, it's too much. It's... it's just not meant to be."

"Bullshit. You're scared."

I don't deny that. I can't. I am scared. Looking at him, I try to hold the eye contact that will tell him I'm strong, not weak, how I really feel inside. "I had a good time, but I'm tired. I think it's best if we both just go to bed. Goodnight, Dex."

I start to shut the door, but his palm goes flat against the thick wood, causing a loud thud. "No, don't do this. I don't know how she got in. But she wasn't there because I wanted her there. Don't let this ruin something good," he says, his free hand signaling between us.

After a deep sigh, all reality hits, and I respond, "She can't ruin what's not there. We're an illusion that's never supposed to be real."

"Don't do this, Rochelle. Please." I see the desperation in his eyes, a panic and sadness. Maybe disappointment in me. "You're convincing yourself that I'm the bad guy, that I don't care, and you know that's lies, lies you're telling yourself to avoid anything that might actually be real."

Wanting this door closed. Wanting the emotions welled up like a fist lingering in my chest to subside. Wanting the tears to stay at bay, I say what I shouldn't to make it all go away. "I don't have to convince myself that you're the bad guy. You do a fine job of that all on your own." With my weight behind me, I slam the door shut, knowing what I said is wrong and unwarranted, knowing that all the good strides he's made over the years to clean up his life—I just took that away in that one line, in a sad attempt to protect my heart. Because no matter what he says to me today, he'll break my heart tomorrow. *That* I do know.

My head is pounding from dehydration and not enough food. I break into the mini-bar to get a bottle of water. After fishing two ibuprofen from my purse, I swallow them and lay back down. With my forearm draped over my eyes, I try to sleep again. It's not working. Tonight was so good... then it wasn't. Damn supermodel in matching lingerie exes. There is nothing wrong with a little cotton every now and again.

Rolling to my side, I try my hardest to block out my confrontation with Dex and what almost was. When that doesn't work, I turn on the TV and watch infomercials until the sun starts to rise. Then I get up and get dressed. After washing my face, I pull my hair back before heading downstairs and outside. Two blocks down and one street over, I find a Starbucks.

I retrieve my coffee when my name is called and find a chair in the corner near the window. With my back to the line that's forming, I drop my head into my hands. *What am I doing here?* I don't have the luxury of being irresponsible. I have children who rely on me to be the exact opposite.

"Stop beating yourself up."

With my back to him, I sigh, not sure how I feel about the intrusion into my head.

"Can I join you?" Dex asks.

Per usual, my heart reacts to the sound of his voice. I slowly look up and nod, giving in. "Why are you up so early?"

He sits across from me, our knees bumping under the tiny

round table. "I don't think I actually went to sleep." Disappointment settles on my face, but he's quick to correct my assumption. "I was alone all night."

"I'm sorry."

"Don't be. If I couldn't be with you, I didn't want to be with anyone else." He leans forward, pushing his coffee to the side, and whispers, "We weren't doing anything wrong. Rochelle, you're a widow, but that doesn't take away the fact that you're young, you have needs. I'm sure you don't want to spend the rest of your life alone."

Sitting up straight, this topic feels heavy for seven-thirty in the morning. "My needs come second to my kids and I don't think my kids need the disruption right now."

"You're a great mother, but you're also a woman. You have feelings and deserve a life of your own as well."

"Dex, why are you here? Why do you want this to happen? Two years ago it was sex in a weak moment. Last night, I was drunk and you're too good looking. But this can't be. I don't understand why you act like it can."

His mouth hangs open enough for me to know I've shocked him. When he gets up, the chair bumps against the window in his haste, but he stops, tapping twice on the table in front of me. I glance up and see once again that I've hurt him when all I meant to do was give him an out. "You know," he starts. "One day, I hope you'll see me for more than a coked-up drummer who used to sleep around."

Just as he starts to leave again, I grab his hand. He looks back at me, the connection slipping from my grip. "I do, Dex. It's me. It's not you."

His hand leaves mine and he disappears, and I'm left with the chiming of the bell above the door echoing in my heart. Memories of him holding me after the funeral come rushing back and the feeling that in that moment, I felt safe, like everything would be okay one day. I found that in *his* arms.

Cory used to be my safe haven, but with him gone... I get up, feeling all wrong that he's gone because he's right. No matter what changes I recognize in him now, I'm still holding his past against him. And I'm still holding onto a future that can never be with Cory. I'm alone. No matter how much I wish I wasn't, I am. That's the reality I need to accept.

I have a guy, a great guy, willing to take a chance on me and maybe it's time I put myself out there and give him that chance. But I have conditions—two, in fact—a brown-eyed and a blue-eyed—conditions that will always come first in my life.

I run after him, out the door and across the street. "Dex?" I call just before he enters the hotel. "Wait up."

He stops one block ahead of me, and turns back. Hands shoved in pockets, head tilted down, but his curious eyes look up to watch me run toward him. Stopping with a few feet between us and with harsh breaths from running, I say, "You're right."

The hope his voice held earlier is all but gone when he asks, "About what?"

"About us."

"What about us?"

"The truth is, I can't be frivolous with my emotions, but you're right, we aren't wrong. What we did isn't wrong. You've changed and though not everyone can see it, I do. It's been amazing to watch your transformation from the guy I knew years ago to the man you are now. But I need time—"

"I understand."

"No, I don't know that you do. I loved Cory. I'm not saying that to hurt your feelings, but it's something I struggle with every day.

He's not here anymore, but I am and I don't want to be alone."

"He left us all. I've tried to hold back, for your sake. To not require you to think about me, but I fucking miss him, every single day. I miss my friend. I know you loved him. So did I. He was the only one in my life I could always rely on. That void will never be filled, Rochelle. I'm not trying to fill his shoes. I'm not him. All I can be is me and hope it's good enough."

"Oh Dex. I'm sorry. I know his death has affected everyone. But it's time I focused on my family. I have to put my kids first. I want to. They deserve that much and more." He nods as I continue. "So I have an offer for you. I'll understand if you're not ready to take us all on. I promise I will. But what if we start off slowly? Maybe you can spend some time at my house when the tour's over?"

"What do you mean? Like hang out?"

"Yes, let's start off as friends, real friends, friends who spend time together because I come as a package deal. You're young and not responsible for anyone else, but when you date me, you date my boys. So what if you maybe came over for lunch or dinner one night? It will give you a chance to see the reality of what you're getting into before things get too deep."

"Your boys know who I am, Rochelle."

"But they don't know you. It's the only offer I can make."

"So two steps back and we slow things down?" A section of his hair falls forward and as much as I want to touch the soft strands again, I don't. "You tell me when," he says, "and I'll be there."

"Deal." I stick out my hand, another offer of my sincerity to give him the chance he deserves.

He accepts the offer. "Deal."

We shake on it, his warmth coursing through my body. When we part, I go to him and wrap my arms around his middle because despite the deal we just made, he needs to know that our time together mattered to me. I tilt my mouth up toward his ear, and whisper, "Just in case you think I'm being completely selfless here, I'm not. I remember every kiss we shared and everything we did that night."

I see his mouth broaden into a smile and he kisses me on the forehead. "Good to know I'm not alone."

"You're not. I'm just not as brave as you."

He pulls back to look me in the eyes. "You're braver than you know yourself to be."

"I'm only brave because you give me strength." I glance down and when I look back up, I feel like we might just kiss again. Licking my bottom lip, I take in a deep breath, but when I release it, he says, "Two steps back for now, but one day, Rochelle Floros, I'm gonna be the man of your dreams."

I don't dare mention that I've already had a few dreams of the naughty variety about him. "What about my reality?"

He walks backward a couple of steps, a self-assured grin on his face. With a cocked eyebrow and two thumbs to his chest, he replies, "Right here. Reality and fantasy all rolled into one, baby."

Putting my hand on my hip, I can't stop the smile he brings out of me. "A bit cocky, aren't we?"

"I'm very cocky, but you already know that from the first time we fuc—"

"Oh my God, I meant arrogant, not your, your—"

"That works too."

"Pfft. Go. Go before I feel the need to knock that chip off your shoulder."

He reaches the door and pulls it open. "We'll be knocking, but it will have nothing to do with chips."

"What about shoulders?" I tease.

"I always knew you were a kinky girl." He goes inside and I'm left standing there like a fool in the middle of the sidewalk with a huge goofy grin on my face.

I pull my phone out and check the calendar. The band gets back to LA in eleven days, so I text *Dex:* ***How about lunch in twelve days?***

*Dex:* ***Going out or staying in?***

I type back: ***I'll cook for you.***

*Dex:* ***What are you going to cook?***

*Me:* ***Are you coming over or what?***

*Dex:* ***I love when you beg. It's sexy.***

*Me:* ***I'm not begging. I'm asking.***

*Dex:* ***Since you're asking so nicely, the answer is yes.***

*Me:* ***You're incorrigible.***

*Dex:* ***I've been called worse.***

*Me:* ***I just bet you have.***

*Dex:* ***Stop bugging me. I need some beauty sleep before we leave for Boston. You think I wake up this hot naturally? Oh wait, that's right, I do.***

I burst out laughing and reply: ***LOL. On that note, Mr. Humble, sweet dreams.***

*Dex:* ***Forget sweet. I'm hoping for wet if I have my way, sweetheart.***

My eyes go wide and my mouth drops open. I quickly shove my phone into my back pocket and hurry inside the hotel. Within minutes, I'm knocking on the door.

He opens his door wide and with a wry smile while acting innocent, he asks, "And to what do I owe the pleasure?"

I walk under his arm and slip inside his room. "I could use some sleep too."

As I strip off my shirt and jeans, he suddenly gets this cocky expression on his face as he lets the door slam shut. "Don't let me stop you from getting naked or anything, but what happened to two steps back?"

In just my bra and thong, I sit down on the edge of the bed. He moves closer as if he has no other choice. His eyes trace up and down my body leaving a trail of goosebumps in the wake of his heated gaze. I lean back on my elbows while he stands between my legs, his fingertips touching the tops of my thighs and slowly sliding down on the inside.

My thighs tighten in response and he smirks. With a teasing smirk of my own, I crawl up the bed, giving him full view of my ass, climb under the covers, and snuggle in before we cross a line we know we shouldn't. I hear his heavy, impatient sigh as I pat the bed next to me. "Well, c'mon. Let's get our sleep on."

His shirt is over his head and off, his jeans dropped just as fast. He slips under the covers and I immediately move to lie against his side. We lay there in silence for a few minutes. I find comfort when I hear his steady heartbeat, then whisper, "How about just one step back?"

"Deal," he says, then kisses the top of my head. He stretches and turns off the bedside lamp and gets more comfortable while I stay wrapped around him. "I think I'm gonna like this stepping back friends business."

# 6

This new plan, the deal I made with Dex, seemed like such a good idea at first. But when I woke up in his arms just before noon, I wanted to stay. I couldn't though. He had to get up to catch a flight to Boston for the next show and I needed to get back to LA.

This was only supposed to be a short trip when I planned it. But something about having his body wrapped around me made me want to see if Janice wouldn't mind keeping the boys another night.

"You should probably go," Dex says, his voice husky with sleep.

"What?" I tilt up to find him smirking down at me. "Why do you say that?"

"Because this feels too good. And if you're not careful, I might have to steal you away and take you with me."

"What if I came voluntarily?"

"That's the plan." The double meaning is exaggerated by his hand slowly running up the side of my body and back down again.

He sits up and rubs his face before pushing his hair back. "So you gonna come?"

"And you call me dirty."

He laughs, then says, "Not dirty, kinky." He leans in really close, his lips against my ear. "There's a difference and I'm more than happy to explore that kinky side with you... and the dirty side."

"You're too kind," I say in response to his words tickling my neck and making me tingle in other ways. "Thanks for volunteering."

And there's that smile again, the one that shoots straight to my heart when he says, "I'm here to please, sweetheart."

I really shouldn't like his arrogant side as much as I do, but I don't bother hiding it. "You're making it very hard to leave this bed."

"Then don't. Stay with me. Stay in bed with me. We'll catch a later flight or rent a car and drive together."

"You're making me an offer I'm finding hard to resist. I want to go. I really do, but I need to check. It would only be for one night—"

"I'll take one more night over nothing."

"You have a show tonight. Sound check, meetings—"

His fingers run along my cheekbone, pushing back strands of hair that lie across my cheek. "Don't think about the time we don't have. Think of what we have when we're together."

I close my eyes under his soothing touch. "I'm scared, Dex. What if this doesn't work out?"

"Don't be scared." After drawing in a slow breath, he says, "If all we ever have is one more night together, the rest of the nights won't matter."

I can tell he wants to kiss me as we stare into each other's eyes. I'm not opposed to the idea myself as our breaths mingle between us. I close my eyes and lean forward, but instead of a kiss, he whispers, "One step back." A gentle reminder of what I put in place as he drags his fingertip lightly over my lips, his gaze savoring them.

"And what if I don't want to take a step back?" I sulk, rejection covering my heart.

"That's my good cuddling skills talking right there. Once I let you leave, you'll realize you were just under my spell."

Now my cynical side comes out. "Cuddling skills, really?" I roll onto my back.

"Yeah, cuddling skills. I'm a master, but it's not something I work on. It's like a gift the ladies can't resist." My silence must speak for me because he adds, "Trust me, once you leave my arms, you'll realize how powerless you really were while in the throes of my amazing cuddles."

"I didn't know guys cuddled?"

"Damn right guys cuddle, but I just happen to be a master, an artiste, an expert in the field."

"Does that make you a cudster or an arddle?"

"I'm thinking it makes me more of a perddle, but that's just a personal preference."

I sit up. "I'm gonna get up now and see if my common sense comes back."

"Wait." He grabs my waist. "Just one more time."

I tilt my head, then start to laugh. "Okay, I'll let you cuddle me one more time." I snuggle into his side and his arms tighten around me. When my body relaxes, my eyes start to close again.

"I win. I'm the cuddle king."

Even though I love being with him this way, I roll my eyes and sarcastically repeat after him, "You win, Oh great cuddler." A minute more in his arms and I finally look up. “Are we still doing this?”

“You’re welcome to stay as long as you like. I’m happy to oblige.”

“What about Boston? Do I get these kinds of snuggles there?”

“If you come to Boston, I’ll give you whatever you like.”

“Tempting.” When his erection presses against my leg, I say, “So are you. Too tempting most of the time.”

He drags his finger slowly down my neck and over my collarbone, stopping just at the top of my right breast. “I’m struggling here, but for you, I’ll live with tempting for now.”

“C’mon, I have a surprise for you,” Dex says. We arrived in Boston just over an hour ago and went straight to the arena for sound check.

Typically, no one would take notice of us because they’re so used to seeing us around, but not today. While I follow Dex down the hall, I see the stares, the looks, the curiosity in their eyes as the stagehands go about their jobs, setting up for the performance tonight. But I’m not bothered by it. He leads me onto the stage where a single chair with a guitar on it sits with a spotlight shining down, lighting the area. “What is this?” I ask.

“I want you to play.” There’s a spark in his eyes that I bet gets women to do whatever he asks of them.

But with the fear beginning to rise inside of me I can’t think about that. With wide eyes, I ask, “You want me to play for you?”

“No, I want you to play for you.”

“On stage? Why?”

"Because I don't think you do anymore and you should."

I stare at him, my stomach tying up in knots, then I try to defend myself. "I'm busy is all. No biggie." I shrug to add to the casualness I'm trying to portray.

"No biggie? You used to love to play," he says. "I remember watching you in the studio on the last album. You come alive when you play."

"I'm busy. I'm tired. I don't have the same passion for it that I used to."

This time he stares at me like he's trying to work through some complicated equation... or maybe he already has me all figured out. Maybe he can see through the façade I try so hard to put on every day. "I don't have to prove anything, Dex." I cross my arms, adamant.

"Nope, you don't have anything to prove. Not to me or anyone else, except maybe yourself."

"I don't understand what you're doing?"

"Don't you?"

"No, I don't."

A loud thud behind me causes me to look over my shoulder. Johnny sits in a chair near the other, guitar in hand. "You lead. I'll follow," he says.

I can't hide my panic. "No. I don't have time for music anymore."

"Wow," Johnny says, looking disappointed. "That's pretty damn sad, Rochelle."

"Sad as it may be, I have different priorities these days."

Johnny leans forward resting his elbows on his knees, chin in hand, rubbing it in thought. "Music isn't something that comes in and out of our lives when it's convenient. Music defines us, filling the holes that others have left behind."

My hands start shaking. “I can’t. I just can’t.” Walking around Dex, I head for the side of the stage and rush down the steps to the exit doors. The sun blinds me when the door flies open. I move to the side, away from the door, and into the shadows. It’s been well over a year since I last played and I remember every second of it. The studio recordings took every ounce of what was left of me. The guys wouldn’t take no for an answer, so I filled in for Cory on the last record. But once we were done, I was done as well. The nightmares started and I haven’t gone near any of the guitars in our house since. That part of my life has been packed away just like the instruments.

“It’s times like these that I still wish I smoked.”

I spy Johnny out of the corner of my eye and my shoulders drop in ease from seeing my friend. “You don’t?” I ask.

He leans against the cinderblock wall and shakes his head. “Holliday would kick my ass. She has this seventh sense that alerts her when I’m screwing up.”

“She wants you to live a long life.”

“Yeah, I guess she does,” he says with a smile that’s more reflective of his love for his wife than for me.

“Holli loves you.”

“We all have the capacity to love more than we think we’re capable of.”

“Are you talking about Holli or me?”

“Might be about you.”

“Since when did my love life become the band’s pet project?” I lightly kick his foot with mine.

“When did you stop playing?”

“The day I left the studio.”

“Why?”

Taking a moment, I look down at my shoes, noticing all the

scuff marks on them. “Music was something I did with Cory, for him, because of him.”

“You played before you met him.”

“I messed around.”

“No, you’re just forgetting the details.” He pushes off the wall and reaches for the doorknob. “That passion still lives inside you.” He pats his chest over his heart.

“Then how do I find it again?”

“It will find you when you’re ready.” The door closes and I’m left there in awe. His lyrics speak so justly of the man behind them and Johnny Outlaw sure knows how to deliver a line.

I go back inside and find Dex in the dressing room waiting on sound check to begin. “Hey, gotta sec?” I sit down next to him.

“For you.” He leans back on the couch, his sticks in hand while tapping rhythmically on his leg.

“I want to thank you for what you did. It was very thoughtful.”

“We’ve had some good sessions over the years. We should do that again... maybe when I come over in a few weeks.”

Bouncing my palm lightly on his knee, I say, “Maybe. I might need some more time with that too.”

His drumsticks pause and he says, “Time is something we take for granted.”

“I think I know that better than anyone.”

The beat continues as he starts up again and says, “I lost my dad when I was eight years old.”

Taken by surprise by the admission, I exhale. I knew his dad had died before I met him, but I didn’t know Dex was so young. My heart thumps in my chest and I place my hand over his hand, stilling his rhythm. His sticks stop and he takes them in one hand, then covers mine with the other.

A guy opens the door and I pull my hand away reflexively. He says, "Sound check is up. The new snare is on the kit and tested, but they want final approval."

I lay back and push Dex up. "Go. I'll be around later after the show."

With that smile that drives me wild, he asks, "You sure you don't want to join us on stage?"

"I'm positive. Thanks for the offer though."

I watch his ass as he walks out the door, simply because he has a great ass. Then I kick my feet up on the coffee table and drop my head back while closing my eyes. The panic has subsided and my heart becomes all mushy thinking about his sweet gesture. Shaking my head, I smile. Dex is a very unexpected, but a wonderful surprise in my life.

TR

I head back to the hotel to change before the show. Lara traveled to Boston on an earlier flight than us and is checked into our room already. Having her there helps keep the drunken lines with Dex from blurring. She knows to hold me accountable for my actions.

After my shower, I lay on the bed as she digs through her suitcase. With a shirt in her hands, she asks, "What do you think about the red, one shoulder number for tonight?"

"With the dark jeans? Sexy."

"Black ankle boots or black shimmer heels?"

"Ankle boots."

"Sex with Dex or kissing only?"

I stare at the back of her head, surprised by her question, but not shocked. When she turns around, she grins with her hand on her hip. "I can tell you're into him. You can't hide the truth from me."

"I like him, but it feels self-indulgent."

She sits on the edge of the bed and I move over to give her more space. "Since when is happiness self-indulgent?"

"You know what I mean."

"Yes, I do, but here's the reality. You are a single woman, whether you wanted to be or not. It's been years. You don't have to forget, but don't do your heart the injustice of never letting it race again either."

"What will people say if Dex and I do end up dating?"

"What people? Because everyone that is important in your life wants you to be happy. If it's happy with Mr. Smooth and Sexy, then even better."

"You think he's sexy?"

"God, Rochelle. You were totally right. He's hot, hotter than even I remembered and I remember him being pretty damn hot. I think his old hairstyle, that ratty bandana, and sunglasses hid that sexy man for too long."

"He smells good too."

Her eyebrows shoot up. "Oh really?"

"Yep," I say, nodding. "He does."

She giggles and that makes me giggle too. It feels good to talk to someone about Dex. It feels good to be unburdened from the guilt that's weighed me down for so long and just feel giddy again.

"Did you sleep with him yet?"

No one knows of our one night years ago, except Tommy, and I'm not telling now. "Lara!"

"I'll take that as a yes. I'm not judging by the way. I'd drop my panties for those captivating brown eyes any day."

She gets up and grabs the red top again.

To move this topic along to something else, I say, "We need to leave in thirty if we're gonna make it to the show in time."

TR

Johnny looks back at Dex sitting on his pedestal as he beats down the end of the song on his drum kit, closing the show. Dex gets up, walks to the edge of the stage and the crowd goes nuts. He launches the drumsticks into the audience and I shake my head. He pays a fine every time he does that, but he still does it because he knows how much the fans love it. He's been warned a million times not to do it, but I kind of love that he still does. Johnny exits the stage first, then Dex, Kaz, and Derrick trailing.

"Good show," I say as they pass. They're usually moody or high-strung after a performance, so I like to give them space until they're grounded again. Lara and I walk to the exit, wanting some fresh air because it smells backstage. A lot of sweaty men moving heavy equipment and lights around will do that.

With my back against the grey wall, I slide down and balance as Lara lights a cigarette. The doors open again and Kaz and Dex are there. They nod in acknowledgment, but continue talking about some screw up that pissed off Johnny. Dex winks at me before telling Kaz, "Fuck, just hit the riff. It's not hard. You do it in rehearsal." Dex lights up, then brings the cigarette to his mouth and inhales. The action is sexier than it should be. I'm not sure if it's the way he holds it or the way his lips caress it, but either way, I can't stop staring.

Through smoke-filled exhales, Kaz says, "No one notices that shit."

"Everybody fucking notices," Dex snaps, aggravated. "Fans

know these songs inside and out. How the fuck do you mess up a song you've been playing for two years?"

"Fuck you," Kaz gripes. "Maybe it wasn't a mess up but my own fucking spin on it."

Dex is quick with his response, "Nobody wants your spin on it, man. They want Cory's."

Kaz takes a drag and then says, "Fuck that music. That music is dead just like him. It's time for us to make our own."

I'm on my feet, moving to the door.

Kaz grabs my arm. "Oh fuck, Rochelle. I'm sorry. I didn't mean it like that."

I yank my arm free and go inside, not running though it's all I want to do. I can't breakdown in front of them. I can't show my weakness, or how affected I still get. I go as fast as I can, now running despite all the strength I try to pretend to have. But I'm stopped and pulled into a dark doorway. I gasp, the sudden impact a surprise and I look up into sympathetic, but warm eyes.

My own eyes start to water, the tears forcing themselves out. Dex pulls me against him. His scent—sweat from the show under a clean shirt—sexy and strong, masculine, but overpowering. His large hand covers the back of my head and he strokes. I breathe him in, finding the comfort I need.

"Rochelle."

We jump apart when Kaz appears. "Rochelle, I'm sorry. I really am. You know Cory was my idol."

Slowly stepping back into the light, I clear my throat and steady myself. "Then treat him with the respect he deserves. He wrote that song, the one you were complaining about, when he was nineteen. It came from somewhere deep inside, somewhere slightly dark. You don't get that. You play notes that you feel forced to play, so you're pushing back. I *do* get that. But The Resistance isn't about you, Kaz. It's about the music and a band as a whole. You play over an hour of new songs. The encore will always be about the hits and what the fans love. So do us all the courtesy of setting your ego aside and playing for them instead of yourself."

I push past him and head for the dressing room, the anger hitting its stride by the time I open the door. "Rochelle?" I hear Dex calling my name, but I walk past Johnny and Kaz, and grab my bag from the floor.

When I turn around, I run right into Dex's chest, his arms around me again and I'm suddenly all too aware of the other guys watching us.

Johnny stands. "What happened?"

Feeling my face heat from them being privy to the intimacy between me and Dex, I free myself. Just a glance at Johnny, then to Kaz, and I see the expressions on their face, the disapproval on Johnny's, confusion on Kaz.

"What the fuck, Dex?" Johnny asks—protective brother voice in place as he straightens his shoulders back.

I try to ease things between them before I leave. "It's okay, Johnny. He didn't do anything. It's me. I just need to go. I'll see you back in LA."

"Rochelle? Wait up," he says, catching up to me in the corridor.

"Dude, really. I'm okay. I just don't want to be here right now." I see Dex out of the corner of my eye, Lara just beyond him coming inside with Kaz. "I'll be fine. I'll see you at home."

Johnny nods, knowing when to back off. "Be safe."

"I will." I walk in the opposite direction, leaving them all behind. With a quick glance back over my shoulder, the scene fades to black as I focus ahead of me.

TR

As I pack my clothes, a light knock on the hotel door makes me pause and sigh. I'm guessing it's Lara or Dex. I'm hoping it's not Johnny. He sees right through me and I don't have the energy to lie to him.

When I open the door, Dex is there. I smile automatically while leaning against the wall. "What are you doing here? Shouldn't you be out partying after the show?"

"I didn't want to go." An urgent kiss lands on my lips, the sweet pressure trapped between desperation and passion. I find the line often blurs when I kiss him as well. "I don't want you to go either." Sliding my hands down his arms to his wrists, he lifts them to caress my neck. "Sometimes we're assholes. It was Kaz's turn tonight. I'm sorry."

"I know he didn't mean it, but when he said it... I don't know anymore," I say, shrugging. "I don't want him forgotten."

"He won't be. He's a legend, Rochelle." His lips replace his hands on my neck. "But let's leave all that for now. Right here together, we can be us—no baggage, no past, no witnesses. Just us, here together."

I kiss him, needing him close. When our lips part, I look into his eyes just as he opens his. I whisper, "No past. Just us with no judgments or expectations."

He kisses me again, then says, "Back in LA, we have to be responsible and do what's right. Once there, we can go back to square one, not for me, but for Neil and CJ. We'll start over, the way we should have two years ago."

"You're okay with that?"

"No," he replies, making me laugh. "But I'll do whatever it takes to spend more time with you. Anyway, your boys seem pretty cool. I mean Neil is named after one of the best drummers in the world, after all. The kid can't be that bad."

I giggle, the lighthearted moment easing the heavy from before. Dropping my forehead to his chest, I ask, "What about tonight?"

"Tonight, you're mine."

*Is this too much too fast? Am I the only one who's concerned about what the future holds?* "Are you worried?"

"Shit yeah, I worry. I worry that this may be the last time I get to kiss you or feel your breath on my skin. I worry that I'll never get to hear your heart racing because you're near me. So yeah, I worry. But tonight, let's not talk about tomorrow or what happens after. Let's just live in the here—"

"Live in the now." I pull him inside by his shirt and let the door slam closed, deciding to do just that. I kiss him again and again while walking backward into the room, leaving yesterday to the past and tomorrow to be dealt with another day.

We tumble onto the bed, our bodies entwined, his lips pressed to the skin of my collarbone. With one knee between his legs and his knee between mine, we move together in a flurry of overdue movements. I tug at his collar, trailing kisses across his shoulder. His strong hands flex and grip as he holds me at the waist and slides them up, his thumb rubbing gentle circles against the side of my breasts.

He moves on top of me, his erection against my stomach, his lips finding and caressing mine. Breathless, I drop my head back. "I want you. I want you so much, Dex. So much."

His hands stop flexing, his lips stop kissing, his body stills while his breathing remains jagged over my cheek. I'm about to say something just as he pauses and looks away. His fingers tap lightly across my ribs and he leans down to whisper, "You deserve more than this."

"No." I release my breath and hold him by the jaw, making him look at me. "I'm good. This is good. The here and now, remember. Tonight is all that matters."

"Rochelle, you deserve dates and flowers, romantic dinners, and for me to show you that I'm good enough to spend time with your family."

"You're good enough, Dex. It wasn't about you not being good enough for me or my ki—" He kisses me, ending my plea. As soon as our lips part, I continue, "Kids. So please don't think otherwise."

Chuckling, he runs his finger down my nose and lingers on my lips, stopping me from talking. "Here's the truth of the matter. If we do this... again, there's no going back to square one tomorrow. Not for me. I won't be able to act like I don't care about you, like I haven't thought about you every day since we were together last. So it's easier to stop now than later."

With a discouraged sigh, I say, "You're stronger than me, Dex."

"No, I just know my greatest weakness is the woman beneath me right now." He rolls over sighing in a way that shows frustration has set in. Turning his head to me, he says, "I want to fuck you so bad, but I also want to do all that making love stuff too. And if we do that, I can't pretend it didn't happen." He sits up and walks to the other side of the room, leaning his back against the wall.

I prop myself up on my elbows, caught by the heaviness of the emotions I'm suddenly feeling for him.

"Go to sleep tonight. Fly home tomorrow." He walks into the

shadow of the entryway. "I'll see you in a few weeks."

I hear the door open as I fall back on the bed, my own sexual frustration setting in. But just when I hear the door close, the weight of his body lands on top of me and he kisses me hard. Surprised, my eyes fly open, but then I go for it just like him and kiss him back with just as much passion. He pushes off of me again and stands between my legs. "I make very few promises in life, but this one I can make to you. Rochelle Floros, I'm coming for you. It's our time, so get ready for me." He turns abruptly and leaves me sitting there stunned... and tingly... and then smiling, my heart full of happiness and so much more for that man.

# 7

Lara came back to the room this morning and found me asleep. She's been giving me a hard time on our morning flight back to LA ever since. "That grin on your face sure was unexpected."

"I wasn't grinning. I was sleeping."

"Well, whatever you were dreaming about had you smiling like a fool in your sleep."

I roll my eyes. "And what did you do after the concert last night?"

She looks away briefly before she says, "Met some friends at the bar downstairs. Once you texted me you were going to bed, I thought it best not to bring the party up to the room."

"Thank you."

"You're welcome. Now what brought on that smile? It was polar opposite of what I expected to find when you left the show."

I figure the truth will hush her up. "I had three orgasms last night."

Her eyes go wide. “Eh, er... wow. Umm, okay. Huh.” She adjusts in her seat and says, “I’m impressed. Did you have these on your own or did someone special, someone like Dex, induce these?”

“All on my own.” I just don’t mention that Dex was the inspiration behind each one. Seems every time I close my eyes, I can still feel his lips on me and the gentle sucking he did to my collarbone.

“Ew, are you gonna cum again right now? Wipe that expression off your face.”

I burst out laughing and slap her arm. “Stop teasing me. You wanted the truth. Well, you got it.”

“I love a great masturbation session.”

“Oh my God, keep your voice down, Lara.”

An older woman in the seat in front of us peers back through the crack between the seats. When my eyes meet her judgy ones, she frowns and turns back around quickly.

Lara shrugs not caring if she’s heard by everyone on the plane or not. “Wouldn’t it be hot to have sex with the pilot while he was flying the plane?”

Shaking my head, I say, “I’m not really partial to planes.”

Her hand covers mine on the shared armrest. “I’m sorry.”

“It’s okay.”

“So maybe you’re more a mailman type of gal. You know, a guy who can really deliver his package?”

My head goes back and I scrunch my nose. “What 80’s porn have you been watching?”

“Not porn, just my imagination... Okay, some porn, but we all watch porn every now and then.”

“Maybe I should watch some,” I say, actually considering the idea.

“If you had three orgasms all by yourself, I don’t think you need porn. Your dirty thoughts are good enough."

"I have some good references."

She leans closer. "Do tell."

"No, I think I'll hold onto them a little longer."

"If it makes a difference, I saw how Dex looks at you over the last few days. You could have him if you wanted."

Looking out the window of the plane into the great blue yonder, I reply, "It makes all the difference in the world." Three more hours on the flight left to go, so I lean my head against the window and close my eyes. "I'm gonna try to get some sleep."

TR

After thanking Janice for keeping my kids, I drag my suitcase into the bedroom. The boys follow me in and we all lay on my king size bed together, cartoons on the large flat screen hanging on the wall. Despite that they were engrossed in the show, I'm instantly smothered in kisses and hugs and I love it. My boys take the opportunity to bounce on the bed, and despite the no jumping rule usually in place, I let them. Their happy faces are worth the potential for broken springs.

"Mama, I love you," CJ says, and I grab him mid-jump and snuggle him to my side.

"Come here, buddy," I say to Neil.

He bounces to his knees and then drops to my open arm, which I close around him. I kiss each of their heads and smile. "I missed you guys so much. Did you miss me?"

"Yes," they say in unison. Then Neil adds, "You were with Uncle Johnny on tour?"

"Yes," I reply, wanting to reintroduce them to Dex soon

hopefully. “And Dex, the drummer. Do you remember him?”

“He gave me the drumsticks.”

“Yes, that’s right.”

“I don’t member,” CJ says.

I rough up his hair. “You’ll see him soon and you’ll remember. You’ve met him many times.” I reach over and declare, “Ticklefest.”

After lots of giggles and catching up on their days while I was away, I start dinner. I want to make something that shows how much I love them, warming their souls while filling their tummies. I decide on homemade lasagna, which they devour, making me happy. We read books and then I tuck them in.

When I lay down in my bed, I turn on the TV. My mind drifts away from the match-making show and I think of Dex, wondering what he’s doing tonight. It was a travel day for them and no performance, so I don’t know if he’s going out or staying in and resting up. It makes me realize that I don’t really know him—his habits, his hobbies, his routine—at all. But I want to and this time I don’t feel bad for that.

I roll to my side and smile before catching up on the show, my nightmares a little less this night.

Why does a simple text seem monumental right now? This should be easy, I tell myself as I pace my kitchen. Looking down at the phone in my hand, the screen glows bright white waiting for me to type something. I feel like I’m asking Dex out on a date. Wait, *am I*? What seemed like a casual get-to-know-you-better plan has suddenly turned into a big date. Oh no. I turn my phone off, not ready for this at all.

Two hours later while lying on the couch, I kick my feet up on the arm and go to my message app again. This time I'm determined. I start to type: ***Hi Stranger, just wondering if...*** Ugh! Delete. Delete. Delete. *Stranger? Really?* Ugh!

***Hi, hope you're doing well. I know you probably need some down time when you get home next week, but I was wondering if you want to come over for a meal. I can cook for you. I'm sure it's been a while since you've had food not delivered by room service. I'll deliver it to the table though and all you have to do is show up. We can hang out, maybe play a board game with the boys. Tag is also a big favorite of theirs. Anyway, let me know.***

I hit send before I can chicken out. Staring down at the rambling message, I'm so embarrassed. If there was a way to take that back, I would.

My phone buzzes in my hand when a message appears. It's a lot sooner than I expected. ***Long time, no talk, Stranger. It's good to hear from you. What day?***

I laugh at the 'stranger' then type: ***You get back on Monday. How about Wednesday?***

*Dex:* ***How about Tuesday?***

I might be blushing that he wants to see me as much as I want to see him. ***Tuesday is great.***

*Dex:* ***What time?***

*Me:* ***5 p.m.?***

*Dex:* ***I'll be there.***

*Me:* ***See you then.***

*Dex:* ***Feel free to text me anytime, dollface.***

*Dollface?* Now my cheeks really heat. *Me:* ***Text soon, champ.*** Champ!!! *What the hell am I doing?* He's making me senseless.

*Dex:* ***Lol. Okay, champ is interesting...***

*Me:* ***Ignore me. Just carry on with your day like that never happened.***

*Dex:* ***I'll try, but it'll be hard.***

My eyebrows rise up when I read 'It'll be hard.'

*Dex:* ***Did I just type that?***

*Me:* ***You did.***

*Dex:* ***I'll forget about champ, but you need to forget about things being hard over here in Dallas.***

*Me:* ***Now that will be 'hard' to do.***

*Dex:* ***Are you sexting me?***

*Me:* ***You're the one sexting I believe. You started it first.***

*Dex:* ***I'll be happy to finish it too. See you next Tuesday.***

*Me:* ***Another funny. Like C U Next Tuesday.***

*Dex:* ***Let's stop while we're a'head'***

*Me:* ***You're right. Stop.***

I laugh and set my phone down on the couch cushion next to me, but it buzzes again. I look at the screen and read: ***Just in case I wasn't clear, I'm really looking forward to seeing you again.***

*Me:* ***Me too.***

Once again, I find myself pacing in the kitchen, nervous. I'm roasting a chicken and I don't even know if Dex eats meat. How have I known him this long and I don't know if he eats meat or not. I think he does, but it's been a long time since we had a proper meal together. What if he's gone Vegan in that time? I poke the parsnips with a fork to check for tenderness and then decide that I should make a salad. It's a healthy meal all around and if he's gone Vegan then he'll have the two sides, at least.

The doorbell rings and the kids go running. I throw the fork on the counter and dash for the door, hoping to beat them to it. Dex knows the code to the yard gate, but I still want to be the one who greets him. "Wait, wait, wait. Let me answer it."

The boys stop and let me in front of them. I take a deep breath and straighten my shirt before opening the door. "Hi," I say a little breathless. I'm hoping he thinks it's sexy. Though I was expecting him, I'm still caught off guard by how attractive he is. I waver a bit, grasping the doorknob tightly to ground me.

"Hi," Dex says smiling at me. He's holding a bouquet of flowers made up of lilacs, peonies, and miniature white roses. "These are for you." Leaning in, he kisses me on the cheeks. "You look beautiful."

"Thank you," I reply, impressed by the romantic gesture and look away as I feel my cheeks heat.

Turning back to his touch, his hand rubbing my arm, I see he has come bearing more gifts. He whips out some Fun Dips for the kids, shaking them in the air. "Brought these too."

"Yay!" The kids jump up and down in excitement, snatching them from his hands.

"That was nice," I say, then turn to the kids. "You can have them after dinner. Not before."

After a round of disappointed grumblings from them, Dex says, "No biggie."

"I'll let you deal with the sugar high later." With a laugh, I turn and nod toward the kitchen. "Come on in. I need to check on the chicken." But I stop and turn around abruptly. "Do you eat chicken? I don't even know if you eat chicken."

"I eat chicken." Relieved, I start back to the kitchen, but he stops me and takes my pinky, and says, "It's good to see you again." Slowly tugging me closer, he wraps his arms around me and hugs me.

I relish the closeness as I wrap my arms around him. "It's good to see you too. Thanks for coming over." I hear him gulp and I gulp in response, but his arms around me feel too good to get hung up in the newness and unknown of what's ahead for us. So I take a deep breath, breathing him in, and smile. "You smell good."

"So do you. You smell like roasted chicken." He chuckles.

Pushing off of him playfully, I say, "That's because I'm roasting a chicken."

"Cool."

"Drink?"

"What are you having?"

I enter the kitchen, but sneak a peek back at him. He's wearing a white T-shirt that highlights his tan arms, fitted around the muscles of his biceps. His jeans are a loose, but not baggy and he has on lace-up Vans. To top it off, I can tell he's freshly showered, not just from inhaling his clean, manliness back in the living room, but his hair is shiny and kind of enviable. But it's the devilish smile on his face and devious look in his eyes that makes me reply, "Wine. You? I have beer, cocktails, soda, water, milk?"

"Did you just offer me milk?"

"Yeah, it's a popular beverage around here."

He just continues smiling. "How about a soda?"

"Sure."

I make our drinks and tend to dinner one more time before leading Dex outside where the boys are running around on the swings chasing each other. We sit in patio chairs and watch for a few minutes before CJ comes over, and says, "I member you."

With a big smile that shows off Dex's dimples, he says, "I member you too, big guy."

"Why are you here?"

I lean forward, taking CJ by the arm and pull him in front of me. Holding him by the waist, I wiggle him. "Dex is here for dinner and to play with us."

CJ's eyes light up. "We like Marco Polo, but Mama doesn't let us play much since we run into things and get boo-boos."

"Ahh," Dex responds. "I can understand. How about tag or hide-and-go-seek?"

"Hide seek," my little guy says, jumping up in excitement. "Let's play. Neil, Hide seek."

Dex stands up, offering me a hand up. I take it, catching his eye on me as I stand. He looks out over the yard and announces, "I'm it. I'll count to twenty and then I'm gonna come find you." He turns to go to the door, pinching my side as he does. "Better hide fast. I'm coming for you."

The words echo the ones he told me back in Boston before I left. And I like hearing them again.

As soon as he hides his face in his hands, the boys and I run for cover. The boys go for the bushes in the corners. They're tiny and can hide in there easily. There aren't many spots for me, so I run to the side of the house and squat down on the other side of the garden. I hear him announce, "Twenty. Ready or not, here I come," and I don't know what it is about this game, but butterflies fill my stomach as I sit in anticipation of being found and trying to make it back to home base untagged.

Peeking toward the corner of the house, waiting, I hear little joyful screams and Neil yell, "I'm safe!" That makes me smile. I know very well that Dex could catch him if he wanted. To my right, I see a Dandelion growing. Just as I reach for it, I'm grabbed, hand over my mouth as I scream, his other arm holding me to him. When he uncovers my mouth, his finger goes to his and he says, "Shhhhh."

I slide up, my back against the wood, and he leans forward. With his arms on either side of my head and his chest barely touching mine, his breath warms me over as if the sun wasn't doing a good enough job of it. "Square one is gonna be hard to do with you looking so edible."

My breath is rough as I breathe in his words. "Square one?"

His eyes crinkle at the corners and being this close to him makes my knees weak. He's so close, so close that I could kiss him. His nose runs along the side of my nose and his lips brush against mine. But he pulls back, and says, "Yes, remember? Square one." Nodding his head, he smiles, knowing damn well I'd kiss him if I had the chance. "We're starting back at square one."

I can't hide my disappointment. "Oh yeah, that's right."

He steps back and looks down at the garden. The last time we were here was on that day I don't like to think about. He says, "I knew it would all be okay." Following his gaze, I see the sprouts of new lettuce growing there. "By the way," he adds, tapping my arm. "You're it." Dex takes off running toward home base, leaving me standing there, my insides twisted in a new emotion, my body already missing his touch.

Instead of dwelling on the fact that I came up with this stupid square one idea, I run around and try to find my CJ. "Where are you, cutie pie?"

Giggles alert me to the corner bush, but the opposite one he ran for earlier. I hurry over and go to the back side, so he can make a break for home base, which he does. Thanks to my slow-motion running, he makes it safely there, grabbing onto Dex's leg and laughing. Dex rubs the top of his head, and kneels down. "You're safe, buddy. Your Mom's still it."

Breathless, I reach the patio. I think we have time for one more round before dinner, so I start to count and everyone else scatters. This time I tag Dex first, making him it, and I'm really starting to think he just might be *it* in more ways than one.

TR

I always wondered why people drank coffee at night, until now. I don't want this night to end. I don't want to miss a thing, not even a moment, so I make us coffee to make it last.

Tonight, I don't get the Dex who filled the tabloids with stories of drug abuse, legal issues, and a myriad of women. And it's not the Dex I knew five years ago or even three. This Dex is attentive and considerate, quiet at times, and contemplative. Our conversations have been lively and his outlook on his life fascinating. He's changed over the years. It's been inevitable with the fame and the money, but he's matured and has this gentle side to him that he's showing me that I'm finding very hard to resist.

But even coffee can't make the night last forever despite my best efforts. Tomorrow has requirements that come along with the new day that I can't delay. Realizing the time, I say, "Wow, it's getting late."

"It is?" He says, looking at me. Dex is lying across the couch, his lids much heavier than they were an hour ago, his smile lazy, but so attractive.

"It's just gone ten. It's quite the life I'm living here in the Valley."

"It's a good life. I've had a good time." He sits up and stretches and that V, the one that I remember so vividly from before, is exposed. "Hey, eyes up here."

*Busted.* "Sorry," I say, though I'm not really.

"It's okay. I like the way you look at me."

Tilting my head, I grin, feeling flirty. "How do I look to you?"

"How *I* look at you."

And with that, silence infiltrates, leaving me speechless. I want to get up and go to him, everything about him draws me in, but I don't because this is the first of many nights I hope to spend with him. I don't want to risk the perfection of our time together.

Standing up, he says, "Thank you for dinner. I don't think I knew you were such a good cook."

"Sheer necessity."

"You can afford a chef."

"I like to cook for my family."

"It's a good skill to have." Taking another step, he adds, "I guess I should get going."

I don't want him to though I know it's the right thing to do. I stand up as well, and ask, "So the first half of the tour's over. Got any plans for your month off?"

"Sleep."

"Eh, c'mon, you get a ton of sleep."

"I don't sleep well on the road. I never have."

I nod, and agree. "I never did either."

"At least you had someone," he says so easily.

I know he doesn't mean anything more than the words themselves, but the reminders are hard to live with sometimes. "Yeah."

Dex comes closer and tugs at my shirt. "Did I just make it awkward?"

"No... okay, maybe a little, but it's real and I can't deny a real moment. Cory was in my life. He's not anymore. I didn't have a say in the decision. But for the record, I still struggle all the time, but it's good for you to see, to know who I am now. I'm not the same girl you met ten years ago."

"No," he whispers, pushing my hair back over my shoulders. "You're not. You're the woman that..." Looking away from me, he backs up suddenly. "I should go."

"Dex?" I turn and follow after him. "What were you going to say?"

He scrapes his teeth across his bottom lip and it's entirely distracting and more than a little teasing. "Square one, remember?"

"I'm beginning to hate square one." I open the door for him, deflated, maybe defeated inside.

With a chuckle, he leans in and kisses me on the forehead. It's quick and gentle, not illicit in the least, though I could use some illicit right about now. "Go to bed and get some rest. And before I go, how's Thursday looking for you?"

"What time?"

"Five o'clock."

"I'll be here with the boys."

He smiles and asks, "How about the three of you come to dinner at my house?"

"Really?"

"Really."

I lift up on my tiptoes and hug him. "We'd love to."

"See you then and if you get lonely, feel free to sext me anytime."

"I'll keep that in mind." I give him a little wink because really, what else can you do but camp it up.

After locking the door and setting the security system, I lean against the wall. I'm all smiles and full of feel-goods from the night and from the man who just left. But I'm left wondering on Thursday, *do we get to move to square two*?

# 8

Wednesday drags. I try to appreciate each day we're given, but it's hard when all I want is for it to be Thursday already. Since it's not, I do what I totally shouldn't do according to dating rules. *I text Dex.*

*Me:* ***Is it Thursday yet?***

***Five minutes later...***

*Dex:* ***I wish.***

*Me:* ***Me too.***

*Dex:* ***Want to go to lunch?***

Too excited, I rush my answer, not caring about old dating rules. *Me:* ***Yes.***

*Dex:* ***I'll pick you up in an hour.***

*Me:* ***I'll be ready.***

Now I try to play it cool and settle the giddiness that has built up inside me while hurrying to my closet to figure out what to wear. Dex makes me want to dress cool like he does, but aside from clothes that tend to lend themselves more for evening wear, I don't own much 'cool' anymore. Not sure where we're going to eat, so I pull a long striped skirt on and a fitted tank top because it's comfortable. It's also warm out, so this way I won't get all sweaty. The last thing I want to be around Dex, is sweaty. Images of the last few times we got sweaty together cross my mind, but I quickly shake them away, well aware that that kind of workout won't be happening today. No matter how much I kind of wish it could.

I finish getting ready and am going to the kitchen to retrieve my purse when the doorbell rings. After grabbing my bag, I'm greeted by Dex's smile, and just like that, my breath catches as my heart skips a beat. "Hi," I say, feeling that familiar heat rise to my cheeks.

His grin grows wider and he says, "Hi. You ready to go?"

"Yep."

In the driveway sits his 1976 Challenger. He opens the door for me then shuts it after I slide onto the leather seat. "The car's looking good," I say when he gets in.

"Sitting in a driveway for almost six months doesn't do any car good, but this Challenger is reliable."

"Where are we going?" I ask.

"Rodeo Drive."

"I didn't take you for the Beverly Hills crowd."

He pulls off my street and says, "I'm not, but my mother is. I need to pick up a birthday present from her favorite jeweler. Mind going with me before lunch?"

"Not at all." I look out the window, then turn to him again. "How are you?"

His fingers stretch over the steering wheel and I see the right side of his lips curl up. "I'm good. I'm glad to see you... too."

"I guess I'm not good at pretending, playing it cool and all that." I roll my eyes, feeling foolish.

"You don't have to be. You only have to be yourself around me. At this stage in our lives, it feels like we've known each other longer than we have."

Dragging my hands down the front of my thighs, I say, "I think we've just lived more life in the time we've known each other than before we met."

"I thought life was so fucking hard back then."

"It's much harder now."

He nods, leaning his head against the seatback, he sighs. "Let's not ever grow up."

I laugh at the irony before the humor is gone. "I think it's too late."

"It's never too late to live in Neverland."

"I thought Neverland was only for boys."

"Hmm... I don't think so." He contemplates the thought before adding, "Wendy was there."

"Wendy wasn't supposed to be there though. Peter took her there."

"Maybe we can just pretend she was meant to be there all along."

Looking down at my lap, I twist the hem of my shirt. His words always seem to have a meaning deeper than what's spoken. "I'll be Wendy," I whisper, playing along with what I hope is the right assumption. "You can show me your world, Peter."

He glances over at me, then back to the road, his brown eyes revealing how he feels. "You look beautiful." Reaching forward he turns on some music. The Nirvana song is loud, the words sad, but like the man sitting next to me, complex and completely captivating.

When we near the store, he slows down, and asks, "Do you want to wait here or come with me?"

"I'll come with you."

He pulls up to the curb and the attendant opens my door. Dex moves to the sidewalk, giving the keys to the valet as he passes. I could be mistaken but it looks as if he's reaching for my hand, then quickly tucks it into his pocket instead. When I'm by his side, I ask, "Hey, what was that?"

While checking out the surrounding area, he says, "That was the realization that Neverland only exists when we're alone. The rest of the world owns everything else."

His strides are long and determined to reach the shop, so I pick up my pace to keep up with him. "It doesn't have to be like that, Dex. Cory and I—"

He stops and looks at me. His demeanor patient, but his expression tainted when he asks, "What about you and Cory?"

*Eeks. Touchy subject.* "Um, I was just going to say that we managed to elude them most times when we went out."

Staring into my eyes, his narrow, but suddenly he checks his watch. "We're going to be late."

"Late for what?"

"Lunch," he says as the door to the jeweler opens and he walks in.

A few minutes later, he's inspecting a broach in the shape of a cat. "My mother loves cats as companions. I think it's because they're aloof like she is. She disagrees."

"I love fireflies."

With a smile, he says, "Why fireflies? They're ugly."

"But at night they transform. They're magical. I've seen them on the East Coast, but I don't think I've ever seen them here in LA."

"I don't think I have either. It's probably too smoggy." He

hands his credit card to the salesperson after approving the custom piece.

"I bet there are fireflies in Neverland."

His hand brushes against mine. "I bet there are."

TR

"You're taking me home for lunch?"

"No, I'm taking you to my mother's."

"In Beverly Hills?"

"Yes," he responds and turns left.

"You're a rich kid, aren't you, Dexter?"

He takes a right, obviously a short cut he knows by heart. "As the band's business manager, you know how much money I've made."

"You're right. I do, but I mean, you come from money. How did I never know this before?"

"I guess you had your mind on other things."

That hits hard. "I guess I did. I'm sorry for not asking about you before now. I should have. I want to know all about you and your family."

Pulling up to the white gate of the nearest driveway, he punches in a code on the keypad. As the big gates open before us, he says, "We're here." After he parks, he takes the gift from the seat between us and looks at me. "My Mother can be intimidating. Don't take her shit."

My wide eyes must show my fear. "How about I just stick close to you?"

"That's good." The mood lightens and we get out.

A butler is standing at the open front door when we approach.

"Sir, good to see you again," he says.

"Good to see you, Charles. You know I prefer Dex to Sir. This is my friend, Rochelle Floros."

"Ms. Floros. It's a pleasure to meet you," he greets me with a slight bow.

"Rochelle is fine," I say, sticking my hand out to shake his. He hesitates before accepting it. I know it goes against their formal training to accept the handshake, but I haven't been around butlers and such since I lived in Boston. Housekeepers, yes. But formally trained butlers, no.

I smile at Dex, so curious as to how he went from this fancy estate to where I met him at that dive down on Sunset. As we follow Charles inside, I whisper, "We've known each other for almost eleven years."

"Eleven next month."

"You knew that?"

"I—"

"Antonio," a woman calls as she comes toward us, the sound bouncing off the marble floors, echoing. She's dressed in a maid's uniform.

I'm kind of blown away by how different everything is here from his house in the Hills, and how I know Dex to be. But we're all shaped from our childhood so I'm interested to see if any of the rich kid from Beverly Hills still remains.

"Judith." His arms open wide. Looking at me over her shoulder, he adds, "Judith was my nanny when I was young. She stayed on as housekeeper afterward." He pulls back and smiles at her. "You're looking good. You working out?"

He's such a flirt.

She blushes with a hand on her hip, and replies, "I have a new boyfriend, so there might be a little workout involved."

"You dirty girl!" he says with a look of approval.

"Stop it." She swats his arm and he playfully ducks out of reach. "Anyway, you're here for lunch with your mother, but unfortunately, she's not here."

The good-natured moment has evaporated and a staleness fills the air. "Where is she?"

"It doesn't matter, Antonio. I've got a wonderful meal and I see you've brought a friend. Hello, I'm Judith." A warm, welcoming smile crosses her face as she reaches for my hand.

"I'm Rochelle. It's very nice to meet you."

She covers the back of my hand with her free one and asks, "Are you hungry?"

Dex cuts in before I can respond, "We're not staying."

Judith rubs his arm. "Don't let her upset you."

"She already did. Where'd she go?"

Judith hesitates then glances to me before she answers him, "The club."

He nods as he walks toward me. "She always did enjoy spending more time with a martini than her own son. Did Gage call her?"

"No, he was due in court today."

"We're gonna go." His pain evident.

"Antonio..." I hear the sadness in Judith's voice. It sounds a lot like the ache in my chest I'm feeling for him.

He takes my hands and starts walking back out the door.

Judith hurries behind us, and says, "I'm sorry she's not here."

"Not your fault. Always good to see you and go easy on your new boyfriend. Not everyone can handle a sex kitten like you in the sack," he jokes.

She laughs. "More like cougar. I haven't been a kitten for many years."

In the car, we wait at the bottom of the driveway for the gates to open. The tension in the car is building but I just want to make it go away and heal the hurt he's feeling. "I'm sorry you won't get to see your mother."

"We're gonna see her."

"We are?"

He nods, not adding to the conversation. Certain topics control his mood like a pendulum. He can be the happiest guy around and then fall to the other side when a heaviness replaces the joy. His mother is obviously one of these topics. Cory being another...

Ten minutes of listening to the engine roar as the wind blows through the open windows of the car, and we're there. Security waves him through. "Are you a member of this country club?" I ask.

"My family has generational privileges."

"Makes sense and very fancy, Mr. Caggiano. I didn't think you golfed."

He pulls into a parking spot and says, "Actually, I do golf. I even played in high school on the team for a year before I quit."

"Why'd you quit?"

"Because I hate golf clothes almost as much as I hate Chad Spears and he was Team Captain."

"Why do you hate Chad so much?"

His irritation is apparent. "Spears is a spoiled asshole." His eyes hook to his right onto mine and he says, "Listen, stay away from him. He's shiny on the outside, all packaged up and manufactured by his producer parents and Hollywood, but he's bad news."

"Are you jealous?" I tease. Wrong move on my part.

Cutting the engine, he stares at me. "I'm not jealous. The girls he dates, they're different when he's done with him. He's a user of drugs, people, and connections. He gets high off of building himself up by destroying others. Bad news, Rochelle. Don't trust him. Okay?"

I've never seen him so serious before. "Fine."

"Promise me?"

"Okay, I promise," I reply.

I'm learning there's a long history there. I mentally note that Chad Spears is another one of those hot topics for Dex.

We walk inside the main building and I follow as he begins walking faster, taking big strides to the patio on the other side. The place is busy, the ladies who lunch dressed in tennis clothes, Diane Von Furstenberg, or silk dresses. I feel out of place, definitely underdressed now.

There's a beautiful woman, flawless skin with chestnut colored hair that is reminiscent of Jackie O. She's laughing with three friends, martini glasses in front of each. He sets the present down in front of her and says, "Happy Birthday, Mother." With that out of the way, he turns around and starts walking away.

She doesn't seem surprised in the least as she calls, "Antonio. Come back here." Her tone is not demanding, but lilted with a smile, maybe to keep up appearances.

"Dex," I whisper, taking hold of his arm before he passes me. "Stop." I nod behind me and add, "It can be different. Give her a chance."

His hardened glare softens before my eyes as he looks at me. When his hand touches my face, he whispers, "You're so damn beautiful." He leaves me standing there in awe of his sweet words and twisted from the sad event.

Her voice reminds me of Katherine Hepburn and other women of society back East, not California at all. "Are you with my son?" she asks, fluffing the bottom of her bob hairstyle.

With big curious eyes on me, I reply, "I am." Maybe more than I'm ready to acknowledge.

"Please send my gratitude for the gift."

Her sentiment feels cold despite the words. "I think it would mean more coming from you."

She's uncomfortable in the conversation by how she shifts on her feet. "He doesn't take my calls," she states with one hand on her hip.

"Maybe because you stand him up. Excuse me. I need to catch up with him." I hurry away, rushing through the clubhouse and out the doors. Dex is sitting in his car, windows down, the engine off. When I approach, he slides his sunglasses down over his eyes and looks straight ahead. Choosing to let this all die down, his emotions showing in his slumped shoulders, I lean my palms on the open window, and say, "Hey, you still owe me lunch."

With a tilt of his head in my direction, I see a slight smile cross his face. "You're right. Get in."

"I didn't know Beverly Hills had burger joints." I take another big bite of my burger.

"It's a little secret. Most people don't realize that not everyone in Beverly Hills proper is wealthy. There are pockets of average working Joes."

Related, but my thoughts veering, I state, "I've thought about moving."

His head jolts and he's facing me. "Where?"

"I'm not sure. Just somewhere else."

Setting his burger down, he appears to have lost his appetite.

He pushes his plastic basket away from him and looks out at the nearby street. "LA?"

"There are a lot of memories tied up in LA, but I feel it might be time for a change of scenery."

When he turns back to me, there's an earnestness found in his unwavering confession. "I don't want you to leave."

His honesty strikes me, causing me to take him seriously. "I have the boys, Dex."

Leaning forward, his whispered words don't hide his irritation, "You keep reminding me like I don't realize you're a package deal."

"I remind you so you can get out before it's too late."

"It's already too late."

His words take my breath, a silent gasp held hostage while I stare into the sincerity of his comforting eyes. Two beats of my pulse and I'm revived, and reply, "You don't know what you're saying."

Under the table, he finds my hand and holds it. "My feelings for you are real. But for you, I'll be your Peter Pan and you can pretend to be Wendy and we'll stay in Neverland until you're ready to see that Neverland doesn't have to live only in our imaginations."

"Dex?" I say, looking down. It's all too much and I push my burger away, feeling a lump forming in my throat. "You say these things in broad daylight—"

"I say what I feel and I feel so much for you."

I sigh. "Please—"

"Please what?"

Sitting up, our fingers falling away from each other, I say, "Please leave the future out there in the distance for just a little longer. I have things that I need to sort through first, right here in the present."

"I'll wait."

Getting up, I set my napkin on the table and walk around the booth to his side. Sliding in next to him, I take his face between my hands and ask, "Did Wendy and Peter ever kiss?"

With a smug smile in place, he says, "All the fucking time."

My smile is unstoppable as I lift up to kiss him on the lips. His strong hands cover my sides, holding me to him, but he pulls back. "We shouldn't do this here."

"I'm sorry."

"Don't be."

"Good. Because I'm really not."

He leans forward this time and kisses my forehead. "Let's go. I need to get you back to the Valley before the kids are out of school." Hearing him say that makes me think that maybe he does realize what comes along with dating me.

In the car, I want to ask him about his mother, but I'm not sure how to broach the subject. I decide direct is best. "Your Mother said to tell you thank you."

Silence.

"Dex?"

"I haven't seen my brother, Gage, in almost a year. He's married and lives in Thousand Oaks. LA's big, but it's not that big."

"Why haven't you seen him?"

"He's a lawyer, a partner at a firm with a steady job and all that, former pride of my family, but he took money from me and I found out three years ago."

"He stole from you?"

Dex's fingers tighten around the wheel, his knuckles going white. "He set up this account and had me sign a contract that I thought was for IRS reporting. It blew up in his face when the IRS contacted my accountant wanting their money. Like I wouldn't find out."

I shift my back against the door, so I can see him better. "Why didn't I know about this?"

With a glance, he says, "You were kind of busy three years ago."

*The plane crash. The funeral. My darkest year.*

"I'm sorry." I say it because my heart aches for him and his betrayal.

With a reassuring smile, he says, "Why are you sorry? You have no reason to be."

"I'm sorry I couldn't be there for you."

"There was nothing anybody could do. I dealt with my shitty brother. Per her usual MO, my Mother didn't take my side—"

"She took his?"

"No, she tried to play Switzerland, but I know deep down if the roles had been reversed, she would have sided with him. He was always her favorite. It was easy to see it. Each summer, I was shipped off to my grandfather's. She took him to the South of France."

"Doesn't sound like it was all bad if you ask me. I mean, how much sun and beautiful azure-colored water can you really stare at all day?"

His laugh is heard over the wind that whistles through the car. "True." When his hand finds mine, he says, "You have a really unique way of looking at situations, Wendy."

"It's a gift, I guess. I just learned that you see a situation how you want to see it, whether it's the truth or not."

"Your beauty shines through."

"Well I'm also learning that you're not just a pretty face and kickass drummer."

Chuckling, he says, "Nope, I also have other talents." He waggles his tongue, and at the sight of that, I clench my legs together. If he wasn't so damn sexy, I might be offended.

Pulling up into my driveway, I say, "Can't wait to see that in action, you big tease."

"It's not about seeing. It's about feeling. And trust me, I'm struggling to wait too." He looks past me, and says, "You're home."

I'm too stunned and now too turned on to think clearly, so I just sit there for a few seconds trying to collect myself from the puddle I turned into on the floorboard of his Challenger. The name of the car feels way too apropos right now. "Yeah, I should go... home, inside, the place I live," I start rambling.

One more stunning smile in my direction, and he adds, "I'll see you tomorrow."

"Yes, um, right. Tomorrow."

I get out and stumble a bit, left a little off balance from his words and a lot off balance by how much he affects me. And just like how the day started, I'm left impatiently waiting for Thursday to get here.

# 9

# Dex

She's become an addiction, and something I obsess over. Living the life I have, living it hard, I've become an expert at both addiction and obsession. I know the difference. Rochelle is the first person I've felt both over.

Now that she's let me in, I never want to go. I've waited so long for this chance. I have to pretend to act normal, but I feel anything but that when I'm around her. I don't want to scare her. I want... I want... I want so much with her, from her, that it scares me. But I play it cool, keeping my deepest thoughts to myself. I'm good like that, the quiet one. I've been called moody, but it's not that. That's an emotion someone wears for show. My moods aren't for show, but to hide, to protect what I don't want any of them to see. If they know how I really feel, rejection can follow and I've had too much of that in my life to survive a rejection from her.

I lie on the couch in the middle of my dark house, letting her invade my thoughts and crawl under my skin, becoming a part of me. She's the sun when it sets and my moon when it rises. My day begins and ends with her on my mind. She asks about me but all I want to do is hear about her. Her days are mundane to her, but are envious to me. Routine. She has this amazing life, her routine as she calls it, and I just want to be there, be a staple, a part of her daily routine. Too much.

*Obsessed.*

I'm obsessed.

This girl, this light, walked into my life and I just had to follow it. At nineteen, she was beautiful. She had brown hair with that just come from the beach look—chin length, a little wild, a little off. Her big brown eyes reminded me of the sun tea that would sit in the window sill when I was a kid. Rochelle didn't belong in that bar, but she owned it the minute she walked in, under-aged and full of confidence.

From behind the drumkit, I watched her, changing my beat to match the rhythm of her vibe. She was unique in the middle of a crowd of trite. As she put her straw to her mouth, my gaze wrapped around her wrist and followed the floral tattoo that had been started but not yet finished. When the band took a break, she climbed right up on stage and said, "You're good. You ever consider playing rock?"

"We play some rock covers sometimes."

"What about rock music that you help create? Original stuff."

Leaning back on my stool, I cross my arms over my chest. "I don't own my drums. It's me and the sticks for now."

She shrugs. "That's cool. It's your talent that caught my ear. Anyway, the bassist has a set of drums you can use if you want to join our band."

Suddenly, she had my undivided attention. Well, she had it

before, but now she's talking drums and a real band. "Why does a bassist have a drum kit?"

"He used to think he wanted to be a drummer, but his talent lies in the guitar."

"And what do you play?" I ask, so damn curious by this tenacious girl.

"Guitar. I'm not in the band, but two of the best guitarists around are. They're gonna be big. This is your chance."

I stand and notice the height difference. She's short and really fucking cute. "Why aren't you in the band if you play guitar?"

"If you wanna sit around here all night yapping, then I'll let you get back to playing cover songs from the seventies that should have never been made in the first place. But if you want in on the next big thing, then come with me."

"You want me to meet them tonight? Right now?"

With a smile, she says, "Yeah, right now. We have a gig in an hour and no drummer."

"You want me to play a gig with them tonight?"

Nodding, she looks at me like I'm the crazy one. "Yep. I saw how you hit. You're good. You've got natural skill. Not all drummers do."

"You actually want me to leave before the end of this gig to go play *your* gig?"

"I sure do. Is that a yes?" She turns and looks around the club. "I mean, I understand how karaoke—"

"Covers."

"I stand corrected. Covers. I totally get that playing covers can sometimes be cool and all, but I'm giving you the chance to be a part of something great."

"Promise?" I smirk.

"Promise. C'mon. I hate being late."

She hops off the stage and I follow right behind her, hoping that 'something great' will include hooking up with her later. Calling across the room to the old guys I was backing, I say, "Thanks guys. It's been fun, but my work here is done."

They don't seem entirely surprised and raise a pint to me.

Out on the street, she takes a helmet off of a Honda Shadow motorcycle and hands it to me. I recognize it from when I worked as a mechanic last year for a few months. I helped rebuild one similar to this. "This is yours?" I ask.

"Sure is."

"It's in good condition. What year is it?"

"An '87. Ever ridden one before?"

She's a feisty little thing, but I can handle her attitude. "Yeah, but I've never owned one."

"You should. There's nothing that feels more freeing than riding a motorcycle." She tightens the strap under her chin, and adds, "There's always a chance of death when you ride a bike. Makes you appreciate the life you have."

Nodding, I try to relate to this girl. I tuck the drumsticks into my Martens and pull my jeans over them. We get on and she warns, "Hold on tight."

I wrap my arms around her waist and we swerve into traffic. *Holy shit!* The girl's a dare devil. Leaning forward, I ask, "So what's the name of this soon to be big band anyway?"

She speeds up and yells into the wind, "The Resistance."

TR

Because of a last minute project Neil had due, Thursday turned into dinner at her place again. Rochelle apologized, but I didn't mind. I actually liked it. I'm already attached to the boys, being around them is fun. And anytime I get to spend time with her is good.

"Whatever happened to that motorcycle you had?" I ask Rochelle as we lay on a blanket in the middle of the backyard. The sun has set, the kids are watching a cartoon, and we just finished a bottle of wine.

"I got rid of it a few years ago," she replies. "It's clear enough to see some stars tonight."

I've learned when she changes the subject, not to push. She's not as open as she used to be, but I understand that the harshness of life changes people. It's changed her in ways I wish I could give back to her. I move to the new topic to keep her in the moment, here with me. "I once heard that only those who see the big picture can focus on the details."

Looking tired, but amused, she turns to me. "What does that mean?"

Seeing the sparkle to her eyes, I give her a smile. "If we see things on a grander scale, we're more likely to appreciate the little things that make it up."

When I look at her, there's a small smile on her face when she says, "Sometimes you say the most amazing things and I don't even think you realize it."

"If it makes you smile, my work here is done."

With a giggle, her hand nudges mine between us. As if the thought just came to her, she comments, "You never ask for anything. Not even on your performer's contract rider. No special requests whatsoever."

I want to touch her, to kiss her again, and reinforce that it wasn't a wet dream. We had sex once and the memory still haunts me. As casually as I can, I cover one finger over hers, and reply, "Nothing I want can be put on a tour rider."

From the look in her eyes, she's analyzing the meaning beneath my words, but she knows deep down what I really mean. Knowing we can't quite go there yet, I add, "Anyway, the guys request enough shit for all of us on tour."

"That's true." Moving closer, she uses my chest as a pillow. I wrap my arm around her shoulders and steal a peek at her boys inside. They look content with popcorn and big smiles on their faces, giggling at the kid's movie playing. These two boys that I've watched grow from a distance might become my responsibility one day... and I'm not opposed to this. I see Cory in their faces. They have Rochelle's heart and spunk.

I can give... *What can I give them that matters?* They have money. They have family. Any toy they could ever want for is easily bought. *What role can I play in their lives that add value? How can I make their lives better by being in it?*

Her voice is soft and cuts into my doubts. "If you could have anything, what would it be, Dex?"

I slip my hand down her back and rub while staring up at the sky again. "Time. I'd want time back."

She sits up, leaning over me while looking down, her gaze soft but direct. "And what would you do if you got time back?"

"I wouldn't waste a minute." I sit up and kiss her, running my hand into her hair and holding her close.

"Ew! What are you doing?" Neil says with disgust in his tone.

We part like two teenagers busted by their parents. Rochelle is to her knees and then standing up in a flash. "I, uh, he was helping me look for my earring." She tugs at her earlobe.

"It looked like kissing," Neil adds.

"It was," she starts again, her voice shaking. "It was kissing but like just a friendly goodnight kiss since Dex is leaving. Yeah, so—"

"Yeah, kiddo, I'm leaving." I stand and look between the two of them. "Thanks for having me over." Rochelle's a mess and Neil seems a little protective of his mother in his stance. That's my cue. When I approach, he opens the door nice and wide for me. I walk inside and he follows with Rochelle behind him. "I'm thinking you can come over this week, Neil, and we can play on my drums. I can teach you some beats, easy rhythms. What do you think about that?"

"That'd be cool," he says, his tone lighthearted again.

At the front door, Rochelle says, "Thanks for coming over."

I'm not sure what to say because everything I want to, I can't with Neil between us, so I turn to leave instead. "Thanks again for dinner. Bye, CJ. Bye, Neil. I'll see you in a few days."

"Bye-bye," CJ yells.

Neil nods. "Bye."

And when I see Rochelle, she mouths silently, "I'm sorry." When I start walking away from the door, I hear her say, "C'mon, buddy, let's get you guys to bed." The door shuts and I'm left standing in the dark under a blanket of stars wondering what the fuck I'm doing. I think I just got in trouble by a seven-year-old.

TR

As soon as I walk into my house, I head for the bar. It's stocked just the way I like it because although I don't make requests on the road, I do in my own home. I pour bourbon over ice and watch as the ice begins to melt on contact. It's the same burning that I usually feel, like an addiction reminding me how it has all the control. I give into it every time, realizing I don't need the upper hand. I just need to feel the burn again.

And the sensation is euphoric much like Rochelle—a burning euphoria.

Outside, I sit in a chair, setting my drink down to replace it with a cigarette. Under the same stars, but separated by more than a few miles physically and emotionally. Deep drags calm my insides as I rest my hands on my thighs and close my eyes.

I need to loosen up.

*Addiction.*

*Obsession.*

*Square One.*

There are more cons than pros when it comes to Rochelle. Just when I thought it might be our time after all of these years, life has happened, making it more complicated. She's a mother. Damn, that still blows my mind. She's a good one, not like mine at all. Rochelle's warm. My mother is cold. About the only thing they have in common is money, but my mother comes from undeserved, family funds. Money I've already started to inherit on a monthly basis from my grandfather's estate since I turned thirty. Apparently thirty is the expected age to have one's life figured out and in order.

I'll take his money and try not to think about him too much. But memories are powerful and hard to force down.

*Theodore Dexter the Fifth was a trip. The most formal man I've ever known. He wore suits to dinner and everyone was expected to follow the dress code when in his presence. My mother obliged him when we stayed there. She would stay for a few days before taking my brother on her escapades around the world. Gage was more presentable by nature, the chosen child to represent The Dexter's. I would stay at my grandfathers for at least two weeks each summer without them. I actually liked the time alone, but when visiting, even my play clothes were discarded after one wearing for not being crisp in appearance. Breakfast was at 7 or you got none. Lunch at eleven. Tea at three. Dinner at six. Bed by eight. The name of the city always felt fitting. Expectations ran high in Diablo, California. They ran high back in LA too, but here I missed my friends.*

*At thirteen, I snuck out of my room after curfew with thoughts of running away, running back home. I figured no one would notice anyway. I cut through the property and passed the guest quarters when I heard some banging. I moved closer, feeling very stealthy at the time. When I got close enough to look in the window, I saw Tres, the handyman I had seen around the house playing drums. I didn't even know he lived here. He was probably in his early twenties and was wearing a black Ramones shirt. A cigarette, or joint, hung from the corner of his mouth. It was dark outside, but he wore his sunglasses anyway. One of the newly hired maids, a blonde who looked like she was his age, danced around with her arms in the air. Her uniform was unbuttoned enough to see her bright pink bra and the skirt rose up as she moved.*

*My journey that night ended there. I sat down in a chair outside the window—watched and listened for over an hour. I was fixated on that kit and the power he put into hitting it as much as I was on seeing her slowly strip for him. They turned out the lights, but a purple lava lamp lit the room enough to see them as they hit the bed. I'd never seen two people having sex. I had magazines I stole from a convenience store down by the public school near us, but never seen a video, much less two people in real life having sex.*

*Tres blended into the darkness. But the blonde was hot and as much as I knew I shouldn't watch, I stayed there until she yelled his name long enough to penetrate the walls. I got up after that and went back to my room.*

*I lied in bed that night, jerked off for the first time to visions of her before falling asleep. When I woke up, I was angry. I had taken piano for five years and I hated it. I hated practicing and the recitals. I hated the formality and having to perform at dinner parties like a chump. I knew it wasn't frowned upon to play piano or any classical instrument, but the drums were, so it made them that much more intriguing*

*The next morning when I thought no one was around, busy at their jobs, I went back to the guest house and went inside. I spent three hours banging away on that drum kit and that was it. I saw how she reacted to him, turned on by the man behind the drums. That could be me. I could turn her on too. I knew I'd found my passion. The secrecy of it all, this crazy, loud, invasive music just clicked with me.*

My legs are burning, causing me to open my eyes in a hurry. "Shit!" I jump up, the cigarette flung from my hand. I grab my drink and pour a little over my burned skin. The lit end had burned a small hole through my jeans and singed some hair on my leg.

I finish my drink in three gulps and set the glass down on the table before going inside. Up the stairs to my room I go, opening the door, and closing it behind me. I walk into the bathroom and turn on the shower, debating if it should be hot or cold; I have a good argument for each right now. I decide on hot, wanting to relieve some pressure. Stripping down, I then move under the water. My muscles not relaxing like I hoped.

My body is tense. I want to fuck. I want to fuck hard. I want to fuck and come and not wonder what the fuck I'm doing chasing Rochelle. I have a phone full of numbers I could call. I don't want them. They are a thousand numbers that are meaningless to me.

They aren't her and my hand is a better option than a poor substitute.

Leaning my head against the slate wall, I close my eyes, remembering her body on top of mine, and how it was wrapped around my cock like a warm blanket. My grip tightens. She was so fucking wet, wet for me. Kisses to her neck became licks of ecstasy. I tasted her sweat, her sweetness before wanting her to come so I could taste all of her.

But Cory's name shocks me back to reality just like it did that day and my dick goes soft. "Fuck!" I slam the shower off and get out, dripping across the floor while walking to the cabinet and retrieving a towel.

After drying off, I get into bed angry. I sit up and punch the fuck out the pillow next to me before throwing it across the room and hearing it hit the door with a thud when it falls. So fucking anticlimactic for how I'm feeling.

Getting out of bed, I grab boxer brief from my dresser and pull them on. I go outside onto my balcony and sit down. The lighter and pack of cigarettes are on the table. I light up, resisting the urge for another drink. I look out over the city of Los Angeles all lit up in the distance frustrated that the best thing that ever happened to me sometimes feels like the worst.

# 10

I reach for my journal, but stop when I realize what I want to write is not what I'm ready to share with Cory. I grab my laptop instead. I write to get it out, to help unburden my heart.

*Love finds most of us fast and unexpectedly, but when it came to me and Dex, it was slow and calculated as if it knew to hold on and wait. I'm caught in the middle of developing feelings for a man that has shown me more than his heart. He's shown me his soul.*

Feeling much like lyrics, I title it 'Dex' and save the document in my Songs folder. The one thing I've learned about giving a part of yourself away is that you may not get it back. Love is a risk and I'm finding that I'm more willing to take it with him. I'm still left questioning if I'm as ready as I think I am, if I'm prepared to have someone in my life that is also a regular fixture in the boys' lives. I have no room for casual when it comes to them, so I need to be sure before jumping into something that could leave us devastated again.

*Me:* ***Hi.***

Thirty minutes go by on this Friday evening before he replies: ***Hi.***

What to say? What to say? *Me:* ***How are you?***

*Dex:* ***Good. You?***

I'm not feeling very liked right now. *Me:* ***I'm fine. What are you up to?***

*Dex:* ***I'm out. You want to join us?***

*Me:* ***Us?***

*Dex:* ***Some friends of mine. You should come.***

"Beth?" I call from my office.

The boys' nanny comes in. "Yes?"

"Can you work late tonight?"

A sly smile works its way across her face. "You going out?"

"I'm thinking I might."

She's always supportive of me. "I'll stay. I could use the extra money and I owe CJ a foot race in the backyard. He's convinced he can outrun me just because I'm a girl."

"Make sure to win big. We can't have them growing up thinking women are the weaker sex."

With a laugh, she says, "Nope, we can't have that. Now you get ready and I'll go tell the boys we get to make ice cream sundaes."

"Thanks for staying."

"No problem at all."

I close my email and shut down my computer before going into my bedroom, phone in hand. *Me:* ***Text me where you'll be in an hour.***

*Dex:* ***I'm glad you're coming out. It's been too long since I've seen you.***

*Me:* ***You saw me yesterday.***

*Dex:* **Like I said, it's been too long.**

And I swoon, holding the phone to my chest as the happy emotions bubble up inside.

Just over an hour later, I'm walking into the outside patio of a restaurant that's located at the back of a well-known hotel. It's a private place that's hard to get into unless you're famous or you're with someone famous, so celebrities like to hang out here.

Dex is seated at a table on the far side of the garden. There are four other people with him—three guys and a girl. With a cigarette in his mouth, he turns my way and a smile appears. Smoke fills the air above his head as he exhales, then stubs out the butt. Standing up, his chair is pushed back. He takes my hand and kisses my cheek, then whispers, "Glad you're here."

"Me too," I reply.

"Sit here. I'll get another chair."

When I sit, the conversation ceases, so I lift my hand awkwardly, and say, "Hi, I'm Rochelle." I recognize two of the guys from parties or somewhere in the past. But the other man and the woman I don't.

She smiles, but it's tight-lipped while she scopes me out to see if I'm competition for whomever she has her eye on at the table. This happens a lot in LA. Men hold all the cards here and too many women indulge that power by presenting it on a silver platter to them. "Enchante," she says, putting her hand toward me like I should kiss it. I take the limp hand, dropping it as quickly as I can.

Dex brings a chair, setting it at the corner of the crowded table. Tilting his head, he looks at me and smiles. It's sexual and genuine all in one. "It's good to see you." When he looks back to the group, he starts the introductions, "Toby, Keith, but not the country singer, Wes, and Firenza. This is Rochelle."

*Firenza?* Sounds exotic. Funny, I didn't hear an accent.

Her chair is bumped up to his, and she leans forward, her arm resting on top of Dex's. "You look familiar. How would I know you?"

Dex sits back, moving his arm out from under hers.

Everyone looks at me, waiting for an answer, but Toby replies, "She was married to the guitarist of the band."

"Which band?" Firenza asks.

Dex sits up, looking annoyed. "The Resistance." His answer is clipped.

She ignores his mood and continues in on me. "So you're divorced, but you still hang on... I mean, hang out with Dex?"

"I'm not divorced. Cory and I weren't marrie—"

Dex's hands hit the table, drawing my attention as the metal feet of his chair scrape across the cement when he stands. "I haven't seen the waitress in forever. I'm gonna get a drink from the bar." He leaves so abruptly that we're left staring at his back as he goes inside.

Uncomfortable being left here with her and confused to why he left, I start to get up so I can check on Dex. Persistent Firenza keeps going like nothing unusual happened at all though. "So you were only dating?" She scrunches her nose at me.

Wes touches her arm and she glares at him when he says, "He died. He was the one who died in the plane crash."

Hearing Cory dismissed so easily by her angers me. I stand, my own chair noisy this time. When I look at her, her expression never changes. It's just as cold and bitchy as a moment earlier. "You're dating his band mate now?"

My eyes meet Wes's and I say, "I'm gonna find Dex."

As I'm walking away, I hear her explaining to the others, "So what, she's dating Dex now. Who's next, Johnny Outlaw?"

I let the bad vibes go as the distance grows between us. She wants to package me up and categorize me so it's easier for her to understand. But none of this is easy to understand and if I don't, then she won't either. Dex is leaning on the bar talking with a tall brunette. She's laughing. He's smiling. I'm stepping to the side, debating. And now I'm apparently spying. *Ugh!* I make my way through the crowd of cocktail tables and patrons, not wanting to confront him, which is exactly what I'll do if I talk to him now. But I still can't resist sneaking a peek at him. He takes her card and tucks it into his shirt pocket before they say their goodbyes.

*Wow.* And here I was stupid enough to think he actually wanted me. *Why'd I even bother?* I just don't fit into his world and by watching him, I don't want to. I can't stay here and continue to be hurt by him or these women.

I continue toward the door that will lead me to the valet. Just as I exit, I hear him call after me. I hand the ticket to the valet attendant and step to the side, pretending to be oblivious to Dex. "Rochelle? Why are you leaving?"

He's got two drinks in his hand and he hands one to me. I don't take it, but glance off to the side to see if that's my car being pulled around. It's not. I say, "You left me out there with that woman who seems to think I'm a gold-digger of some sort while you come inside and collect other women's numbers. And you're surprised I'm leaving?"

"I didn't want to be rude. She works for Gucci and wants to talk to me about the potential for a campaign."

"She should be talking to me then. I'm your business manager. Why'd you leave the table?"

He stares at me and I stare right back. Then he sets the drinks down on the valet podium and reaches into his shirt pocket, pulling out his pack of cigarettes. Flicking one up, he takes it and taps it on the inside of his wrist before lighting it and taking a deep inhale.

Finally, he says, "I don't want to talk about Cory."

"I didn't bring him up. I was only correcting *Firenza's* rude comment."

"I don't want *you* talking about Cory tonight."

"Then you should have answered for me so I didn't have to."

He inhales again. With a slow exhale above my head, he says, "I wanted you to meet some of my friends. That's all."

"Your friends are assholes."

"Not all of them."

"No Dex, you're right. Not all of them. Just her. And who is she exactly? I seem to be lost on her connection to you."

He drops the cigarette to the ground and says, "We used to fuck."

My heart is set on fire as he crushes me with his flippancy. I glare at him, then spit, "You sure it's past tense?"

"I'm not having sex with her anymore. Why are you so bent out of shape?"

I double blink in shock at his attitude toward me. This is the Dex I've always known, his cocky side getting the best of him. I shouldn't bother, but I do. "By how territorial she seemed during the interrogation I got, she might be under the impression the two of you are still fucking."

With a shrug and an arrogant grin on his face, he says, "What can I say, she wants me."

"Ms. Floros," the valet says, tapping me on the shoulder. "Your car's here."

I turn and take the keys while tipping the valet. "Thank you." Without another word, I begin to leave, but I'm startled and spun around, then pinned against my car by Dex's firm body.

"Don't leave," he whispers just a breath away. "Stay."

"Why?"

"Because I'm not fucking her anymore and the only reason that I'm not is you."

"That's not charming."

"I'm not trying to be charming. I'm trying to be truthful. She knows I like you. You're a threat to her."

"I'm not gonna get into some catfight over you."

"You don't have to. We can ditch them or join them and I'll set her straight. Whatever you want, I'll do. Just stay with me." Our locked stares soften into gazes as our defenses come down, and he whispers, "Please stay."

His vulnerability is a turn on, so several heavy heartbeats later, I lay my conditions down for him. "Fine. I'll stay, but I want you to set her straight. She made me feel like I should be ashamed."

"She doesn't matter to me." He takes my hand in his. "Only you do." Leaning forward he kisses me, taking my breath away along with any doubts I had about us.

And with that, I give my keys back to the valet and we walk inside holding hands. He leads me back to the table, but we remain standing. Looking directly at *her*, he says, "We're not gonna do this anymore."

"I'm sorry, darling," Firenza replies, batting her eyelashes. "Do what?"

The table falls silent and he says, "Fuck. I'm not interested in anyone but Rochelle."

Her face falls when he says it so bluntly, and she starts reaching for anything to keep her in his good graces. "But she's like a groupie, going through the band."

"Shut your mouth," he demands, hitting his hand down on the table. "You know nothing about her. The only reason I'm even bothering to tell you that you and I are over is that I respect her enough to do it." He starts walking with me behind him, his grip wrapped tightly around my hand. "We're leaving. The crowd sucks tonight."

This time at the valet, *he* tips and takes the keys from the attendant. "I'll drive." I slip into the passenger seat and he waits to leave until I'm buckled in. The tension is high in the car, but not sexually like I prefer. He's mad and I'm not sure what to say, so I stay quiet.

By the route he's driving, he's taking me to his house. I hope his mood lightens when we get there. Before we enter his community, he says, "I want you to stay the night with me."

"I don't have a sitter for the night."

He doesn't say anything else the rest of the ride.

When we walk in, it's dark inside, but the pool lights are lit, drawing my eye to the backyard. "It's a beautiful night. We should go for a swim," I suggest, drawn to the blue lagoon.

When I look back to him, his eyebrow is raised and a devious grin lies across his face. "You don't have your suit."

"I can go in my underwear."

"Or go naked."

"Yes, or go naked but I'm thinking my bra and panties will be safer."

He unlocks the doors and opens them wide. "Safe from what?" he asks, following me outside. After kicking off his shoes, he unbuttons his shirt, exposing his sexy abs.

When the shirt is tossed to a nearby chair, I reply, "Safe, safe, safe. What were we talking about again?"

"You were saying how keeping your undies on would be safer."

"Oh yeah, that's right." A new skull and roses tattoo resides on his shoulder and I look at the style of it, reading the words under it—solum bonum decessura. I don't know what it means. I'm distracted again as he undoes each button on his jeans, making me inhale an uneven breath. *Safer*. I'm not sure if he's gonna be safe from my sexual attacks when he's that hot. His words make me look up when he asks, "You gonna get undressed or what?"

"I'm enjoying the show too much. I might just watch you instead."

"Shirt off, woman."

"All right. All right. Fine." I pull my top off and place it neatly on a chaise. Turning my back, I check him out over my shoulder.

He's at the bar and music starts playing though I don't see any speakers. *Nirvana's* "In Bloom." "I never knew you liked grunge so much. Jane's Addiction, now Nirvana."

"Soundgarden, Stone Temple Pilots though it's debatable about their grunginess. Bands of that time like Red Hot Chili Peppers have kick ass drummers. Rock is great but I like the rhythms that straddle the hardcore rock and the grunge era." He pulls bottles of liquor onto the countertop. I pop open the top button of my jeans as he pours two shots of tequila. With his jeans hanging low on his hips and wide open in the front, I feel my self-control slipping away as he comes toward me. "You never did get a drink at the bar."

"Salud," I say, taking the shot and downing it. "No lime?"

"No." His reply is direct, then his tongue drags up the corner of his mouth and I stare. My heart starts thudding in my chest as I move closer to him. He asks, "We should swim, right? It's safer that way."

"We'll end up the same either way."

His right hand touches just where my bra ends and goes lower exploring my waist. "How so?"

When his fingers dip into the back of my jeans, I reply, "Wet."

"*Fuuuck*," he curses under his breath, looking up and taking a step back.

"I'm trying."

His hands slide into his hair, his frustration scene in the move. "Shit. You can't say things like that and expect me to stand here and not react."

"It's the tequila talking. Ignore me."

"Trust me. I've tried to ignore you. It's impossible."

With a sigh and roll of my neck, I say, "I'm thinking it's hot tub time."

"I'm thinking the pool to cool off." He takes his jeans off and dives in.

I take mine off and walk to the edge and sit down, dangling my feet in. He swims closer and grabs my ankles. Bearing my weight on my wrists I lift up as he tugs me down slowly until the front of my body slides down against his. Dex kisses my stomach as I slip into the chilly water.

"Why do we play these games anyway? I want you, Rochelle. I think that's clear."

Clear is not the word I would use for his erection. Rock hard might fit the situation better. The liquor warms my body as it infiltrates my senses and relaxes me. I wrap my legs around his waist, but lean back on the ledge, keeping my body afloat by holding onto the side.

"It's not just a matter of want between us."

Moving closer, his hands slide to my ass as he presses harder against me. "You're right, but we've got the basics covered. Aren't you ready to try more?"

Slipping my arms around his neck, I readjust, the wiggle making my body tingle. "It's not just about us. It's not even just about the kids. There are things, people involved that I don't want to hurt and you asked me not to talk about that tonight. So let's not. Let's just leave it for another day and have another shot."

There's a gleam in his eye reflecting the pool, maybe more as he looks at me. "Okay, more shots then."

He perches me on the side of the pool and I lay back as he jumps out. Staring up at the sky, I try to orientate myself by the constellations I'm used to seeing at home. Just as I start to think I'm turned around, I find the big dipper and a comfort settles in as does Dex. He sits down next to me and I ask, "What does your tattoo with the skull say?"

In Latin, he says, "Solum bonum decessura."

"What does it mean?"

"Only the good die young."

"When did you get it?"

"About a year ago."

"Do you want to talk about it?"

"No," he says, moving into a push-up, his face over mine. "I'd rather kiss you." He lowers down and kisses me. It's sweet, gentle, and wonderful, which is exactly opposite of how I really want him to kiss me.

I'm going to make figuring out what this is a priority tomorrow. Others may get hurt when I give this a real shot, but I can't live tethered to the past. Just when he's about to get up, I grab him, my hands at the back of his head and bring his lips to mine. I kiss him how I want to be kissed, and how I know he wants me to kiss him.

When our lips part, I intake the night air, savoring him on my lips. When he sits up, I do too before moving into the pool to face him. The shot is set on the edge, we clink our glasses, and finish the drink.

He lies on his stomach, resting his head on his crossed arms. "What time do you have to be home?"

"Midnight."

"That's two hours. Wanna make out?"

A laugh escapes, filling the serene surrounding. "Heck yeah, I do." Lifting up, I get out of the pool as he rolls onto his back. I stand above him, offering him a hand to get up. He accepts and stands, but quickly pulls me over to the hot tub. We climb in one at a time and I sit, settling on his lap. His hands hold onto me as his head dips back a bit, his eyelids growing heavy, as his focus on me intensifies. "You're so fucking sexy." He licks his lips. Watching him makes me clench, wanting those lips on me.

With one hand on my back and the other on my hip, he bucks beneath me, then brings me to him, our lips pressing together. Our words are replaced by the bubbling water, kisses, and soft sighs of pleasure. His tongue is strong and dominant, wanting to be felt, to feel, and I oblige.

Large hands cover my breasts and he squeezes gently. I take control as our kisses find purchase against our craving bodies. I run my fingers through his hair, and my nails down his back. His muscles dance under my touch, each tensing and releasing.

With his arms wrapped around the back of my shoulders, his hips join mine. The friction leading to a deeper desire, a desire I try to lessen to save us both the dissatisfaction we're gonna end up with. But it's impossible to hold back when he's giving so much.

*That spot. That spot. That spot.* The perfect spot being teased and coaxed until I tug his hair, pressing myself against him as I tighten my legs around him. My head drops back and his breath is warm as he covers me with hot kisses. His hands grab a hold of my hips. "God, Rochelle. I want you to be inside you. I want you so much."

Goosebumps cover my skin as his words become the only air I need. As I'm coming down from my own bliss, I want the same thing. I want him so badly. Before I can say anything his movements become erratic, his fingers digging into the flesh where my hips meet my ass. "So close," he says, his forehead against my collarbone. “Oh fuck. Yes.” My shoulders are grabbed again and I’m pushed down on top of him.

His arms fall away as he leans back, closing his eyes. When he opens them, he grins, it’s lazy and beautiful. Bringing me closer, he kisses me just like the first kiss tonight—deep and sensual, passionate just like the man.

“Sorry about the hot tub,” I tease.

“Don’t be. It was hot,” he puns.

“The orgasm or the water?”

“Both.”

“I agree.” Feeling very comfortable here.

TR

My body is relaxed and my eyes heavy as he walks me to my car. “Do you want me to drop you off so you can get your car?”

“No, I’ll get it tomorrow.”

His hips press into mine, my car solid behind my back. I say, “This was a good night.”

“A very good night,” he replies, kissing my neck. “When do we get to do it again?”

“Is tomorrow too soon?”

“Not soon enough.”

# 11

If Dex didn't already have a piece of my heart, he has it all now. Watching him teach Neil how to play drums is beyond endearing and makes my heart clench. I've not seen Neil's attention on one thing last this long in a while. I can tell he likes Dex and Dex's patience is admirable. I hear Dex say, "Let's try it one more time on this drum. What's it called?"

"Ummmm...the tom-tom?" Neil answers.

"Right. Good job."

CJ runs in, alerting them to our presence. Dex looks up and winks at me, then asks, "You wanna join us? I have an acoustic guitar over here."

"Maybe." I'm still unsure, but being here in his music room makes me want to play... just a little bit.

CJ slips under the drum set and is pounding the bass with his hand until Dex grabs him and tickles him before placing my little whirlwind of energy beside him. He hands him a stick and says,

"Hit the middle, not the rim. Okay, CJ?"

CJ bangs once and hits the rim, then asks, "The shiny part is the rim?"

"Yep. Don't hit that part."

I walk behind them, letting my fingers drag over Dex's shoulders as I pass. Picking up the guitar, I strum once, then start tuning it until I'm satisfied. Lots of banging on the drums distracts the boys, but I see Dex sneaking peeks at me while a small, knowing smile crosses his face. His lure worked and I took the guitar bait, too tempted being here in the easiness of his music room to resist. Sitting down on the edge of a recliner, I stroke the neck of the guitar, sliding my fingers up the slick wood and back down again. I position my fingers and start strumming again, but this time a melody I know by heart, my own song that I've been working on in my head and writing down on my laptop.

When I look up, my gaze meets Dex's and I don't stop, fighting the feeling to hide the music away. The notes come to me by memory, easy in their flow, the music dancing in my head, leading my hands. Then I stop. This is the part where I always stop, my head getting in the way of my heart. It's too heavy.

"You okay?" Dex asks, his furrowed brow showing his concern.

My breaths quicken as I struggle to control my emotions. Trying to halt the panic, I close my eyes and forcefully slow my breathing. I block out the fact that I know Dex is watching me freak out and try to concentrate on regulating each breath instead. When I reopen my eyes, Dex is kneeling before me. His hand covers my knee, but he doesn't say anything.

"I'm okay."

He nods, then stands up. "C'mon guys, let's go get cookies in the kitchen." Drumsticks are dropped with a careless clang and both boys race for the kitchen. Dex says, "I'll give you a few minutes."

As soon as he's gone, I take a deep breath and then another. Standing up, I pick up the drumsticks so it's not messy in here, having a strong desire to busy myself. I place the guitar back on the stand and turn out the lights. When I return to the living room, I see them outside, the boys running in the large grassy area to the left of the pool. Dex is sitting under the patio, two juiceboxes and two glasses on the table next to him.

I walk out the open door and laugh, "You have juiceboxes?"

As I sit across the table from him, he turns to me, his sunglasses covering his eyes. "I stocked up on kid essentials. I have popsicles too."

His sweet gesture sweeps me up in the moment and I smile. "Thank you."

"No thanks needed." We turn our attention to watching the kids, but he asks, "How long have you been getting panic attacks?"

"I'm not sure you want to hear about it."

"If I'm asking, I want to hear about it."

"I had my first when I went into labor with CJ."

His attention is now fully on me. Turning in his chair, he rests his elbows on the table. "Do you know what brought it on?"

"Hindsight says I do..."

He lifts his sunglasses to the top of his head and looks at me, really looks at me. "You know, I was thinking about Cory. I know I've said it before, but I feel I need to say it again." He glances away briefly then back to me. "I'm sorry. I'm sorry he died. I think about him all the time. I hear him when I play. It's still hard for me to talk about him, but he was a great man, Rochelle." I feel the tears welling up in the corners of my eyes, so I look away. After a calming breath, I feel strong enough to look back at him. When I do, he adds, "He was lucky to have you."

Turning back around, I say, "Dex—"

"I never told you this before, but as much as I loved him..." He pauses and gulps, his Adam's apple bobbing twice in his throat.

I cut him off this time. "Don't say it, okay?"

We stare into each other's eyes, holding the moment a few seconds longer. Pulling his sunglasses back down over his eyes, he gives a small nod before sitting back and looking out over the yard. From his profile, I can see his mood shift through his expression. He stands suddenly, grabbing his glass and going inside.

Following him in, I say, "I'm sorry. It just feels too personal—"

Anger covers his words. "It is fucking personal. It's personal to me. You go back and forth between square one and practically having sex with me in the hot tub the other night. Maybe I'm unclear as to what the fuck is going on between us, but I know how I feel. So I guess you need to figure your shit out and let me know so this doesn't end up messier than it needs to be."

"Shit? It's not shit, Dex. It's my life. I don't have to explain this to you. I owe you nothing."

When I turn to leave, he says to my backside, "Go ahead. Leave. It's safer that way, much like wearing your underwear in a hot tub."

"You're an ass, Dex."

His comeback is swift and tinged with arrogance. "A sexy one if I interpreted the way you stared at me the other night correctly."

I give my best pointed look. "You can interpret my stares however you like, but that doesn't change the fact that I think there's more truth to the tabloid tales than you like to admit."

"Really, Rochelle? We're going there? Because how I see it, we can skirt the issue all we want but somehow we keep ending up..." He steps closer and I stay strong, unwavering as his hands grab my hips and our mouths are only separated by our height difference. In a whisper, he says, "Right. Back. Here." His lips press against mine, and my eyelids close as my mouth meets his in the middle.

"You're right," I say as my heels touch the ground again, my anger subsiding. Every time. Every time, he proves over and over how weak I am to him. I give in feeding his ego and say, "Fine. I like you." I add a shrug to make it come off more casual, but he sees right through me.

A huge, obnoxiously cocky grin appears. "What? Rochelle Floros, did you just say you like me? I think I just kissed the pissiness right out of you."

His teasing and the poke to my side makes me roll my eyes and smile. "Yeah, don't hold it against me. I'm weak to a good kiss."

Swiveling my hips against his, he raises an eyebrow and says, "It won't be your like for me that I hold against you. Trust me on that."

I swat his chest. "You are so bad."

Leaning down, he kisses my neck, then whispers in my ear, "Which is what you 'like' so much about me."

"Mama, I fell down." Surprised by CJ, I turn just as he tugs the bottom of my shirt. "I need Band-aid."

Dex bends down and picks him up. "I got one, buddy."

"It hwerts," CJ replies, then pouts his bottom lip out.

Dex sets him on the counter and pulls out a first aid kit from the cabinet. "Show me the damage," Dex says.

I lean against the counter and watch, fascinated to see how this goes. CJ points to a small pinkish scrap on his left knee. There's no blood, but Dex treats it like a medical emergency, all for show, for CJ. "Oh man, I think we'll be able to save the leg, but we definitely need a Band-Aid on the situation. Let's get you all fixed up."

And there goes my heart, melting for the sweetness of this man.

First he cleans the boo-boo, then he puts antibiotic ointment on, topped with a big Band-aid. "Better?"

"Mama kisses it. Makes it heal faster."

I smile hearing my youngest say that, but it works. Dex bends down and kisses the bandage. "You think you'll be able to run like that?"

CJ smiles and nods. Then he melts my heart by leaning forward and hugging Dex. I see the surprise on Dex's face, but he takes my son and hugs him back, his expression one of appreciation. My heart blooms with emotion in the moment. CJ turns to me when they part and says, "Do we have time to play?"

"Ten more minutes, then we need to go. Okay?"

I watch as he runs off yelling to Neil how they scored ten more minutes.

Dex asks, "Only ten?"

"I need to get them to bed on time tonight. They start day camp tomorrow."

While cleaning up the medical mess, he asks, "What about you?"

"I have two meetings tomorrow. Proposals for a tour next year. The events team wants to do something different."

He turns, his eyes narrowed with irritation. "Next year? We don't even know if we'll tour next year. Damn, we leave to finish this tour off in two days."

"Tours take a lot of time to plan. It's good to hear the ideas. Doesn't mean the band is doing it."

With a heavy sigh, he puts the kit away, then looks at me. "So I'm leaving. Eight shows left."

The topic of him leaving is not one I like to think about right now, but I try to convince myself otherwise. "Only eight shows. It'll be okay."

"You're better at this than I am."

"I've had more practice."

"I've had none."

"None?" I ask. "You've never left a girlfriend before? That can't be right."

Walking around me he stops in front of the back door. "I've never cared about anyone enough when I left to tour."

"So what you're saying is that you like me too."

He chuckles. "Yes, I like you, as if that wasn't already clear."

TR

The next day everything changed. It's strange and kind of amazing how that happens. You think you're finally figuring things out, but you're not and stuff gets twisted... and tainted. No matter how you fight against the inevitable, fate finds you just to make sure you never forget the pain of the past.

It all started off with a knock on the door just as I was about to load the boys into the car to take them to camp. Janice stood there, a frown on her face. Tears in her eyes.

"Janice," the name rushes from my mouth. "What's wrong?"

Her eyes settle on the kids behind me. "I forgot about camp. Can we talk when you get back?"

"Yes. Yes. I won't be long." I call the boys to come with me as Janice hugs them each before we leave. "I'll be right back."

The day camp is just down the street from my neighborhood, so it doesn't take long to get there, but my thoughts are consumed with worry. I've not seen Janice so distraught since... since her son died. I gulp, the lump in my throat heavy with fear. The fear is something I try to swallow down in front of the boys. I don't want to scare them.

After checking them in and making sure they're all set, I head back home. When I open the door, Janice is pacing the living room. She looks up, and the devastation I saw earlier has morphed into anger. "How could you do it? How could you disrespect my son like this? Hurt your children?"

"What?" I ask, taken aback as the door closes behind me. "What are you talking about?"

"It's on the internet."

"What is?"

Another knock disrupts and I look at her like she might know who it is. Janice crosses her arms over her chest, and turns her back to me. The knocks turn to pounding and I rush to answer the door. It can only be someone who has my code, so I don't expect to be surprised again, but I am when I open it. "*Dex?* Hi."

"Hi," he replies looking uneasy.

"What are you doing here?"

Janice's voice carries over my head. "You chose him, a drug-addict over my son!"

"What?" Shocked by her statement, I turn back to her. "I don't understand—"

Dex says, "Rochelle, she knows about us."

Glancing back to him, I ask, "What does she know?"

Janice screams. "I saw the pictures online. Do you know how humiliated and hurt I am by what you've done?"

I'm shaking my head, my hands starting to follow suit. My breathing quickens, shallowing when all I want is to take a deep one.

Dex steps forward. "Janice, I know you don't like me, but my feelings for Rochelle are genuine." He enters my house with his hands up in surrender.

She continues to shout, the anguish she's feeling heard. "I don't care about your feelings. I care about my son!"

Dex still approaches her slowly. "I loved Cory like a brother—"

"Don't you dare insert your despicable self into my family like that when you have done nothing but cause the band trouble! Cory was always there cleaning up your mess of a life and this is how you repay him?"

Her anger and Cory being dragged into this stabs my heart. My thoughts start to twist, so I reach for the nearest wall for balance. With my palm flat against the sheetrock, I close my eyes, but hear Dex say, "I'm not the same person I was before, Janice. You only know what you read and that's not the truth anymore. Believe me. Our kiss was innocent, but sincere."

My world is spinning—guilt, anger, sympathy, Dex, Cory, Janice, the kids as she yells, "I saw the posts with you and Rochelle kissing in public like it doesn't matter, like you don't care about anyone but yourselves or how this would make me or the boys feel. So much damage was done with your 'innocent' kiss."

I collapse to my knees on the cold tile, my hands falling forward as my mind begins to blur.

# 12

A steady beat infiltrates my dreams. I fight the awareness that brings me from the darkness to a more lucid state, the sound louder. *Beep. Beep. Beep.*

My eyelids flutter open at the sound of the machine next to me. The soft light above feels too bright until my eyes slowly adjust. Janice is there, her hand on mine. "Rochelle. Dear."

The last moments before I blacked out come rushing back to me. The beeping picks up as my heart does. "Dex." I cough to clear my throat. "Where is he?"

Her hand leaves mine. "Rochelle, you shouldn't be thinking of him. There are photographers outside the hospital, waiting for you to comment on this 'story.' It's time to end this crazy behavior. You need to think of your children."

"What story?" I start to sit up.

"That's why I came over this morning. There are pictures of you and Dex kissing outside a hotel."

"No."

"Yes, there are. And do you know how much that hurt to see? My son has not been gone that long and here you are gallivanting around LA at seedy motels like he never existed." A tear falls down her cheek.

My body aches, but my mind is stronger. "Janice, I can't believe you think that. You know I loved Cory."

"Loved? Past tense? Well, I still love him, present tense, and always will."

My hand goes to my head as it starts to throb. "You're twisting my words."

She steps back, appalled. "Your actions are twisting your reality. You have small children to raise. If you prefer to sleep with a drug-addict playboy, then do so, but I won't sit by and let my grandchildren bear witness to it." She walks out, her heels clicking loudly down the corridor.

There's a pang in my chest, the pain of her words hit me hard. Maybe she's right. I'm being selfish right now. *What am I doing? Choosing to do what I want seems in complete opposite of what I should do for the boys, or does it? Has Dex changed? I mean really changed?*

A nurse walks in and asks, "Ms. Floros, I'm Anne. Do you know why you're here?"

"I'm thinking I had a panic attack, but this one felt more like a heart-attack."

She leans against the foot of the bed. "I see you've taken medicine for them before. The doctor has already called in a new prescription for you." With her clipboard down at her side, she asks, "Do you know what might have brought this one on? It was severe enough for your loved ones to bring you to the hospital."

"People were fighting..."

With a small nod of understanding, she asks, "Are there ways to eliminate some of that stress?"

I gulp, then reach for the water pitcher. She comes around and pours a glass for me. "I don't know. Maybe. I'm not sure. I guess I didn't realize... I'll give it some thought."

"Take this seriously, Ms. Floros, and consider ways to reduce stress and conflicts. Those are some common triggers for panic attacks. Make sure to eat healthy and to exercise regularly." She removes the IV. "Exercise can help reduce the toll that emotional stress can cause. I don't want to see you back in here again."

"Does that mean I'm free to go?"

Swabbing the area, she covers it with a small white bandage. "You are. You just need to sign a few forms at the desk first. Your ride is waiting for you at the nurse's station."

Wondering who's waiting for me, I look up and ask, "Who's my ride?"

She looks down at her clipboard. "Dex Caggiano."

TR

It's LA, so the hospital has a private back drive for these types of media situations. I'm thankful for that. We sneak out that way. The dark tinting of his black Bronco keeps the paps on the street from getting any photos worth using when we pass.

We don't speak until the coast seems clear, then begin to relax though an awkwardness stretches between us that's never existed before. Pushing through, thinking about what the nurse said, I start, "Dex, we should talk before we get to my house."

"Yeah," he replies, sounding resolved. "You might have more paps there, so I shouldn't stay."

"I mean, we need to talk about today, the panic attack. Janice. This. Us."

His hesitation is heard when he replies, "Okay."

"I can't hurt her like that. She's been there for me since Cory's death. I was there for her. It wasn't easy, but she was the only one who seemed to truly get how I felt. She's wonderful to my kids and loves them. I've never seen her like she was this morning. She was distraught and *I* did that to her. I hurt her like that by betraying her."

"You didn't betray her by kissing me. She wants you to keep playing the role you've played for years—the widow, but you're more than that, Rochelle. You're a woman, a mother, a musician, a business manager. You are more than a one-dimensional person. She needs to recognize that. It's not just about her."

"I need to focus on my kids, Dex. They don't have a father. I have to be both mom and dad for them, and lately, I feel like I'm failing."

"Us dating—"

"I hadn't had a panic attack in years and now I've basically had two in the last two days. Both times were with you. Do you find that coincidental? Because I don't."

He pulls over to the side of a street that leads to mine. "You're building this up in your head like you being happy goes against feeling bad that Cory died. They aren't related."

"Janice—"

"Janice is turning what we shared into something bad. You're letting her into your head." He takes my hand, holding it as if it might be the last time—firm grip, thumb trying to soothe.

I pull my hand away slowly, leaving all the feelings we were developing behind in the palm of his hand. "The timing is wrong."

"Bullshit!"

Startled, I jump in my seat.

Lowering his voice, he says, "That's a cop out. I know you feel something for me. I see how you react because I also feel it when I'm around you. There's something here and you're just scared."

"Scared of what?"

"Scared to have a life without Cory and thinking you have to justify it to others. The problem with that is when you start justifying it, it will make you feel like your love for Cory was less. It wasn't. It's just different. He's not here, Rochelle."

"Stop it. Stop talking about Cory and take me home."

"Now you want to stop talking about him?" He looks surprised. "I can't win with you when it comes to him." He shifts the car into drive.

"This is not a competition, Dex."

Disappointment slides onto his face. "Then why is he being shoved in my face every time we make a move?"

"This is one of the reasons why we won't work. We see things very differently."

"One of the reasons? Name another because from where I sit, we fit like two puzzle pieces clicking together."

"You're a *supposed* recovering addict. You have sex with anyone who offers. You—"

"That's it. Right there. You play like you know who I am, but you don't. That's why the lies are so easily believed. I can tell what you're doing. You're giving me an out that I don't want. You're allowing yourself to believe the worst about me to ease your conscience, but it won't—"

"You know what. Not everything is about you and your past. You lost a band mate and friend, but I lost my soulmate!"

My breath chokes in my throat after I say the one thing that would hurt him most. His eyes die inside as he stares at me. As usual, I'm the one who needs to make him feel better about everything. But I can't this time. I'm too tired to help anyone else right now. "I was the one left in the wake of this tragedy to pick up the pieces for everyone around me, and pretend that everything is all right so they can go about their days not worrying about me." I shift in my seat, taking a breath, then hit my hands against my thighs as I yell, "Everything is not all right! *I* am not all right!"

I see the street in front of my house is clear. *Thank God!* But right when Dex pulls up in front of the locked gate, a car parks right in front of us with a long lens aimed in our direction, so I react by ducking down. "Oh my God! That's exactly why we can't do this. They don't want me. They just want your latest conquest. Well, guess what? That's one role I don't want to play. I have to think about two little boys and protect their future."

"Protect their future from me? Protect them from me? You're twisting this. I care about those boys. I love them. I would never hurt them!" Throwing the SUV in reverse, he backs up around the corner, then turns, heading in the opposite direction from the paparazzi. "I can protect you from them. You just won't try. You're protecting your heart so hard that you're losing the ability to feel anything except numb."

Unfortunately, they're right behind us when I peek up and over the back of the seat. My head hurts, my heart is racing, and my eyes have filled with tears. "This is the stress I can't have in my life. I can't have you, Dex. I'm sorry. We can't happen. It's not good for me. *You're* not good for me. We're not good for each other."

He struggles to keep his tone steady, but I hear the shake in it. "Don't make rash decisions, Rochelle. You just got released from the hospital. You're tired. In the grand scheme of things, this is nothing, but *we're* something. We matter."

I grab either side of my head while shaking it. "Stop saying that.

We don't. I can't think of only myself and enjoy it while hurting others in the process. It doesn't work like that." I look up and add, "Just like now. Just like I'm hurting you. But it's you or everyone else. That's how I see it and the only options I have to choose from."

He makes the block and then pulls up to my driveway and punches in the code. "Are you telling me that you don't want to date me because it will upset others or because you don't believe I've changed? Because you've said both, which makes me think you're reaching for anything and hoping it sticks." The gate closes behind him and he parks.

"Don't belittle my reasons."

"They're not reasons. They're excuses and you know it, but I'm gonna let you go live with those excuses. Just remember these are the choices *you* made. I was here, wholeheartedly for you." His breath deepens, a mixture of anger and sadness battling in his eyes. "This fence isn't tall enough. You should go before they come back."

I open the door, determined to walk away without damaging him anymore. When I step one foot out, he adds, "Go find this happy-ever-after you're so desperately searching for that I can't give you. And maybe one day you'll see that you're throwing away that ending before you even realized you had it."

His words make me panic, worried he's right. "Dex, it doesn't—"

"I can't make you believe in me." He revs the engine while gripping the steering wheel. Looking away from me, he says, "You either do or you don't." He backs up and the gate starts to reopen.

I release a heavy sigh, feeling the anxiety of the paparazzi showing up again and the weight of the pain caused from this conversation. His window is down, so I walk the few feet to him and start to lean in to say, "Pleas—"

"Go inside. This conversation is fucking over. Just like we are!"

The shock of his words coaxes my anger back up as I stand there. He leaves skid marks on the street from peeling out so fast. Pissed, I turn my back and go inside before any photographers show up.

As soon as the door closes behind me I see Beth. She's sitting on the couch reading a book to CJ and they both look up. "Hey, are you okay?" she asks. "Janice called me."

"No. I'm not. Can you stay a bit longer so I can clean up?"

"Sure, no problem."

I kiss CJ on the head. "Hi, Sweetie. Where's Neil?"

Beth answers, "In his room, practicing on that drum pad Dex left for him earlier."

*Dex.* "I'm gonna take a bath."

"Okay, the boys have eaten. There's still some casserole in there if you're hungry."

"Thank you."

I stop by Neil's room on the way to mine. "Hi Buddy."

He doesn't look up. "Hi Mom."

"Did you have fun today at camp?" I ask, seeing the black and grey pad on the floor in front of him.

"Yeah. Now I'm practicing my rhythms. They're para somethings but I can't remember, so Dex told me to call them rhythms. He says if I learn these three, I get to start on a song next time."

"Oh." Looking into the hopeful face of my sweet son makes my whole body ache. I almost tell him there won't be a next time with Dex, but I don't, not wanting to upset him. No need to have all of us crying over Dex. "I'm gonna take a bath if you need me."

"'Kay."

I start the hot water on the tub before stopping to look at myself in the mirror. It's hard though. Breaking people's hearts is not something I enjoy doing and I feel ashamed for hurting him. I take my clothes off and slip into the tub, hoping to wash away the pain of breaking my own heart in the process of Dex's.

The water soothes, but it doesn't relieve. When I get out twenty minutes later, the pain is more than skin deep. It can't be washed away that easily. I'll leave it up to time to heal the rest while I focus on my family.

TR

***Dear Cory,***

***I can't control my heart. As much as I try, the beat goes on. There's no power in that. The heart holds not only the power over our souls but the key to it.***

***I had this epiphany at three in the morning. I wish I could sleep, but my brain has other plans like torturing me with too many thoughts, regrets, and memories. Why this doesn't happen at three in the afternoon boggles my mind. It is what it is though.***

***XO***

By seven, I was tired and a bit delirious. I missed Dex already and it hadn't even been twenty-four hours. Not only that, but he was right. I *was* thinking of him fondly. When we let go of the anger, we find clarity in the remains.

Beth was here early to take the kids to camp and I was drinking my coffee before getting dressed for my meetings that got moved from yesterday to today. A trip to the hospital is usually an acceptable excuse to reschedule.

Janice's voice travels from the living room, calling my name. I put my makeup brush down and go out there. I haven't called her since the hospital, but I'm still hurt by what she said. When I walk out there, she's standing near the door, timid. With a half-smile she says, "I'm sorry about yesterday."

I love this woman, so it's hard to stay mad at her. Walking to her, I open my arms. When we hug, she says, "You're a wonderful mother to Neil and Cory Junior. I was upset thinking you were over my son."

Stepping back, I say, "I will never be 'over' Cory. But he needs to live in my heart because he's not here to live in our home. To be truthful with you, I'm lonely, Janice, and doing something for myself doesn't make me a bad mother. It makes me human. I can't wear black for the rest of my life. I still wear the ring, but I'm almost thirty and I don't want to spend my life alone."

"Just don't pick him."

"Dex?"

"Yes, you have to be careful who you bring around the kids, Rochelle. He's a bad influence."

"He's not. You're wrong, he's changed. You're reading tabloids and gossip magazines and believing them blindly. I know the real him."

She steps closer and takes my arms gently. "I love you like a daughter. I care about you, but I also know you're in a vulnerable state and can be easily taken advantage of if not careful. Dex is no good. There's always some truth found in those stories."

"Hearing you repeat it doesn't change how I feel about him. I can't help who I fall in love..." I stop, gasping. My hand covers my mouth and I turn away from her.

"You *love* him?" The words hit me in the back like tiny daggers.

The air is sucked from my chest as my own words sink in. "I... I might," I reply more for myself than her.

Upon this realization, I'm on the move. I run to the front door and slip on my Havianas. "I have to go."

"Where?"

Looking at her, seeing the shock in her eyes, makes me want to stay, but I can't. I'll talk myself out of doing this or she will. "We'll talk later. I'm sorry."

I run outside to my car. I'm five minutes down the road before I realize I didn't finish putting on my makeup, but I know he won't care. I see the way he looks at me. He more than likes me. He practically it said yesterday. I'm not sure I would call my feelings full blown star-crossed lovers love yet, but it sure feels like the beginning of something 'spectacular.' I need to talk to him, to talk this through with him, to apologize for everything I said. His plane for the last leg of the tour leaves in an hour, so I know he'll be up, but I've got to hurry.

After tapping in the code to his gate, I park next to a white convertible BMW. Makes me wonder if he got a new car though I've never thought of him as a BMW kind of guy. That will throw the paps off his trail for sure. I knock twice before finding the door unlocked. When no one answers, I walk in. I see a martini glass with a few shot glasses on the coffee table and get a sick feeling in my stomach, making me pause at the bottom of the stairs. I ascend them slowly, my gut telling me to go back to my car and call first. I go, my curiosity winning out. When I reach the second level, I walk to his room, finding the door cracked open. I push it the rest of the way open with one finger and my jaw drops along with my heart.

Platinum blonde hair, long, tan legs stretch across his bed, her breast exposed though the sheet does me the favor of keeping the rest of her body covered. *Firenza.*

Her blue eyes look up from the phone she's been reading, and she smiles. Elbowing Dex's back, she says, "We have company, Tiger."

"Rochelle?" His voice follows me as I turn and run down the stairs, but Dex catches me before I reach the front door. Looking down, I make sure he's not naked, not needing the gross reminder of what he was doing, which was very clear as he likes to say. "Let go of me, you bastard."

He has the nerve to be angry with me when he asks, "What are you doing here? You wanted nothing to do with me, so why are you here?"

Like a sucker punch, his words hit me in the gut, making me nauseous. Stepping back, he releases me. When I look up at him, his eyes are glazed and bloodshot.

"I came over here to tell you I was wrong. That I thought that maybe we were meant to be like you led me to believe."

A different emotion takes over his expression completely, and he says, "Rochelle... please." He gulps while reaching for me again. "I didn—"

"You didn't what, Dex?" All the adrenaline, the anger I had a minute before has left, leaving me defeated and deflated. "I thought you were right, but Janice was. Guess a 'tiger' can't change his stripes after all."

"Don't do this. You told me you didn't want to be with me. You said I was bad when all I've done is bend over backwards to prove to you that I'm good. You pushed me away."

I'm tired of crying, but they come anyway. "Not judgment, disbelief that one argument led to this. I stayed home and cried, hurt, confused, but alone. You call a fuck buddy over after telling me 'We matter.' We obviously don't or you wouldn't have had sex with her, and *her* of all people."

"It's just push and fucking pull with you. I get you've been hurt, but you chose to live with the pain than to move past it with me. I'm only doing what you and Cory's mother say I do. It's like manifest motherfucking destiny or some shit. So fuck this. I'm done."

We stare into each other's eyes, neither of us relenting until a cleared throat grabs our attention and we look up. Firenza stands on the top of the staircase in a tank that looks a lot like one of Dex's. "Come back to bed, Antonio."

When I look back to him, the disgust I feel far outweighs my weak emotions that I once felt for him. "And here I thought you were the good guy..."

There's a shift in his demeanor. I may be physically right here, but he knows my heart is already gone. Reaching for me, his voice wavers when he says, "Rochelle?" Regret colors him. "I didn't mean..."

Fear takes over in his eyes as I back away. The pain in my chest makes me want to run, but I won't let them win, refusing to let either of them see me breakdown. I open the door and start to leave, making it halfway to my car before I stop, and say, "As your business manager, I should remind you that your flight leaves in thirty minutes."

"Fuck!" I hear him yell before the door slams closed.

I get in my car and yell the same thing but for entirely different reasons.

# 13

When I open the door to my house, Janice is there and stands from the couch. I thought she'd be gone, wishing she had. I swipe at my eyes, hoping she doesn't see my tears. "Rochelle? Are you okay?"

"No," I reply, walking past her and going to my room. I slam the door closed and lay down on the bed, wishing for this day to go away, wishing I could go away for a few hours from myself.

I'm tired of being strong. Curling into a ball on my side, I finally drop the act I've put on for everyone else and cry. I give myself an hour to recover, but my heart is refusing the deadline. No matter how much I remind myself that I have to get ready for the meetings, I still struggle to pull myself together. This ache in my chest makes me think I'm mourning more than just the loss of Dex. Cory is always on my mind. I used to be happy. I used to carefree. I used to have a heart full of love. Now... I miss him. I miss the ease of our life together.

I went numb while holding my newborn. I should have gotten to enjoy my sweet baby being born. But that was ripped away from me when I was told of the plane crash. A numbness took over, then anger that welled up inside of me, squeezing the life out of me, making each breath hard to take as if the world was lacking oxygen.

The anger is so easily to identify with, but I pushed it down, not wanting to upset anyone, not wanting anyone to think I didn't love Cory. I loved him with all of my being. But he left me in a world I don't feel equipped to live in or maybe it's just my emotions that are hard to live with. I reach for the framed photo of me and Cory that sits on the nightstand. Taking it in hand, I run my finger over the glass. I see love when it was pure and simple. He made it so damn easy to love him. When I smile, I have a moment of clarity—Johnny, Dex, and Tommy mourned Cory's death. His family has mourned. Mourning doesn't mean forgetting... I will never forget him, but I need to mourn him.

Now I'm left questioning whether it was fair to start things with Dex under these conditions. Not being in the right state of mind, I'm in no mood to have to justify my reaction today. We had sex. We made out. We were coupling. That much is fact. So for him to jump into bed with someone else after a fight... I don't know if I can forgive him for that.

Thinking about him, makes me want to call him. And wanting to call him makes me feel pathetic. I check for any messages, just in case before setting my phone back down. Now I'm even more disappointed that he hasn't called or texted me. *Ugh!*

I try to convince myself that it's because he's on his flight, but deep down I know it's not. What pisses me off the most is that I want to hear from him. I want him to tell me this is all a misunderstanding and that what I walked in on wasn't what it looked like. But I know better no matter how much I try to change the image in my head. He also didn't deny it. I need to stop being stupid and focus on business.

TR

By the second meeting of the day, I'm bored. "These ideas are unoriginal," I start in. "I don't want the band doing the festival circuit. Anyway, I'm not seeing a need for them to tour next summer unless they have a new album out and right now they aren't due to go back into the studio for three months. Give them another two months to work through the tracks that haven't even been written and then we might have new music for them to promote. But it's going to be a hard sell to talk them into it now without tour ideas that wow them."

Nick is the home base assistant to Tommy. He says, "They're tired right now. Getting burned out like all bands nearing the end of a lengthy tour. Tommy says we shouldn't even pitch the idea to them until they're home and rested."

"I wouldn't even broach the subject unless we're solid with something original," I say, "Johnny likes real ideas, something he can visualize. We'd need to present it on paper, through art. Also, this tour needs a better concept for the drum kit. Dex..." My heart starts beating heavy in my chest. I clear my throat while looking down. Focus. "Umm... Dex likes his platform rounded and it's been square the last two tours."

MaryLee, the set designer, leans forward and asks, "Why does he like a rounded platform?"

I turn my attention to her, trying to hold any personal reaction I might have. "He thinks it shows off his drum set better. The curves highlight the curve of the kit. It's a personal thing, not something I think makes a difference to most, but he'll want input when it comes to the drum arrangement on stage."

She taps a pen against the table, looking to others for additional suggestions. When none come, she says, "What about we highlight Dex on the tour. He can have a sliding stage that moves front and center when he has a solo, then moves back into place?"

Nick agrees, "I like that idea."

I add, "It can move up and down maybe."

MaryLee sits ups. "That's a fantastic idea. We can showcase him."

Nodding, I say, "Get more ideas going. The album will set the theme, but we need these new concepts to really pull it off and get them enthused to sign on."

MaryLee asks, "When do you want the concepts?"

"We have time. Two months. I want a model made to see how the platform will work and to show the guys. Thanks for your time. We'll talk soon." I get up and leave, restraining myself from rushing to the elevators. As I ride down, I begin to wonder if I've screwed up my job now as well by sleeping with Dex. Any idiot would know this outcome was predictable, but I still fell for his act. That's just it. He said it himself—He was trying to prove how good he was. It doesn't come second nature to him. That's why he has to prove it. Good people don't have to prove it because they show through their every day behavior.

As soon as I'm in my car, I think about the time under the stars—big and little pictures—the details, and the kiss before we were caught.

I was a fool for going to his place. The second he had a chance, he dropped the good guy act and slipped right back into his wolfish self. He's probably breathing easier now that he's taken off the sheep's clothing.

Needing gas, I pull off to a gas station on La Cienega Boulevard. After it begins pumping, my thoughts drift back to the gathering at my house after the funeral. So vividly, I remember how he felt wrapped around me, and the smell of his breath against my neck as I cried, when he gave Neil the drumsticks, and how he replanted the lettuce knowing it was more about the metaphor than the vegetable.

Firenza invades the good—her arrogant smile, tearing me apart as she stood there mostly naked and called him by his first name like she has a right to. I almost prefer he fuck a nameless stranger, a groupie, instead of her. She knew I was a passing fancy and nothing more than a challenge he'd taken. Everything about her tone, words, and body language knew she would be with him again.

"Come here often?"

I look up and see Chad Spears standing on the other side of the pump getting gas. "Hi." He repeats himself, "Hi. Sorry to interrupt the deep conversation you seem to be having with yourself."

I laugh, suddenly embarrassed. "Yeah, deeps thoughts and all while getting gas. You know how that goes."

"Sure. I always come up with my best ideas while waiting at the gas pump." He smiles. "You're causing quite the stir these days."

Sighing, I ask, "Online?"

"Seems so. The girl who fought so hard to stay out of the headlines is now making them."

Glancing at the meter, I have a few more gallons to go before it's full. "LA sucks like that. I guess I'm not sure why there's interest in me at all."

"A beautiful widow, a tragic tale, and a bad boy. Makes for good gossip."

"Tragic is right."

"You still seeing Dex?"

My shoulders tense, my answer clipped. "Nope."

His pump clicks off before mine. He locks up his tank, then comes around to my side and leans his back against my Escalade. "How about that raincheck?"

It's the most sincere I've ever seen him. No guard or pretenses, no audience to perform for or like he's trying to impress me. Just a genuine smile and a gentle tone. He reminds me of teenage guys who haven't been defeated by rejection and not tasted enough success to have an attitude yet.

My pump clicks loudly and I reach for it, but he takes the handle before I can and puts it back in place. As I put the gas cap back on, I waiver, thinking I may have judged him because of Dex and maybe that's not fair. "I do owe you a drink."

Looking down at his watch, he says, "I'm late for a meeting, but how's Friday around three for you?"

I'm tired of trying to please everyone else. Chad Spears is not my future, but he may be fun with no commitment, maybe exactly what I need. Wondering if I'm trading one bad boy for another, I decide I don't care anymore. "That works."

"Cool." He hands me his phone. "What's your number? I'll text you."

"Here. I'll do it." I take the phone and program my number into it.

"So," he says all flirty and looking better than he ever has on a red carpet. "Friday?"

"Yeah, Friday."

With a little wave, he walks back to his sports car and I walk around mine to get in. One more glance in his direction and I smile before he drives off. I follow behind but turn the opposite way on Le Cienega. I immediately turn on music so I don't have the quiet to over think what I just agreed to. It's a drink at three, basically the same as a business meeting. The music gets louder, so I let the date and all the heavy thoughts stop and try to enjoy someone else's rhythm for a while.

TR

Spending time with my boys renews me. There are no other beings on earth that bring me more happiness or make me more proud. As Neil reads to his little brother, I hold them on either side of me, loving the sound of their voices and giggles. After 'The End' is read, I give them a bath, letting them play in my jetted tub, which they love. My mind occasionally wanders to Dex, wondering if he's thinking of me, like I have him. Wondering if he cares how much he hurt me.

By eight o'clock, I'm wiped out just like the boys. My mind even more tired than my body. My heart still bruised. I crawl under my covers and check my phone on my nightstand. There's a text from Tommy: ***We need to talk. Call me after the show.***

Crap.

I look at the time again. The band is playing in Florida, so they're on Eastern Standard. They should be halfway through the show if they started on time. I text back: ***I'll call you in two hours.***

I can only imagine what he needs to talk about at this time of night. I'm sure Dex has told his side of the tale by now and I'm probably the bad guy for breaking his heart. I cringe thinking I might have to talk about this, but they should hear my side before their judgments settle in.

Grabbing my files from the end of the bed, I open them wide, then spread out the contracts for the new offers that were sent over from the main office. Action figures. *No*. Wine... um, *No*. Not their style at all. Private jet company. *Too flashy*. Watches. *Maybe*. A tour book. *Maybe*. A documentary. *Maybe*. A line of athletic wear. *No*. I gather the maybes and stack the rest back up and place them in the No folder. I'm gonna have to present these in the next two weeks to the guys, which means traveling to see them. As much as I think I can be professional around Dex, I also know my heart isn't ready to see him.

His betrayal has tainted our past and all of the things that made us special together. Everything has changed for the worse. We weren't special. *I* wasn't special. I was used like so many before me. He had no intention of love, but I believed his words. Now I believe his actions. They speak louder. I just hope I can bear to be in the same room as him.

Logging onto the tour schedule, I look at the dates and cities. Miami in nine days. Nine days to wean my heart away from him. Nine days to mentally prepare myself to see him after our fight. Nine days to forget the past and try to move forward like we never happened. Nine days.

Ready or not, I'll go because I have to. I'm damn good at what I do and I'm not gonna let little things like broken hearts and hurt feelings get in my way.

TR

My phone rings just after ten-thirty. "Hello?"

Tommy's voice is gruff. "Hey Rochelle, I need talk to you about Dex."

Bracing myself to the mattress the best I can, I wearily reply, "Okay, but I think it's only fair that I get to share my side of it."

"Your side of what?"

"What happened betw—Wait, what were you going to say?"

"His kit got damaged in transport. He got through the show by using a floor model from Guitar Center. It's not gonna work for the tour. It's not made for that kind of stress. I'm sending over the contact information for the set maker. Call them first thing in the morning and see if they can rush the frame, bass, tom-tom, and snare out overnight to the next city. Philly. Philly's next."

"What happened? And what about the rest of the equipment?"

"The hi-hat and other symbols are fine. A local stagehand put the set down on the dock and a backloader didn't see it. Bent it to shit. Dex is pissed."

"He should be pissed. Will the current set work if the other won't make it?"

"For the next show, yeah. But he was hitting pretty hard tonight. I don't know if it will make it for two shows. It's not as heavy as his usual. Oh and maybe give him a call tomorrow. He seemed out of sorts today. Left his clothes because he was late for the plane. Said he didn't have time to pack. Maybe you can send some clothes too."

"Geez, Tommy, let me just drop everything and go shopping for Dex," I reply sarcastically. "He forgot his clothes? What happened to *you* managing him during the tour?"

"C'mon, Ro. Do me the favors. I can only do so much from here and keeping a tight leash on the guys is doing me in already and it's only the first show of this leg."

"What do you mean?"

"Dex is wasted because he's upset about the drums. Johnny left after the show. Derrick and Kaz are dragging me out with them. I'm thinking I need to go to keep an eye on them. You know how those two are when they party."

"Partying with the guys sounds like real torture, Tommy," I say, rolling my eyes. "But don't worry. I'll handle everything in the morning."

"I knew I could count on you."

"No need to suck up. I already said yes. Don't you have some bars to get to?"

He laughs. "Yup, getting right on that. Thanks for the help."

As soon as the phone disconnects, I lay in bed and turn on the TV, trying to distract myself from the fact that I have to return to Dex's house in the morning. *Damn him.* There's just no escaping. As soon as I decide to get out, I'm dragged right back into the lion's den... or tiger and lair in his case, according to Firenza.

# 14

I'm not happy about going back to the scene of the cheating crime, but I'll do it for Tommy. Even though it's really for Dex. I swallow my pain, blaming myself for getting involved with him in the first place, and go inside with a huff.

His house is quiet, the house manager only coming twice a week while he's on tour to check on things, organize mail, and dust. I help pay the bills while the guys are gone, so I know all of this. I know too much these days. I shut the door behind me and stand there, smacked by the conversation I was caught in the last time I stood in this spot. The disappointment that he could give us up so easily, that he could move on so fast, weighs my feet to the spot, hesitant to go further. I steel myself and head upstairs not wanting to waste any more time than necessary here.

His bed is made this time. I'm sure with fresh sheets, but the memory still remains. My senses tormented by the memory. Firenza taints that same bed that I once had sex with him in. My stomach rolls, so I take a deep breath, gripping my arms around me and focus on the job at hand. I direct my gaze to his nightstand where his charger sits, no phone attached, and I wonder if I should pack it. I walk over, reaching behind the stand to unplug it, knowing the answer already. The corner of a photo tucked under a leather book catches my eye.

I reach for it and pull, sliding it out from under its hiding spot. My breath doesn't catch, it stops altogether as I stare down at a photo of me.

I don't remember when or where it was taken. There's a light reflecting in my eyes, the area around me has a red glow, maybe an after party from eight or nine years ago judging by my hairstyle. Two corners are bent and finger prints cover the glossy surface. I don't know why Dex has it, but all that strength I gathered to get through this task suddenly evaporates. I sit on the edge of the bed and stare down at it. It's a smile I don't recognize as one I usually have, not posed for the camera, exposing an inner happiness, one not manufactured *for* others but instead *by* others.

Tucking it back under the well-worn leather book, I'm tempted to open the book. It looks like a journal though so I don't. My thoughts are still on why Dex has this picture of me and it raises questions. Too many to work through right now.

"Ms. Floros, hello?"

I turn around and see his house manager. "Hi, Marguerite. Um..." Suddenly I feel the need to explain why I'm here as she looks at me curiously. "Dex needs clothes overnighted to him. He was running late, so Tommy asked me to come here and pack a case."

"I can help you. I know where everything is."

Relieved, I say, "That would be great."

She goes to his closet and pulls down a duffle bag and has an arm full of T-shirts when she walks back out. "These are his favorites. I keep them together. That way he can find them easily. Maybe three pairs of jeans?" She sets the stuff down on the bed.

"Yes, that will work." I start to put the shirts in the bag as she goes back to the closet for more clothes. Peeking over at her, I say, "I saw a picture on his nightstand."

She stills, her hands stopping on a stack of jeans. She recovers quickly though and says, "Yes," and nothing else.

"It's of me."

"Yes," she replies when she returns. She sets the jeans down, her eyes lowered as well, almost seeming to avoid my questioning ones.

Wanting to pursue it more, I ask, "Can you tell me about it?"

"I'm not sure."

"You clean his room. So you know it's there. Has he ever mentioned it?"

"Ms. Floros—"

"Please call me Rochelle."

Her kind smile reappears. "Rochelle, I've only ever had instructions, not explanations."

"That sounds like Dex. He's not the best at explaining his actions." A dig I should have probably saved for him.

Walking to the dresser, she shuffles around and I continue packing the bag. She looks over at me and says, "It's to remain there."

I stop what I'm doing, and ask, "What is? The photo?"

"Yes, those are my instructions. He wants it there, except when he knows he's going to be having company. Then I'm supposed to put it in the drawer."

"Those are pretty specific instructions."

With a small smile, she says, "Yes, they are."

She doesn't need to explain anymore, the drift is caught in her expression. After adding his boxer briefs into the bag, she puts two handfuls of socks, then disappears into the bathroom. She's not gone long, but long enough for me to slip over to the nightstand and grab the picture. I tuck it into the bag, hidden from view just as she returns with a toiletry case and sets it inside the bag. It's zipped closed. She grabs a little lock from the closet and fastens it. "Women steal his clothes. They all want a piece of him," she says, protectively.

Grabbing it off the bed, I turn and head out of the bedroom. "I'll ship it from the office address so they won't know it's his."

Following me down the stairs, she says, "He cares about you."

I stop with three steps to go and look over my shoulder. She seems like she might want to say more, but I don't. "Thanks for helping me pack, Marguerite."

"You're welcome."

Outside, I toss the bag in the back of my SUV and drive away feeling more confused than when I arrived, as if that was even possible. After I ship the duffle bag, I call the makers of his preferred drums. Cost is not a factor so they'll hit the road themselves and have them delivered and setup for the show tomorrow. He'll be happy. Tommy will be happy. And I can go back to dealing with my work.

***Dear Cory,***

***I don't want to talk to anyone else about this, so I hope you don't mind my nonsense. I should be working. Should being the operative part of that sentence. But I have so much on my mind. I was just thinking the problem with plans, like working, is that your mind and heart don't care***

***about the day-to-day routines. They care about things that affect them and make them work harder, beat faster.***

***Today I had a fascinating conversation with Marguerite, Dex's housekeeper. The conversation has played*** on repeat all afternoon and pretty much the entire next day.

***I found this photo he had...*** I sigh. ***You know, I shouldn't bother you with silly stuff like this. I miss you.***

***XO***

I close the journal and think on the photo. A photo of me that he keeps on his nightstand only adds to the bewilderment I have over this whole situation. What Marguerite said about the photo makes me think that maybe there is something more to this story. But my more logical side cannot come to any solid conclusion to why he would lie to me. So I am stuck—*do I believe what Marguerite said or do I believe what I saw?*

TR

I arrive at the café a few minutes early, but I'm impressed that Chad Spears has arrived even earlier. "Hello," I say, approaching the table.

"Hi." He stands and comes around to pull my chair out for me. We greet each other Hollywood style—a faux-kiss to the cheek. "You look beautiful," he says.

"Thank you." I sit down as he takes his seat across the small table from me. "Have you been waiting long?"

"No, less than five minutes." The waiter approaches and Chad asks, "Champagne, Rochelle?"

"Are we celebrating?"

"Yes."

"Champagne will be great then."

The waiter walks away in a hurry, eager to please. I'm sure everyone is eager to please Chad since he's famous.

Chad leans his elbows on the table and says, "I'm glad you met me."

"You mean met you as a person or here today? Ha!" I joke.

"Both." He smiles. Holding the menu, he asks, "Have you been here before? It's early, but I'm hungry. Are you?"

"I haven't been here." Looking around, I add, "I like it. And I can always eat."

The bottle of champagne arrives and our glasses are filled as menus are set down in front of us and specials announced. When we're alone, I lift my glass and ask, "So what are we celebrating?"

"Us. To us and finally cashing in that raincheck." He's a charmer all right. Our glasses tap together and we drink. As I'm setting mine down, he asks, "How have you been?"

"Good. Busy with life. You know how it is."

"Yeah, I head out next week—"

The waiter appears and asks, "Do you know what you'd like to order?"

Chad turns to him, but with a glance to me, he asks, "Rochelle?"

"I'll have the Waldorf salad, light on the dressing."

Chad orders plain grilled chicken and steamed veggies before turning his full attention back to me. "So as I was saying, I head out next week to start a project in Toronto."

"Oh," I remark, picking up my glass. I drink and listen as he talks about this movie for some indie director that he thinks could lead to an Oscar nomination for him. My mind wanders, remembering this is why I always got along with musicians better—they are less talk and more action.

My hand is grabbed and I look up at him. He says, "Okay?"

"What?" I ask, surprised. Busted for not listening. Oops.

His brow is furrowed as he pleads, "When she gets here, pretend to be my girlfriend. Okay?"

I realize I had not heard whatever led up to this question and thinking he realizes it too because he says, "This chick, she's all over me all the time. She'll come over here in a minute. Pretend to be my girlfriend. I've been trying to shake her for months."

I feel bad for not paying attention and readily agree. "Oh. Sure. Okay."

When he looks over my shoulder, he says, "She's coming." I start to look back, but he stops me. "Don't look! Keep your eyes on me."

"Chad, darling," I hear over my right shoulder. "I didn't know you were still in town. I would have called."

Looking up, I recognize her as a popular LA socialite who lives to make tabloid headlines and not much else. He stands to greet her, effectively pulling me up with him. They European kiss—one on each cheek. She lingers and he tugs me closer. As she backs up, he wraps his arm around my waist and kisses me on the cheek. "Have you met Rochelle Floros?"

His arm snuggling me close doesn't seem to faze her. Like Dex, maybe he just has a whole slew of fuck buddies. She replies, "I don't believe I have, but I've spent a lot of time in New York and Miami recently. I'm Dotty Greensberg."

*Dotty Greensberg?* I stifle a laugh and offer a hand instead. "Nice to meet you."

"Rochelle is my girlfriend," Chad states confidently.

I remain quiet, trying to channel the fake girlfriend role I've been asked to play.

"Girlfriend?" she asks as if the word is foreign to her, a glare directed at him. "So this is a new relationship?"

"Yes," he replies. "Well, it was good to see you, Dotty."

The waiter walks up with our plates.

She gives her best smile trying to hide her heartbreak. It's obvious she likes him, but I've learned that it takes two or someone always gets screwed. "Yes, I should go. I'm meeting my agent at the bar."

Chad releases me and I sit down, the charade almost over. They polite kiss each other goodbye and he sits down smiling. Putting his napkin back in his lap, he says, "I think that went well."

"Yeah, seemed like she believed you." Believe. Believe. Charades... Dex. I drop my fork.

Chad asks, "What is it? Your salad?"

Was I set up? Dex wants me to believe he slept with Firenza. Maybe he didn't... or maybe he did. If he didn't, why would he want me to believe a lie? He tried to say something, but I cut him off.

"Rochelle?"

I look back up at Chad.

He says, "You keep disappearing. Am I that boring?"

"No," I say, shaking my head. "I just have a lot on my mind. I'm sorry." Trying to keep my mind from reeling in conspiracy theories, I attempt to keep my attention on Chad.

"No problem. So how's the band business?"

We fall into light conversation, easier than I expected it to be with him. But after spending time with him one-on-one, I have a feeling he doesn't do deep conversation. He loves to talk fashion and gossip. I listen most of the time, not able to add too much to either of those topics. After we eat, I call it a day wanting to go home and think about things.

While waiting for our cars at the valet out front, I say, "Thank you for the meal and drinks."

"Thank you for joining me. So I mentioned I'm leaving soon, next week in fact, but I have this party to go to on Sunday. Would you like to go with me?"

"Oh... *like on a date*?"

"Yeah," he says, smiling. "Kind of like what we just went on."

My head goes back. "Was this a date?"

"Was it not?"

My embarrassment is felt through the heat of my cheeks. "I'm sorry. Yes, of course. I just thought of it as more friends hanging out when you asked me."

"I know you have a lot going on with the band and you know, your other things—"

"My kids?" I fill in the 'other things' for him.

"Yeah, your kids. But I like you—"

"*But* you like me? You mean in spite of my kids?"

"You'll have to give me time. I've not dated anyone with kids before."

I try to end his failed attempt to explain things as the hole he's digging gets deeper. "Chad, I think we both can see there's no romantic chemistry between us. I know about your history with Dex and I don't know if that played into why you asked me here today, but let's just stay friends. I had fun. We don't need to ruin it with starting something that's obviously not gonna work for either of us."

He's not sad. He's not relieved. But he's grateful. "I would have slept with you, you know."

I laugh. "Geez, I appreciate it, but I'm all good in that department."

My car arrives first. “Thank you again.” I smile as I walk away. “Break a leg on that new project.”

With a nod, he says, “Thanks.”

And that was the beginning and end of my relationship with Chad Spears. As soon as Dex came to mind, the date was already over in my mind. So now I need to figure out what the deal is with him and why I’m holding on so tight to the possibility. He’s only caused me heartache, but deep down, way deep down, he might be worth the pain.

# 15

I fly to Miami on a Monday. After a week of meetings, packing, and work, I leave my boys in the care of Janice and take off for Florida. On the plane I go over the files one more time, making sure I can answer any questions the guys might have regarding the deals. The flight is a little turbulent and sickens my stomach. While cleaning up in the bathroom, I look in the mirror. My hands are shaking and I'm a little pale. I should have gotten a prescription, but deep down I know I'm not just upset from the flight.

I've lost a lot of sleep the last few nights. I had nine days and seemed to have squandered them away, not feeling any less hurt than I did then. Screw Dex. I don't owe him anything and he owes me nothing. We are back to being completely platonic. Just how we should have stayed all along.

I flash my pass and go backstage, finding Tommy near the backup amps on stage left. Hugging him, we don't bother talking, since the band is performing, and neither of us wants to shout.

The set change and break happens after this song. As soon as it ends, the band hurries off stage, knowing they have ten minutes to do whatever they need to do—whether it's use the bathroom, get a drink, or make a phone call. They run down the stairs that are near us. Each one of them smiles at me as they pass, except for Dex who eyes me but keeps walking. We follow them into the dressing room, Tommy shutting the door behind. Like a coach, he goes over what's working and what didn't, including one of Johnny's guitars that broke a string while he was playing.

I try to give Dex his space by standing across the room. As much as I kind of want to reach out to him, I don't. I'm conflicted over this whole mess we've found ourselves in and burned he picked someone else up so soon after our fight. *Am I being unreasonable?* I don't even know. I'm a girl and sometimes reason takes a backseat to feelings. Sucks, but I'm not unique this way.

Without my eyes leaving my feet, I feel the weight of his gaze on me, a stare that caresses my curves, reminding me of where his hands once were. When I dare look over, the warmth I'm so used to seeing has left... what is there, I'm unfamiliar with, so I turn away.

"When's the meeting?" Johnny asks me after he finishes drinking his water.

"Lunch tomorrow. My suite."

He nods. "Let's go." They all stand up and Tommy opens the door.

Just as Dex passes, he whispers without looking, "Thanks for the clothes."

"You're welcome."

I don't get any visitors tonight, stuck in my room alone. I chose not to go out with Kaz and Derrick. Tommy called it a night and went to bed as soon as we got back. Johnny was meeting friends for a late dinner and Dex disappeared. I have no idea what happened to him and I try not to spend my night guessing either. That could lead to disastrous thoughts of groupies and drugs. I'm not ready to go there right now, so I turn my attention to the fact that he's made a huge impact on my life in such a short amount of time. When he spent time with Neil after the funeral. The way he 'fixed' CJ's boo boo. When he looks at me like he can't bear to lose me. All of these memories are little Band-aids on my heart. I sigh.

I just can't seem to stop thinking about him despite my better judgment. I was unsuspecting, but not blind and yet, it feels like this man I've known forever came out of nowhere and swept me off my feet.

Maybe I'm being ridiculous or maybe he's made a bigger mark on my heart than I originally thought. *How much pain can one heart bear? Am I willing to take another beating? Is Dex worth it?* The mystery that he's laid out before me makes me wonder what he's up to, which is driving me bizonkers. *Why can't I just get clear-cut answers? Why must it all be a guessing game when it comes to him? Why is he lying to me? Or is he telling the truth?*

I turn on the TV and fall asleep after watching three Friends episodes in a row.

TR

The next morning, I head downstairs to the coffee stand in the lobby. I'm waiting behind three other people desperately in need of caffeine like me. The one at the front can't seem to figure out their cup sizes, so the barista is going through explaining and taking way too long to do so. I check my phone for the fourth time since I have the meeting in less than thirty minutes and at the snail's rate of this line, I might not get my coffee. That doesn't bode well for anybody.

"Can I buy you a cup of Joe?"

I recognize the smooth voice before I see him. Turning around, I say, "Make it a latte and you've got yourself a deal."

Dex doesn't smile, but he doesn't look unhappy to see me either. "You always liked your lattes. Mocha as usual?"

"Yep." I find myself swaying between my anger from his actions and the traitorous side of me that wants to take his side and let him back in, just a little bit.

"Surprised you're talking to me."

"It was only a yep. Don't get your hopes too high." I roll my eyes.

"I'll take one word over the silent treatment."

When I look up, he has the most sincere smile on his face. He's hard to resist. "Anyway, I thought you weren't talking to me after our fight, so we're even."

"I'm sorry."

"Let's not get too deep. Haven't had my first cup yet."

He chuckles lightly. "Maybe later then."

I shrug and looked toward the baked goods display. "Yeah, maybe later."

A guy in line starts saying, "Dude... dude. Oh shit. Dude."

I see him pointing at Dex and Dex instantly tenses, so I offer, "How about I buy you a coffee this time and I'll see you at the meeting?"

"Deal." He steps out of line quickly and hurries away before the fan can fully comprehend that he was standing next to greatness.

"Dude," the guy says again, this time into his phone. "He was right in front of me..."

I finally reach the front of the line and order the coffees. I decide to buy a to-go container for the guys just in case they haven't had any. When I reach my room, I struggle opening the door with my hands full, but Kaz shows up and helps.

We go inside and I situate the coffee in the living room portion of the suite near the couch. He settles in and closes his eyes. I let him rest. I know how touring tears you down physically, remembering the old days when I toured with Cory.

Everyone arrives on time, some not as happy with the ten o'clock meeting time, but it is what it is. And what it is, is business we must get done. I go over the proposals with them and they decide which ones to move forward on and which ones to eliminate.

As a group, they seem satisfied, so I am. When they leave, I start making calls and getting contracts sent over. I log onto the latest batch of paparazzi photos taken of the band members that their press agent sent over. It's the usual boring stuff which I like to see. Nothing salacious. Nothing newsworthy in their personal lives. These are the kinds of pics that don't get bought by tabloids or blogs.

But when I scroll to the fourth page, I see me—me and Chad Spears from our kind-of-sort-of date. *Shit!* My heart starts pounding and my hands start shaking while I reach for my phone. I immediately call Rory, the band's public relations agent.

He picks up on the first ring. "I've been expecting this phone call."

"Can you kill the pics?"

"Too late. They were sold to two sites last night. That's when I found out about them."

"Make them go away, Rory." I beg, "Please."

"Rochelle, you should have given me a heads up. I could have done something then, but now, it's too late. I'm sorry. I can look into the story they'll post with it and try to use some tactics to get them to go easy, but it's Chad Spears. He sells magazines. He gets people clicking online. You being a widow of a famous musician and with him gets *even more* hits."

"I can't... These photos will upset people. Cory's Mother for one."

"And Dex."

The way he says it so casually as if the whole world knows our secret makes me cringe. "What do you know about that?"

"Everything. That story of you kissing at the bar—another time you should have forewarned me."

"I'm new to this. Cut me some slack."

"Slacks been cut. Now it's time to play hardball. I'm gonna send you an email that I usually send my clients when I first bring them on. It's how to stay out of the headlines when you don't want to make headlines. I suggest you memorize it if you don't want the attention. If you do want it, I can help you out there as well, but I'll need some forewarning next time."

"I don't want the attention. How much time do we have before this story comes out?"

"Less than twenty-four hours I would say, but probably closer to an hour. The online blogs are fast with this kind of news and it's already a few days old."

Looking out my room window, I stare at a nearby building that's blocking the sun, casting a shadow over the hotel. Very ominous. Very fitting. I sigh, dropping my head down.

"Hey Rochelle, I'll do my best," he says, his voice sympathetic. "I've already got calls into them."

"Thank you, Rory. I appreciate it."

*Shit! What have I done?* I need to tell Dex before he hears about it.

A hard knock on the door foreshadows things to come. I stand slowly, the weight of a thousand waves pulling me back, begging me not to answer. I have to though. I peek through the peephole and my fears are confirmed. When I open the door, Dex walks in and straight for the window. His body is stiff as he paces back in forth. I remain standing near the door. "Hi," I say, a fake happy tone failing me.

His eyes hit me like daggers when he asks, "Do you want to talk about anything?"

Cowering a bit, I reply, "Not really."

Turning his back on me, he nods and stares out the window. His voice is alarmingly calm like lava boiling at the base of a volcano. "I only asked you not to date one person." When he looks at me again, he narrows his eyes and asks, "Do you remember who that one person was?"

It's not a question and we both know it. "Chad Spears," I answer begrudgingly.

"God damn it, Rochelle." He closes his eyes as if he can calm himself by not seeing me. When he opens them again, he shakes his head. Instead of saying anything else, he comes toward me, closing the gap in a few long strides. But he doesn't stop. He keeps going and leaves the room. The disappointment I feel is abruptly halted as the door flies open before it has time to latch. His body is pressing against mine and he kisses me. I push back but he holds tightly to him. And just as fast as he kissed me, he stops. Brushing his lips against mine, he whispers,

"That was the last time I will ever kiss you."

And then he leaves me standing there breathless and agitated.

# 16

Here I stand, just seconds separating us, in shock as my door slams closed, automatically locking with a thud. *The last kiss he'll ever give me?* The last kiss *he'll* ever give me!

*His egotism is exasperating.*

The nerve of him swooping in here and kissing *me* like I was the one who wanted it. He took it without my permission. It was him... *clearly.* And now I've been rendered speechless while my lips continue to tingle even after he's gone.

The one thing I didn't count on when I was planning this trip was how I would feel about Dex. Sure, I'd let a million scenarios play out in my head, but they were ones based on harsher realities. When I saw him, all of those thunderous emotions weakened. I had somehow forgotten how handsome he was or that he has this innate ability to win people over with just his smile. The boy is gifted and no heart stands a chance against him. Obviously, I'm no different. Compound that with his nerve to threaten me with kisses or lack thereof and my mood sours.

Frustrated, I fist my hands and go to my computer to look up flights. *Screw this!* I don't need this added headache, this added heartache. Tommy can get any additional contracts signed. For my own sanity, I need to get the hell out of here.

A knock matching the last one sounds out and I stomp my way over. I glare at the back of the wood door gathering my anger together and ready to direct it at Dex. I swing the door wide open and spew, "How dare you—"

"How dare I what?" Johnny asks, his eyebrows knitted together.

"Oh!" I lean, easing back. "Hi. I thought you were someone else."

"Clearly."

I roll my eyes when I hear that damn word again.

He walks in like he owns the place. "Are we gonna keep pretending like no one knows what's going on between you and Dex?"

Exhaling heavily, I reply with sarcasm and a tilted grin, "Sounds good to me."

He sits at the desk, kicking his feet up next to my laptop. With a glance over at the screen that shows the different airline options, he asks, "Going somewhere?"

"I'm leaving."

"Tomorrow."

Shaking my head, I say, "No, tonight, Johnny."

"You can't tonight. I don't have anyone to eat dinner with."

"You have the band, Tommy, thirty stagehands, fans, radio DJ's, press—"

He chuckles. "Yeah, sure. I'll call up the press and ask if anyone wants to have dinner with me."

Lowering his feet, he leans forward and looks down. I sit on the edge of the bed, still trying to calm down, and wait. I'm not sure if I'm going to get a lecture or what, but I let him lead the conversation. After a minute or so, he says, "I'd like to have dinner with you and talk." His voice is softer and sincere, more Jack Dalton than Johnny Outlaw. "Will you have dinner with me?"

Our eyes meet and my anger starts to dissipate. "Just like old times. Almost." Cory's not here.

"Yeah," he says, knowing exactly what I mean. "Almost."

Always a sucker for his charming side, I guess I'm staying the night. "I will. But I don't want to talk about Dex, okay?"

"Okay."

TR

"So when did you and Dex start up?" Johnny asks right before taking a bite of his steak.

I set my fork down, but continue chewing the bite in my mouth before speaking. "You said we wouldn't talk about him."

Pointing his fork at me, he says, "No, you said you didn't want to talk about him. I want to talk about what's going on with you. The band knows. Hell, everyone on the tour knows. You guys can't hide your relationship for shit. Like, you're the worst secret lovers that ever were. I mean—"

"All right. All right. Stop it. First of all, we are not in a relationship. Secondly, we are not *secret* lovers."

"I know. That's my point. You suck at hiding these things."

I sigh, rolling my eyes. As much as he's frustrating, he's kind of funny too. "Stop teasing. We aren't lovers at all."

"Have you had sex?"

"Johnny!"

"You've had sex with Dex." His face scrunches in disgust. "And besides that rhyming, gross by the way. I'm totally judging you for that."

"You sound like Holli."

He shrugs, not ashamed. God love him.

As he drinks his beer, I say, "Look, I'll tell you what we're not. We're not lovers, secret or otherwise. We're not friends because we can't seem to do that without other stuff getting in the way—"

"Like your attraction for each other?"

"Settle down, Mr. Quicky with the Comebacks. No, I meant all of this baggage both of us are lugging around."

"Maybe it's time to lighten the load, Rochelle."

"I can't. I'm held to different standards. Impossible standards."

"Not by me. I don't like the idea of you and Dex. I mean Dex can't do better than you, so I see why he's in it. But as for you, Dex is pretty much rock bottom. So what's your excuse?"

I look around the restaurant. It's a traditional steakhouse and dim, candles on the tables, and us in a booth in the corner. I spin my wine glass around a few times before lifting it and taking a sip. He's stopped eating and is waiting for my reply, but I'm not sure what to say, so I go with the truth, tired of hiding my real feelings. "I'm lonely."

And there it is, a soft sigh accompanied with a side of sympathy written all over his face. "That. What you're doing right there, Johnny, that's what I don't want. Not from you. Not from anyone."

Leaning back, he drops his hands to his sides. His eyes fixed on mine. "I want what's best for you and the boys."

"I know. I do too. But I'm starting to feel like what's best for me as a woman may not be what's best for the boys."

"Dex isn't that bad. I mean, he's actually kind of cool. We've kept him around for a reason."

With a light laugh, I say, "I know that too, but Janice doesn't. The tabs don't."

"Fuck the tabs. We don't live our lives to justify our actions to them. Sometimes we fuck up and sometimes the day turns out better than planned. We just have to do the best we can. As for Janice, I know I don't have to explain her angle. You're well aware of that. But she loves you and she loves those kids. You guys are all that remains of her son, so she's gonna be tough on you. Probably not accept some guy strutting in like he's gonna replace Cory."

Looking down at the burgundy table cloth, running my finger along the fold wrinkle, I release a deep breath. "Dex didn't strut, but I treated him like he did."

With a slight nod in understanding, Johnny says, "I have a feeling he's underestimated a lot."

"But we shouldn't. As his friends, we should stick by him. I've seen how much he's changed over the years and I doubted what I knew to be true because of my own fears of being judged."

Johnny shifts when the waiter arrives, and asks, "Would you like to see our dessert menu?"

"No, thank you," he replies and then I repeat the same.

When we're alone again, he leans in. "From where I sit, you have a choice to make."

"I pushed him away," I interrupt. "And then he slept with someone and I caught them, so there's no choice to make anymore."

His face contorts. "Hmmm."

"For some reason my gut tells me he didn't, but he wants me to believe he did."

"What?"

"Exactly. It's a mess." With another sigh, I say, "We're a mess."

"Back up. He slept with someone, but didn't, but wants you to believe he did?"

"I don't know for certain, but something like that."

"You guys are twisted." The check arrives and he glances over it, sets his credit card down in the folder, then scopes out the restaurant. The waiter swipes it from the table, leaving us alone again. Usually by this point at dinner, he gets anxious to leave because word has spread that he's in the restaurant. It will be a miracle if we get out of here without him stopping to take a pic or signing an autograph or twenty. Looking down at his watch, he says, "It's almost eleven, but I'm up for an adventure. How about you?"

His excitement is contagious, so I ask, "Like old times?"

He smirks. "Yeah, but without the cop chase."

Nodding toward the door, I say, "Let's go."

Thirty minutes later, the band—all four members—Tommy and me, are piled into a light blue minivan heading away from South Beach. The food I just ate feels heavy in my stomach, the awkwardness of the situation not sitting well with me. I did not have enough to drink to pretend to be cool.

"Where are we going?" Kaz asks, shifting uncomfortably next to me.

I elbow behind me lightly. "Stop moving. You just jabbed me in the boob." I'm half on his lap and Derrick's right leg. Dex is on the other side of Derrick crammed against the far door.

"Sorry," Derrick mumbles.

Tommy laughs from the front seat. Dex leans forward and hits him on the arm, sneaking a peek at me in the process. Johnny hands his phone to Tommy and tells him to put on some music. Classic Aerosmith starts playing just seconds later; the melody calming the giggles and grunts as we settle in. Music is the thread that stitches us together. I feel Kaz's foot bounce to the beat. Out of the corner of my eye, I spy Dex drumming his fingers on his legs.

The van crosses over a large bridge and then turns off on a small street that veers toward the beach. When Johnny parks, we all stagger out of the van, enjoying that we can stretch our cramped up legs.

The beach is isolated. More of a fisherman's beach than a sunbathers. The headlights shine forward, lighting the water as it crashes down on the sand. I take my shoes off and walk forward wanting to get lost in the sounds of the music, the ocean, and the dark sky above.

Kaz and Tommy are nearby. Derrick is on his phone and walking down the beach. Johnny lays down in the sand halfway between the water's edge and the car. And Dex—I turn back and see him sitting on the hood of the dated rental. He's a silhouette of darkness, smoke wafting into the wind before it has time to settle above his head. He's watching me. Unabashedly. His gaze seeking me out and taking hold, making me want to go to him. The water covers my feet and splashes up the side of my legs. The bottom of my jeans are rolled up but still get wet.

As "Dream On" by Aerosmith kicks in, I trek back. When I pass Johnny, he lazily asks, "You sure?"

"Yeah," I reply and keep walking. Dex's legs are parted, his forearms resting on his knees. He's wearing sunglasses not to hide his eyes, but to hide his emotions. He can't hide though. Just like me, there's more to this, more to us than he can admit. I lean my back against the grill, resting on the bumper and keep my eyes forward.

His knee bumps me and I turn to look at him. In a hurry, he slides down the hood, his feet hitting the sand. I stand and he looks at me. Lifting his sunglasses up, his expression more pissed than any other. With a slight roll of his body, he's pressed against me, his arms on either side of me, his palms flat on the hood. His head is on my shoulder, and he says, "You're inside of me, the blood that fills my veins, the aches that my heart feel, and every good decision I ever made. That's what you mean to me. I can't stay away from you and I don't want to." Lifting up and looking me in the eyes, his lips brush against my cheek without leaving a kiss, and he adds, "You're the melody I can't capture and the notes I can't hit. But I can't fight your pull, always gravitating toward your world, to you." Just when I think he might kiss me, going against his promise from this morning, he pushes off, leaving me in awe of not only his words, but the man himself. The underlying passion we fight so hard against is back in place, denying us both any peace until we give in again.

With my mouth left agape, it's times like these I wish I smoked. I steady myself as I walk back to Johnny and sit down silently next to him. His arm goes out and I lie back, using it as a pillow. Our life experiences have bonded us. He's become the only man I can rely on in my life. One of his best qualities is he knows when and when not to push. He stays quiet, letting the waves fill the air instead.

Derrick is the next to join us, sitting down on the other side of me. Tommy and Kaz leave the laughter down at the water and sit next to Derrick. I see Dex in the distance throwing something into the ocean; a seashell is my guess.

Despite his actions, he still fascinates me. Physically, he's so beautiful, and could easily be mistaken for a model down here in Miami. But his insides are conflicted. He's a lot like me in that way. I know there's good inside. I've seen it in him. But sometimes, we can't fix people. He wants to live one way, but his image comes into play and he battles that demon daily. I realize regardless of our pull, as he calls it, our efforts might not be enough. He might have to be the one who finds his own peace instead of me giving him what he needs. I may not be able to do that.

I sit up just as Dex sits down on the other side of Johnny. No one says anything, and a different song echoes through the windows of the van. Kaz is smoking a joint. The smell reminds me of our days as a garage band. We were all about fucking up just so we could say we lived life to the fullest. Cory was always the most responsible of us.

I look over at Dex and he looks away. It's then that I finally get it. All of this with Dex isn't about him. Sure he has his issues to deal with, but this is about me and my issues as well. I can have fond memories of Cory, which I always will. But he's not here sitting on the beach with us or to guide us to safety anymore.

*Dex is.*

Dex with his smile that hides the good from the rest of the world and saves it all for me. Dex with his mysterious side and secrets and intriguing reasons for lying to me. I may be glorifying him, but deep down, I feel he's lying to protect me, not to hurt me. Revelations like these make me anxious and want to share them, celebrate them, but not with the guys here. I can't act like an emotional girl around them. I'd lose all my cool kid cred if I do.

I stand up and dust the sand off my ass. "Dex, walk with me." I don't ask. I make my demand as I start walking toward the water again. He's behind me trailing, so I slow down and let him catch up. "I can't keep doing this with you."

Looking over, he's pulling another cigarette from his shirt pocket and a lighter from the front of his jeans. He lights up, then tilts his head back and blows. "It's a self-fulfilling prophecy."

"What is?"

"I am."

Hoping my words are not lost to the wind, I whisper, "You don't have to be."

"I don't know any other way."

I bend down and pick up a seashell. When he squats down next to me, I say, "You do. Just sometimes you get lost."

"I need you to help me find my way back."

My eyes meet his and in the moonlight of Miami, I reply, "Okay."

He nods. It's small, but it's an understanding passing between us, an agreement between two hearts.

# 17

*I didn't know what I had agreed to with Dex, but I left Miami knowing it entailed more than just words. Actions and support would be included. In what way, I would soon discover.*

Burnout is a big problem for bands on the road. Fortunately, they had a four day break in New Orleans, which I'm sure they needed. The headlines didn't thrill me. Gossip blogs had posted photos of them playing an impromptu concert at Preservation Hall. A few drunken pics on Bourbon Street bothered me. They didn't say Dex hooked up with anyone, but how would they know really.

A knot forms in my stomach just thinking about it. It's a grounded fear since we haven't dealt with the Firenza issue. Something is off with that situation. When I replay that morning back in my head, the whole thing just doesn't sit right with me. Naturally, Dex having sex with *her* doesn't sit right, but something about how he acted toward me in front of her still makes me doubt what I saw with my own eyes.

The way she nudged his back... and how he had his back to her in the first place.

The look in his eyes, the fear, wasn't one of fear of losing me, but more of shame.

He makes me feel weak when I need to be strong because I know he cared about me. But emotionally, I'm in no position to ask the questions that need to be asked, not strong enough to hear the answers. So I need to stop guessing at what his motives were because that's the one thing that was clear. I punch my pillow to fluff it, wishing I could stop thinking about why he hasn't called me either. *I'm weak.*

Resting my head down on the couch, I try to block out my thoughts by listening to the boys playing in Neil's room, hoping to sneak in a quick nap.

But as soon as I close my eyes, I hear, "Mom."

Gradually opening one eye, then the other, I find myself face to face with Neil and CJ. Neil flashes four postcards in front of me. "Dex is home. I want to go to his house and play."

"How do you know?" Sitting up slowly, I take one of the postcards. "What is this?"

"We got letters from him."

"What? You did? When?" I flip Chicago's postcard over and read: ***Hey Buddies, I'm in the Windy City today. Looking forward to hanging with you guys again. Take care of your mom, Dex.***

Stunned by what I'm seeing, I anxiously pull the next postcard from his hands—Atlanta—and read: ***Neil, the crowd at Chastain Park was so cool. One day I'm gonna bring you to a concert so you can play drums with me on stage. CJ, hope you're keeping up with your alphabet. We'll practice hitting rhythms to the alphabet song when***

***I return. Take care of your mom, Dex.***

The handwriting is messy, but legible—a lot like Dex these days. Grabbing postcard three, I read: Nashville: ***Hey Buddies, miss you guys. I've bought you each a surprise, but you have to be good for your mom to get it. I'm gonna check with her too, so no fibbing. Hope you're practicing your paradiddles and rhythms. Take care of your mom, Dex.***

Neil snatches them away from me. "Mom, these are mine. Dex sent'em to me."

Somewhere while reading postcards two and three, I started holding my breath. My chest now aches as a consequence when I exhale. "When did he send them?" I ask.

"I dunno." CJ grabs Atlanta from Neil and runs around the couch singing his alphabet. Even he knows what they say. Beth or Neil must have read them to him. Neil sits on the coffee table in front of me. "Beth gave them to us."

She leaves my mail in the basket in the kitchen, but I forgot to check it over the last few weeks. Too much other stuff on my mind. "Why didn't you tell me about them sooner?"

"Am I in trouble?"

"No," I reply, shaking my head. "Why would you be in trouble?"

"I dunno. Just asking cuz you're using that voice you use when I'm in trouble."

I relax a little. "Sorry. I'm just kind of blown away that he sent you guys these. What does the last one say?"

Neil turns it over in his hands and my heartbeats pick up when I see the city name on the front—Miami. He reads, "Dear Neil and CJ, almost home for a short break in the tour. One more city to go. Keep practicing. If you have the single paradiddle down, I'll show you something called a fill. See you soon and take care of your mom, Dex." He looks up at me and adds, "See? He should be home."

The only city left is New Orleans. "Did Beth check the mail yesterday?" I ask, standing up.

"I don't think so. Can I?"

"C'mon, let's walk down and get it."

With both boys in tow, we walk down to the other street where the neighborhood mailboxes are situated. I let Neil open it with the key. He feels very important given the task. I reach for all the mail and pull it out, a letter slipping to the ground. CJ picks it up and says, "For you, Mama."

"Thank you, kind Sir."

I flip through the mail and as soon as I see New Orleans on the front of a postcard, Neil grabs it. We start back for the house and I ask Neil to read it to me.

"Hi Buddies, almost home. Can't wait. I'm super tired from traveling. Forget everything I taught you. Go to law school instead."

Neil looks up at me and asks, "What's law school?"

"It's where you learn to become a lawyer." Pointing at the postcard, I say, "I think he's being sarcastic, just joking with you." I wrap my arm around his shoulders and give him a squeeze.

"Oh." Neil looks at the card confused, but then continues reading. "I'm home for four days and then off again. Looking forward to hearing your progress. Take care of your mom, Dex."

Maybe it was the smile on Neil's face and watching CJ gallop down the sidewalk, or maybe it was that Dex was keeping his word to my kids and they were smiling. I'm thinking it's both, but no matter where this warm feeling inside derived from, I love it. Seeing my kids happy makes me happy. As we enter the house, Neil takes off running and says, "Gotta practice. I want to learn what fills are."

"Teach me. Teach me. Fills." CJ runs after him.

I dump the mail on the island in the kitchen and start sorting it. When I come across the letter with my name on it, I glance to the return address. There isn't one.

CJ comes in singing, but stops and says, "That's like the other letters."

"What other letters?"

He points to the basket in the corner that holds the mail that I still need to go through. "Those."

I walk over and look inside the basket, then pull out two other letters that match the one on the island. I see the similarities in handwriting when they're together like this and I smile, knowing they're from Dex. Each is postmarked to correspond with the tour and cities listed—Chicago, Nashville, and Miami.

I need time to process the fact that he's been writing us for weeks and I'm just now finding out. As much as I want to rip them open and read each and every word, I don't. I won't be able to give them the attention I want with hungry kids begging for food at my feet. My heart is beating out of control, but dinner needs to be made, so I set the letters aside and ask, "CJ, you want to be Mommy's helper with dinner?"

"Yes," he says excitedly.

"Okay, you grab the lettuce and I'll get the carrots and tomatoes from the fridge. You can help with the salad."

TR

The letters call to me throughout dinner, a cartoon, and book time in CJ's room. I kiss him on the head and turn out his light before making my way into Neil's room. Snuggling with him, he reads aloud to me from his adventure book. I help on the tough names and big words, but he's a really good reader. When it's time for lights out, he asks, "Will I get to see Dex again?"

His tone makes my heart sting and not knowing how to answer, I go with my gut. Looking up at the stars on his ceiling, I ask, "Do you want to see Dex again?"

"Yes. I like his gameroom. He has cool video games and the drums are awesome."

I slip out of bed and tuck him in. "What else do you like about him?"

"I like that he's a grownup, but cooler. Some grownups talk to me like I'm dumb. He doesn't."

Smiling, I reply, "That is cool. Get some rest and I'll message him." I kiss him on the head, then turn out his lamp. Shutting the door behind me after several I love yous, I leave and head back to the kitchen.

I pour a glass of wine while keeping an eye on the letters that look so harmless sitting there, but taunt me relentlessly. The hotel envelopes only add to the intrigue. After taking a few sips, I grab them and go into my bathroom and start the water. As the tub fills, I set them down on the vanity and undress. I'm shocked by my own willpower. Once the water is high enough to cover me, I take the letters and climb into the tub. I open them in order. The first is from two weeks ago, which makes me realize I should go through my mail more often.

Chicago. The paper is crumpled a bit and the inks slightly smeared near the hotel logo at the top.

***Dear Rochelle,***

***I don't know what I'm doing, but still feel the urge to do it. What does that say about me?***

***Maybe I can't change. Maybe at thirty, I am who I am.***

***The thing is, I'm not sure who I am anymore. I've lost interest in my own life. But your life—I can't stop thinking about you. You undoubtedly have my complete attention. Sometimes I damn you for it.***

***I never told you much about me. I don't know why I'm feeling the need to do it now. It's probably the bourbon talking.***

***Did you know that I didn't learn to ride my bike until I was eight? I borrowed a neighbor kids' bike and taught myself on the driveway since there was no one else to do it. My brother was too busy with his friends to teach me.***

***I've got more money than I can blow through. I was never meant to be rich. Besides my money, I'm the son to a mother who inherited more than she could spend in a lifetime and a father who built an empire on the backs of using cheap labor with low expenditures. I never fit into their world. I never belonged.***

***But I belong in The Resistance.***

***Sincerely,***

***Dex***

I exhale with sigh. Reaching for my wine, I take an unsteady sip to calm the torrential emotions brewing. My heart and head hurt for him. He's exposed himself to me in the short letter and I'm left here in shock and hurting for him.

Nashville. I open the second letter, not knowing what to expect from this one. It's neater—the handwriting and the hotel stationary. Quality paper.

***Dear Rochelle,***

***I've always wondered what it would be like to live somewhere else, somewhere other than LA. Is thirty too young to have a life crisis?***

***I might be having one.***

***Nothing seems to stick or gel, or anything else with me these days. Except one.***

***And Johnny knows.***

***I didn't tell him. I hope you believe me. He mentioned you in passing, but I know he was really letting on that he knows. I didn't confirm his suspicions. But I didn't deny them either. It felt wrong to do either.***

***Did you know at fourteen, I found out my mother was raped by her uncle when she was fourteen. I don't even think I knew what rape was at that age, but I found out. I also lost my grandfather later that year. He had a heart attack. My mother refused to attend his funeral, so I went alone. Later, I wished I hadn't gone at all. I got drunk for the first time at fourteen right after his service.***

***I smoked my first cigarette at fourteen. I lost my virginity at fourteen. I smoked pot for the first time at fourteen. I did coke at fifteen. I totaled my first Porsche at sixteen. My second at seventeen. My third at nineteen and then I***

***was kicked out of the house. I got my first job at nineteen playing back up for a cover band down on Sunset for fifty dollars a night.***

***You walked into my life at nineteen…***

***Sincerely,***

***Dex***

Dropping the letter to the floor, I sink further down into the water not able to process everything he's told me, struggling since the tears slipping from my eyes take precedence. Of all the years I have known him, I never knew even a quarter of what he's shared with me in these two letters. *Why is he telling me now?*

My hands are pruning and the bath water is cold. I stand up and dry off, draining the tub. Carrying the letters into the other room, I set them down on my bed before getting into my pajamas. Checking on the boys, who have both fallen asleep, I kiss each one of them on the head, then tiptoe out afterwards.

But my stomach is twisted and my heart pounding, worried what the last letter will say, so I wait to read it. While I brush my teeth I think about everything he revealed to me. It makes the stuff with Firenza seem petty in comparison. His past defines who he is now just as mine does. And the one thing I've learned is, there is no escaping it.

I climb under the covers and take the letter in hand along with a deep breath. Miami. Stars. Beach. The last kiss ever. Dex has lost his way and I'm not sure if I've helped or hurt him in the last couple of months, so I open the letter and hope for the best.

Miami.

*Dear Rochelle,*

*I thought LA was soulless until I came to Miami. I've been to Miami many times, but never stayed sober before. Just an observation.*

*I knew you were coming, but I didn't know what to expect. I thought I had a grasp on things, but you stir something in me, emotions I have trouble burying. These little confessionals have been freeing for me.*

*If you ever need to unload some burdens, I'm here for you. I know I'm probably the last person you would trust with such gravity—I should apologize. I worry my apologies hold no value with you anymore.*

*I'm going to try anyway. Here goes... Wait for it...*

*I'm sorry. I'm sorry for so much. If we ever get to that stage of trust again, I won't blow it.*

*But there was something about Miami. On the beach, you outshined the stars.*

*Just something else I should have told you then. I was just too distracted by my own ego to say what my heart was feeling.*

*Something else I should have told you in one of those other letters is I started hanging out with Chad Spears at fourteen. I'm not asking you to stay away from him anymore. I have no right to do that, but know that I'd still like you to.*

*Sincerely,*

*Dex*

*Holy shit!* Fourteen. Fourteen. Fourteen. Everything goes back to when he was fourteen. All the bad he's had happen started at fourteen. With my thoughts and heartbeats running rampant, I can't deny the urge to call him any longer. A text will not suffice. I grab my phone from the nightstand and do it before I can change my mind. After three rings, he answers and I can hear the hesitancy in his voice, "Hello?"

"Hi." My own voice shakes a little from the uncertainty that lies between us.

There's a momentary pause. I hear a TV or music in the background being turned down. "Hi."

I blurt, "I got your letters." I anxiously wait to hear his response, but typical Dex it's not what I expect.

"I'm not sure what to say to that."

"You don't have to say anything, Dex. I just want you to know that I got them all tonight. I didn't know any of that in Miami. I wish I had."

Always expect the unexpected with him. "Can I come over?"

"Ummm... I'm in bed already." I regret it as soon as I say it, so I quickly cover with the truth. "If you want."

"It's late," he says, the moment passed. "How about you bring the boys over tomorrow? I promised Neil another lesson."

Feeling like we might be able to find our way back to each other, I relax down onto the mattress after turning out the light, and reply, "How's noon for you? I can bring lunch."

"Noon is good."

"I should get some sleep. I have an early morning phone call to the U.K."

"Goodnight, then."

"Goodnight, Dex."

I hear him take in a breath, then say, "Sweet dreams, Rochelle."

"Sweet dreams."

We both remain on the phone, the silence that felt distancing before now feels bonding. Eventually, I crack and giggle. "Are you going to hang up?"

"No, I like hearing you breathe."

"Funny that. I was listening to you breathe."

"You're weird," he says, "Why would you do that?"

"Why am I the weirdo when you were doing the same thing?"

"Okay," he adds, "We're both weirdoes. Now hang up first."

With a smile on my face, I reply, "Goodnight for real this time."

"Goodnight for real this time."

We both hang up, or at least I think he hung up when I did. I call back just to make sure. "Hello?" he answers like he doesn't know who it is.

"I didn't hang up on you, did I?"

"Yes, you did. Now do it again because I don't want to be the one who does it."

"You're a dork."

Right before I disconnect, I hear him say, "You're beautiful."

I immediately call him back again. When he answers, he laughs. "Yes, I called you beautiful."

"Just checking. Thank you."

"Goodnight, Rochelle."

"Goodnight, Dex."

This time I hang up and set my phone down on the bed. The problem with Dex is that no matter how much I should be mad at him for all the shit he's pulled over the years, I just can't seem to keep myself in that state. He's not the bad guy he likes to portray himself to be. Call me sentimental, but I see through the act to the man himself.

# 18

The reports were everywhere on TV the next day. *"Chad Spears has been involved in an accident. He's currently recovering from surgery after breaking his leg on the set of his latest movie filming in Toronto. His camp has issued a statement that he is resting comfortably and claim trailer cables were the cause of his fall. They are currently considering a lawsuit..."*

When I told him to break a leg, I didn't mean to literally 'break a leg.' I'd like to say I feel bad, but since our lunch and the tabloid explosion it caused, I don't. Rory found out that Chad was the one who called the paparazzi to stake us out. He's also dating the woman he told me was stalking him. He used me as a pawn for publicity. And I totally fell for it.

Because of his douche move, I opt not to send him a Cheer Up bouquet and head over to Dex's as promised the next day. The kids run in as soon as Marguerite opens the door. She laughs as I justify, "They're excited to be here. Sorry for their poor manners."

She makes it easy on me. “It’s good to have happy children.”

I take her forearm and give her a gentle squeeze. “Thank you.”

“You’re welcome. Dex is in the gameroom if you’d like to join him.”

“I’ll put the food in the kitchen first.” I follow her into the other room and set the basket on the table along with my purse. The blue skies outside his window make his backyard paradise even that much more appealing.

“Can I get you anything to drink?” Marguerite asks.

“A glass of water would be great. Thank you.” I walk to the back door and stare out over the lagoon like pool and large grassy area beyond it.

A few moments later, she hands me the glass. “Thank you.”

“You’re welcome. It’s so lovely to see you again. How are you doing?”

I turn with a smile. “I’m well.” When her eyes soften in the corners sympathetically, I add, “I’m okay… most of the time.”

She nods. “I hope it gets better. I know Dex was really looking forward to today.”

“I was too.”

“You should join them. I’m just gonna tidy up in here.”

“Okay. See you later.” I slowly make my way through the living room and down the corridor, feeling nervous. When I approach I hear laughter. Dex’s first, then the boys. It truly is wonderful to hear all of them happy. I peek around the corner and spy on them for a few minutes, but Dex catches me and winks. With a smile, he says, “C’mon in. See what your muskrats have gotten up to.”

I walk in and find a seat, near them, but just out from the spotlight shining down on the drums. Crayons are all over the floor with loose construction paper scattered at their feet. Dex whispers, “Hi.”

"Hi."

My gaze is drawn to him and as he strums the acoustic guitar in his hands, he says, "You doing okay?"

"Been better," I reply so only he can hear.

He starts playing a song. Louder than he was before and I suspect he's doing it so the boys won't hear us. "Me too."

CJ holds up his green paper and shouts, "I drew our house in blue and me with the dog I want."

My eyes go wide. "You want a dog?"

He smiles so big and says, "I want a black dog with a long tail. Can we get one?"

Dex adds, "Tell her what you want to name him, CJ."

"Spot."

I look closer at the drawing. "But the dog you drew doesn't have any spots."

He nods as if that says it all. I smile because he's adorable. "I love your drawing. Great job."

Neil holds up a yellow piece of paper and then starts to explain, "This is the tire swing. Dex is on this side and me on the other side."

I point at something, then ask, "What's this?"

"Those are the drumsticks."

A flashback of years earlier crosses my mind and I look to Dex. I see a deeper emotion in his caramel-colored eyes. I just wish I understood the emotion better. I ask Neil, "Are those the drumsticks Dex gave you?"

"Yeah. He just gave me these too." Neil holds up drumsticks that have his name inscribed on the side and The Resistance on the other.

CJ holds a pair up too. His look similar but are less worn. "Me got some too."

I ask, "Wow, did you use these in a show?"

Dex leans forward. "I used CJ's in Denver from the first leg and Neil's are from Atlanta."

"Chastain Park," I say, remembering his postcard.

He nods. "The show was amazing. You should have seen the crowd."

"Maybe that's the difference. You could see the crowd the way the place is setup."

"Yeah, maybe that's it. But I could feel the energy too. It was good."

I love seeing him so excited about a show. After Cory's death, we all went through a transition, including Dex. I was worried about the guys. "You've found your groove," I say.

"When it clicks, it's magic."

*Magic*. Staring into his eyes, his words seep under my skin, filling holes that felt empty before. And for a brief moment in time, our unbreakable bond suspends us between time and memories, leaving us in the present full of peace and happiness.

"Dex show me a fill," Neil says, our moment interrupted for the best of reasons—the kiddos.

I see Dex sigh and although I know he's happy to work with Neil, his disappointment that the moment is gone is seen. He rubs the top of Neil's head, and says, "Okay. Let's get down to business." He sends a smile my way before giving the kids his full attention.

I stand. "I'll go unpack lunch and get it ready. Meet me in the backyard shortly." I head to the kitchen. Marguerite is in there making fresh orange juice. "Hi," I greet her again. "Would you like to join us for lunch?"

"No, I need to leave and pick up my grandson soon. I've made juice for the boys before I go."

"Thank you." I move over to the counter where she's working, lean against it nonchalantly, and whisper, "About Dex. I've been wondering if you know anything maybe I should—"

"Dexter is a complicated man." She stops juicing and looks at me. "People always want to put him in a box, easily categorized, and he's fighting against it."

"He's complicated for sure," I reply, turning to look out the window for a moment. When I turn back, I dig deeper. "Why is he fighting so hard?"

"Because it's not his box." She starts juicing again. "As for you, you're trying to figure out something when it may not be time."

I bite the inside of my cheek, wanting to stomp my foot and get all the answers now. "Why can't I know? Why won't he let me in?"

"He already has. That's what scares him most."

She makes it sound so simple. *Maybe it is.* If I give him more time, maybe he'll give me the answers I need.

# 19

I find myself staring at Dex throughout lunch. He catches me several times and winks, but doesn't seem to mind. I think he actually likes when I watch him.

After lunch, the boys are given the run of the house and take off before he even finishes his sentence. He leans forward on his elbows, the two of us alone outside. That's when I feel it, just like the night before when I was on the phone with him—a little fluttering in my stomach. I stand, taking my glass of water with me, and walk to the edge of the cement patio. "How long have you lived here?"

"Six years," his reply is relaxed, much like him.

I can tell he's watching me now. When I check, my suspicion is verified. "It's very homey. I like it here."

"I like you being here." Sitting down across from him again, I look at him, searching for signs of anything that will give me the answers I need. As soon as I look away, he says,

"I didn't have sex with her."

My head jolts back in his direction, the flutters replaced with dread. I tuck my hands under my legs to keep from revealing how this conversation really affects me.

"I feel like shit for lying to you, Rochelle."

"Why would you lie about it? It makes no sense why you would hurt me like that?"

His gaze drifts away and he swallows hard.

I stand, not able to contain my emotions over this anymore. Walking toward the pool, I stop and yell, "I opened my heart to you. And you hurt me, Dex!"

He follows me and even though I want to back away, needing the space, I stay. My conflicting heart spiting me. He stops a few feet away and stares into my eyes. Keeping his voice low, he says, "Let me heal you."

The racing starts, the flutters back, but my rational side takes charge. "I can't. I can't let you back in."

"You already have. You just won't admit it. I'm in there," he says, glancing to my heart, then back up. "I'm in there and I refuse to leave."

It's my turn to gulp heavily, touched by his words. "Why did you lie to me?"

"To protect you. I may be in your life, but it doesn't mean I deserve to be."

"I don't know how to respond when you say things like that."

"I don't need words."

"Then tell me what you need. What do you want from me?"

"Everything."

My breath catches as we stare into each other's eyes. He's serious. He's impossible. He makes me want to give him more than I should. "You want too much from me." Looking down, I shake my head, needing to stand my ground. "I can't give you everything. I don't know how to be enough for you."

"You're enough. I found that out the hard way."

I cross my arms over my chest. "Actually, I found out the hard way. You knew what you were doing when you brought her back here. I'm the one who was blindsided."

"I'm a cliché, Rochelle. I never claimed otherwise."

"You fall back on the perceptions, then complain that no one sees the real person behind the façade. You can't have it both ways." I walk to a nearby chaise and sit, needing the support under such a heavy conversation.

"See?" he says, smiling. "You know me better than anyone. After the letters, you also know more than I've ever shared with another person." He comes and sits next to me. "But what you fail to realize is you're the only person that I want to see the real me. And for you, I'd do anything. So when you told me I wasn't good enough, you're right, I wasn't... and I wanted to prove that by fucking Firenza."

"And?" I glance down, then back up.

"And I discovered that you were in here." He says, touching his chest briefly. "You weren't a fantasy anymore. You had managed to take the one real thing I had left—"

"So you couldn't fuck her because you might lo—"

"Yep, I like you, more than you're ready to hear right now. So we're gonna take this round slower again."

Surprised by his arrogant assumption, I sit upright. "Who says there's going to be another round?"

His fingers take hold of my chin, keeping my face focused on his. "I do."

Backing away, I snap, "That's either extremely romantic like in the movies or totally creepy. I haven't decided yet. Anyway..." I shrug, trying to regain control of the situation. "...You leave in two days."

"We can get into a lot of trouble in two days." Now he shrugs, instigating me by acting like it's not big deal. "You know, if you're up for some fun and stuff. I don't know. Maybe you can't handle fun anymore."

With a challenging eyebrow raised, I say, "I'm not falling for your ploy, Mr. Caggiano. I'm not dumb and I thought we were going to slow this round way down?"

"Friends who get into trouble together don't go slow. They set their own pace. Speaking of trouble, Spears was all over the news."

"I wasn't going to bring him up, but yeah, I heard about the broken leg."

"Karma's a bitch."

"I might have had the same thought." He stands before me and offers me two hands. When I take them, I whisper, "What are we doing, Dex?"

He gently nudges me and smiles. "Hanging out, pretending we can go slow when all I want to do is go fast with you."

Falling for his boyish charms, I nod. "Me too, but let's settle on medium for now."

"Medium it is."

The alarm on my phone chimes, the magic that was returning gone in a flash as reality sets back in. With a heavy sigh, I say, "I need to go. I have a couple of calls and a lot of work to do this afternoon."

His shoulders drop just a little, but I notice, the disappointment apparent though his voice hides it. "I have some errands to do." He starts walking and I go inside with him.

I shut the back door and say, "I wish I could stay. I like when we're this way."

The right side of his mouth lifts, a slight crinkling on the outside of his eyes reveal his inner emotion. "I like when we're this way too." Taking my hand in his, he brings it up and kisses the underside of my wrist. His lips smooth and purposeful as his eyes lock onto mine.

The boys come running through the kitchen, circling us, then back out, but he still has my wrist to his mouth, savoring it. My heart is too weak to be broken again so soon, so I ask, "How many times do we do this before we accept the truth?"

He lowers my hand, but holds onto it. "As many as it takes."

That's when I know we aren't over. But for the safety of my heart, the business, and until I figure out this game of life I'm playing, we need slow bordering on medium.

Walking into the living room, he says, "Guess you need to get going. I'll help wrangle the boys."

I stand there a moment longer watching him walk away and smile at him. His heart connected to mine once again. "Thanks."

TR

Later in the night, just as I climb into bed, my phone rings. My smile is probably heard over the phone and I'm too tired to hide it. "Hello."

"Good evening, Rochelle," Dex says, his own voice smooth and seductive with a light playful undertone.

If I wasn't smiling already... "How are you?"

"Really good. And you?"

The casual chitchat makes me happy. "Oh, you know, busy but good."

"You're busy right now?"

"No," I reply, "I just got into bed after a busy day."

His voice gets deeper and I hear him settling down. "I like the thought of you doing that."

"The having a busy day part or climbing into bed?" I tease.

He chuckles. "Am I going to see you tomorrow?"

"What'd you have in mind?"

"Take a ride with me. Up the coast."

My lips part and a silent gasp chokes my immediate response. "Dex..."

"As friends," he adds.

I'm pathetic and give in way too easily, wanting to see him more than I've convinced myself otherwise. "What time?"

"I'll pick you up at seven tomorrow evening."

"Okay."

"Goodnight, Rochelle."

"Goodnight, Dex. Sweet dreams."

"Sweet dreams."

The pause makes us both laugh. Knowing we have plans makes it easier to hang up though. "I'll see you tomorrow," I say.

"Tomorrow."

It feels a lot like I'm getting dressed for a date. Beth has preached to me several times this afternoon that, in fact, two friends can hang out together without it getting too deep... or sexual. I'm not fully convinced, but I'm willing to try again. Because he's easy on the eyes. Oh wait, damn it. Okay, I'm not convinced at all that two people who have great sexual chemistry can remain only friends.

I kiss the kids goodnight and say goodbye to Beth just as Dex calls me to meet him outside. After closing the front door behind me, my mouth drops open when I see him. "Oh good lord!" Rolling my eyes, I shake my head. This is gonna be impossible with him looking so damn sexy in his leather jacket and old jeans, tight T-shirt, and motorcycle. What? Rushing forward, I stumble over my words, "What? How? Where'd you get her?"

With two motorcycle helmets in his hands, Dex straddles the bike with a big ole smirk on his face. "Wanna go for a ride, sweetheart?"

"Hell yes, I do." I go through the gate, making sure to set the alarm before shutting the door. I take a helmet and put it on. After securing my license and credit card in my pocket, I zip up my jacket. "I'm ready."

I start to swing my leg over the back, but he stops me. "You're driving."

Lowering my leg back down, I look at him incredulously. "Really?" I ask, hopeful.

"Really. You were once a badass on a bike. Show me that girl again."

"I like your version of trouble."

"Good because I have more where that came from."

"I'm counting on it." I get on and he settles in the seat behind me, then wraps his arms around my middle just as I rev the bike. When we take off, I realize I'd forgotten how exhilarating riding a motorcycle can be. Also, how scary. I'm rusty as I try to balance better.

Gaining speed, a feeling of freedom takes over. It's a similar high I imagine runner's get when they hit their stride—a feeling of invincibility, power, and liberation from your worries. On a bike, I only have to think about my surroundings, to be conscious of others, and let my worries drift into the wind behind me.

About an hour later, Dex has me stop at a public beach past Malibu, but just shy of Santa Barbara. "The sun is setting. Let's take a walk on the beach." We hang our helmets and kick off our shoes, before I bend over and roll up the bottom of my jeans. The sand is big, gritty, and warm from the hot day today. Walking toward the ocean, Dex stays quiet beside me, seeming to have his mind on things other than the sunset.

"Wanna talk about it?" I ask while pulling my hair back into an elastic band.

"The bike is a gift."

Shocked by his doozie of a statement, I stop walking and turn to him. "For what?"

"I thought you should have it."

Glancing back to it, I feel the debate beginning. "You can't give me a motorcycle, Dex."

"I just did."

"Take it back," I demand, putting my hands on my hips.

"No. Why should I?"

"Because it's too much. We're friends. Friends don't give each other gifts like that."

"What do friends give each other then?"

"I don't know." I shrug. "Like sweaters and stuff. Maybe a trinket box or flowers, but a motorcycle is too expensive."

"I don't even know what a trinket box is." He points back to the bike, and says, "And that bike was not expensive."

"It's like my old one?"

"Yeah. An '87 Honda."

"Okay, it's not expensive but it's still too much."

"The thought is too much?" He laughs and takes my hand in his. "Let's walk." And we do. The sun is dipping into the ocean, reflecting like magic dust on the surface. He adds, "I bought the bike because of what it represents."

"I'm lost, Dex. Tell me what it represents."

"You know what you once told me about riding motorcycles?"

I shake my head. "No, I don't remember. It's been too long since I had one to remember my philosophies on the subject."

"I remember. You said, there's always a chance of death when you ride a bike, so it makes you appreciate the life you have."

Standing just before the water can touch our feet, I say, "That's deep," which makes him chuckle.

"Yeah, it was pretty profound at nineteen. It means more today."

I start to laugh, but I don't continue when I realize he's being serious. Instead, I turn my head to face into the wind and close my eyes. When I reopen them the sun is almost gone. "I got rid of my bike when I got pregnant with Neil."

He nods. "Makes sense."

The horizon is the only bright spot left. "How'd you remember what I said after all these years?"

He comes to stand between me and the view. "Because it changed my life... you changed my life, Rochelle."

"See," I say, backing away. "You do that. You say these things to me and make me feel special when I haven't earned it. I'm not special."

"You're special to me."

"No!" I turn on my heel and stomp my way through the sand, kicking it up in the process.

"You can't just yell no and walk away, Rochelle. It's not that simple. *We're* not that simple."

He's right. We're not. Coming to a halt, I stop with my back to him and drop my head down, feeling the emotions beginning to wash through me. Smothering my weaknesses, I spin around and point my finger at him. "You can't do this to me anymore. We're not together. Dex."

"I was going to have sex with Firenza so you would hate me. So you wouldn't come on rides with me up the coast at sunset or come by with your kids. I wanted to fuck her to make you fuck off." He comes closer and I stand there stabbed by his words. "No one believes in me. No one. They believe in my drumming, but not in me. You're right. I'm no good, Rochelle. I'm no good for you or your kids. I'm not the one you should be standing next to if a photographer snaps your picture."

"I don't understand this back and forth with you."

"I didn't either and then I woke up this morning and realized I've suffered enough. You've suffered enough. But when we're together, it's all good. We stop suffering and the rest of the bullshit falls away and... You need to know that I see you as pure and good. You're loved by everyone. You're perfection to me." He stops in front of me and wipes my tears away. "So this slow or medium or whatever it is, it's okay for now, but one day I'm gonna be good too. I'm gonna be good enough for you."

"Don't tell me these things—"

"I'm not gonna tell you, sweetheart. I'm going to show you. One day I'll deserve to be the one standing here."

No matter the anguish I feel, I'm captivated by this man. "And until then?"

"Stop dating jerks like me." He walks around my stunned body and heads for the bike.

Running to catch up, I say, "So you brought me out here to tell me to stop dating assholes?"

"No. I brought you out here to watch the sunset. The rest is a just a perk."

I don't bother stifling a laugh. He may be cocky, determined, too sexy for his own good, but he's also wise. Tossing him the key as I pass by him, I say, "You can drive back."

"You sure?"

Grabbing my helmet, I say, "I'm sure." And I am. I'll let him drive this relationship for awhile and we can start with the motorcycle.

I wrap myself around him, molding to the back of him, resting my head to the side. I rub the soft leather, then my hands slip inside the unzipped front to find the cotton blowing over his stomach. Squeezing tighter, his shirt waves up, and my hand is against the firm muscles. My legs tighten around him, the rough back of his jeans hitting me and making me want him. I'd forgotten how much motorcycles turned me on, especially when riding with a hot guy.

His hand covers mine and I close my eyes, enjoying the feel of being this at peace again. Letting my mind go back to the beach, I think about what he said and the side effects of our relationship. But I realize, they're not side effects. They're consequences of our actions. And like all actions, we have a choice to make, a price to pay, and a lesson to learn—consequences.

It's not until I'm lying in my room in the middle of the night that I finally connect the pieces Dex has given me. Two to be fastened together, interlocked in this puzzle we call life—Dex will never feel good enough as long as others remind him of his faults. And for me, just like at nineteen, it took a bike to remind me to appreciate the life I have.

I reach over and turn my phone off, the call I wanted never came, but an epiphany or two did. I fall asleep and dream of the beach and a crooked smile that is perfect to me.

# 20

It wasn't the merry-go-round of emotions that usually woke me up, my own inner turmoil disturbing any peace I found in sleep. *Nope.* It wasn't even an alarm jolting me awake. Two little wiggly monkeys giggle at my side, under the covers, and I roll over, waking up with a smile. "Good morning, guys."

I'm greeted with more laughs, giggles that tell me they think they're getting away with something. I throw the comforter over my head and trap us all underneath. Wide eyes and big smiles warm my heart. "Who's up for an adventure today?"

"Me," both Neil and CJ repeat several times, vying for my attention.

I flip the covers back down and say, "So what are we waiting for? Let's go."

They take off toward their bedrooms and I go to my closet, pulling on comfy jeans and a T-shirt. After brushing our teeth all lined up in a row in my bathroom, we slip on our shoes and head to the SUV. As soon as we're all inside and buckled, I ask, "Who wants to go to the zoo?" They both start jumping up and down in their seat with excitement. I add, "But first, we're gonna get some doughnuts."

Sitting on a bench watching my monkeys watch the zoo's monkeys makes me smile. They've been to the zoo many times over the years but today feels special—a new sense of freedom is felt that I didn't carry even as recently as yesterday.

It makes me want to call Dex and thank him, but like he said, he's not ready. He needs to find the good in himself, a good that I see so clearly now.

Ultimately, Firenza never mattered. I built her up to be something bigger in my head, someone better than me. She's not. She's just struggling to find the good within herself, just like Dex. She thinks hooking up with celebrities and chasing rich men will make her happy. But I kind of live by the old adage—a woman who marries for money earns every cent. Her happiness won't be found in someone else's wallet.

She is a consequence to mine and Dex's actions. We're at fault equally. But despite this new outlook on life, the bottom line is that Dex didn't have sex with her because deep down, he loves me. He didn't say it, but I feel it. I smile, knowing one day Dex and I will both heal and be whole again. And maybe, just maybe, if the stars align, we'll be together. I walk over and join the kids, being silly, and enjoy the great life I've been given.

***Dear Cory,***

***The beginning of October came and just like every year in LA, the weather changes to slightly milder from its usual state. Waking up early to get the kids to school never gets easier, but it does free up more of my day for work. Add CJ playing soccer and Neil taking private drumming lessons and my week is full.***

***Btw – Neil kicks ass on drums. At his age, I can confirm that he's living up to the Neil Peart moniker. You'd be proud.***

***Despite the crazy, I love the days when I get to play mom and spend time with them, but I'd miss the connection with the band.***

I laugh lightly as I write: ***Who knew I'd end up in the business world after fighting against it for so long. But you know what? I'm good at my job. Damn good, and that makes me feel great. As silly as it sounds, my family is proud that by all appearances, I'm a respectable member of society these days instead of a 'groupie with tattoos' like they once called me.***

***The tour ended over the summer and the band has been writing music again. Johnny told me last week they have five solid songs for the new album, but refused to share until they're "ready." The offers have been pouring in and***

***now the band seems to be doing a lot of appearances. I remember you preferred to stay home. I still do too. Scheduling has fallen on my shoulders to keep them organized. It's a lot of work, but I love the extra responsibility.***

***We really didn't think they could get much bigger, but the fans proved otherwise. The Resistance earned two gold records and three awards for Band of the Year, Album of the Year, and Sexiest Band of the Year. Yeah, I've had to temper their egos for that last one by reminding them of their awkward teenage years from when I knew them when... You would find it really funny. Anyway, I guess that's it for now.***

***XO***

I tuck my journal back into my nightstand drawer and lay there, staring up at the ceiling. The quiet leaves too much space to fill and my mind drifts to Dex. I call Holli, hoping for a respite from the wondering.

She answers, always happy to hear from me, "Hey there."

"Hey, it's not too late is it?"

"Nope. Just having a glass of wine outside. It's beautiful out tonight."

"Where's Johnny?"

"He went back into the studio after dinner. Did you want to talk to him?"

"No, I called for you."

She says, "It's good to hear from you. How have you been?"

"I need to talk to someone..."

"Alright. You sound serious. Everything okay?"

I release an unsteady breath, then say, "I miss Dex."

There's a long pause. I'm sure she's taking in the information. "Why do you miss Dex?"

"I need to tell you something, but you can't tell anyone else. Okay?"

"Okay," she answers hesitantly. "You can trust me. You know that."

"I know. That's why I'm calling. Look it's no secret that Dex and I were getting close... I'm sure Johnny told you."

"Johnny didn't tell me, but I heard some roadies talking about it."

"Oh great. Now we're fodder for roadies." I roll my eyes.

"It was all good gossip if there is such a thing as good gossip. As for Johnny, I've wondered why he didn't tell me. I'm thinking he hasn't come to terms with the idea. You know how protective he is of you—"

"And how he used to feel about Dex."

"I think he's made peace with him ever since he completed the last visit to rehab. When it comes to you and Dex being together, that may take more time."

"Here's the thing I don't understand," I start, snuggling under my covers after rolling away from the lamp on the nightstand. "We've struggled, Holli. This doesn't come easy for me and he's just as lost as me. Put us together and sometimes we're like peanut butter and chocolate and other times we're like oil and water."

"Did you just compare your relationship with Dex to food?"

"Don't judge. I'm hungry and I want all the bad things to inhale right now because I feel this crazy sadness, a sadness that's different from the one I had for Cory."

"I know the sadness, Rochelle. I know it well because I feel it too. Every time Dalton tours or has to make an appearance out of LA, I feel it." Her voice gets all girly-mushy on me when she says, "Awwww, you miss Dex."

Naturally, I respond like the girl I am and pout. "I do. I miss him. I don't know what happened, but he pulled away when I thought we were moving forward. We were going slow, but making progress."

Holli sighs softly, then says, "I'm sorry. I wish I knew what was going on with him. I only see him occasionally when the guys practice and record here."

"Can you talk to him about it?"

I think about what I would say to him if I could talk openly. "Maybe. But when I've seen him lately, it's with the boys. He still spends time with them here and there, but never stays to spend time with me."

"Are you worried about him relapsing? Hiding something from you?"

"Not really. I'm more worried about the fact that I can't stop thinking about a man who seems to have stopped thinking about me." I laugh at the end though I'm not really amused, just trying to cover my awkward real emotions.

"When our hearts are involved, we're always at risk. But there's no fun in safe."

"Nope, there's no fun in safe." I look at the ring of flowers wrapped around my wrist and remember how free I felt from the ties of my past. These flowers represented the life I chose, not the one my family had chosen for me. "Yeah, if I'd played it safe, I'd be married to a banker or insurance broker in Boston, attending luncheons in Chanel suits."

She laughs. "I love a good Chanel suit, but not on you. You're way too vibrant for something like that." She pauses, then says,

"How long has it been since you spent time together, just the two of you?"

"When he told me he was going to show me how much he cares."

Holli's smile is heard through the phone. "Well, time will only tell, but I have a good feeling about you two."

"I appreciate you listening. Oh, and while I have you on the phone. Lunch soon?"

"Definitely. I'm in town next week, but leave for a week after that for a shoot in New York."

"Awesome. We'll catch up next week."

She says, "Anytime, my friend. Bye."

"Night."

Laying there, I acknowledge my feelings instead of hiding from them. I miss Dex. I miss snuggling with him and taking drives up the coast to watch sunsets. I liked him in my life and I think my heart just got used to him being around. It leaves me thinking about the promise he made to me on the beach in Miami, wondering if it was fleeting in the moment, just like the sunset that night.

I bury my face into the pillow, refusing to sit here and wallow. After a minute, I roll over and turn out the lamp and go to sleep.

# 21

Three months after our ride up the coast and two days after my call to Holli, I receive a letter. The return address lists Caggiano as the sender. I flip it over in my hands a few times before sitting down on the couch and dumping the rest of the mail on the coffee table. The letter remains next to me for a good five minutes before I brace myself for the worst and open it.

***Dear Rochelle,***

***I thought the days without you would get easier than being tortured with your untouchable beauty. Each passing day offers a new form of cruelty and I have to stop my reflex of reaching for the phone and calling you, driving to your house, or writing you a letter.***

***I've failed as you can see. I'm starting to think that it's not about proving myself good***

*enough so I can have more of you, but more about learning to enjoy what simple pleasures I'm given—your smile, for instance. I could write a song about the way your smile brightens my soul, filling it with light and hope, something pure that never existed there before.*

*Your eyes—the way they pinch at the corner when you're frustrated and widen when you're happy. The golden brown brings new meaning to the word brilliance.*

*The laugh that makes me want to become a comedian just to hear it more. The olive of your skin that makes me crave to lick every inch as well as caress it. These days I'd settle for a simple touch.*

*Your beauty exudes all that you are on the inside. I find myself wanting to consume your every breath and mark you as mine. Weaknesses I'm struggling to overcome.*

*But when you hit bottom, sometimes you're given the gift of clarity. Me without you is never the answer. I need you. The way you make me feel... it's good enough. It makes me better because you're around. It made me realize that when I'm with you, I'm good enough.*

*Love,*

*Dex*

I reread the letter seven times before I run around my couch, my world full of hope again as I hold it to my heart. I love being a mom and responsible, but sometimes it's just good to be a giddy girl again.

"Dance party, Mama," CJ says, running after me.

I bend down and smile, then kiss him on the head. "Yes, we should have a dance party." Grabbing the remote, I flick on the music and then find an upbeat pop song. He jumps on the couch and I set the letter down on the table before standing on the hearth and shaking my booty. "Neil?" I call out. "Come dance with us."

I turn up the music just as he peeks his head around the corner. With a smile on his face, he comes in and jumps up on the hearth with me and starts dancing too.

Later that night in bed, I reread the letter and wonder if I should write back or call or do nothing. I'm not sure, but maybe he's telling me what he can't say to me in person. Maybe that's why I don't see him much these days. He's struggling to respect the boundaries I put in place. And now it's my turn to respect him and to protect him. I tuck the letter in my nightstand and go to bed with a smile beaming from my heart.

TR

The following day, around 10 a.m. my gate buzzer sounds. I get up from the kitchen table where I have a bunch of files spread out and answer it. Depressing the button, I say, "Who is it?"

"FedEx. I've got a package for Rochelle Floros."

I look through the camera and see the delivery guy standing there with a small box in his hands. Buzzing him in, I watch as he sets it on the front step and knocks. I open the door and sign for the package before closing it and locking it behind me.

I never have packages delivered to my home, so the whole thing is odd until I see the sender's name—Caggiano. I hurry into the kitchen and reach for the scissors to open it. When the flaps are released, I see a Disney hat with mouse ears on top. My name is stitched on the back and the note attached reads: ***Wear Me.***

Following directions I put the hat on and then dig out the card. A Magic Kingdom ticket falls to the counter. The card says: ***Please meet me at 8:30 tonight, the front gates of Disneyland. Ask for Bob Hervine.***

*Disney at eight-thirty? What is he up to?* I'm too intrigued to not go. Looking at the time, I have hours before the kids are home. I pick up my phone and call Beth. She answers after the first ring every time, which I love. "Hello?"

"Hi, It's Rochelle."

"Hi, how's it going?"

"Good. I wanted to see if you were free tonight, around seven?"

"Sure," she replies. "You got a hot date?"

I pause to think about it, then reply with a laugh, "I'm not really sure."

"I'm happy to come over. I don't have any classes until ten in the morning, so feel free to stay out as long as you like."

"Thank you. I'll see you tonight."

I walk into the bedroom and start rummaging through my clothes to figure out what I should wear. When I go into the bathroom, I burst out laughing that I'm still wearing the mouse ears. I set the hat on my bed along with a sweater just in case it's chilly and sneakers on the floor since it's Disney and I'll be walking a lot. I'd prefer sexy, but for an amusement park, I'm going practical.

TR

I ride the tram from the parking lot to the park. Walking up to the front gates, I'm wondering how I'm ever going to find a Bob Hervine at this hour when it's dark. As my ticket is taken, a Disney Cast Member says, "Wait right over here please. Bob will be with you momentarily."

*Well, there you go.*

"Ms. Floros?"

I turn around to see a stocky man with a rotund belly coming toward me and a huge smile on his face.

"Yes," I respond. "I'm Rochelle."

"I'm Bob. Nice to meet you," he says.

I shake his hand. "Nice to meet you as well."

He starts walking, but stops, and says, "C'mon. We're on a tight schedule."

"Oh." I hurry to catch up with him. "Sorry."

"No need to apologize, but Mr. Caggiano has planned something very unique and timing is everything." He's walking very fast, so I double my pace. "Mr. Disney built Main Street..."

I get a guided tour, although told very fast, of each main structure we pass and then through the castle. "The fireworks are about to begin." He smiles. "So we have to hurry. Magic is in the air."

"Magic?"

On the other side of the castle, the first fireworks shoot into the sky, lighting it up. I watch in awe of the grandeur of the huge display. Bob taps me on the shoulder, and says, "Don't look there. The real show is over here."

I follow the direction he gestures in and see Dex standing under the sign, Peter Pan's Flight. His smile is coy, a bit nervous looking, which is so unlike his usual confidence. I walk over, taking my time, letting him sweat it out a bit. "Hi," I say.

When he greets me, his smile grows. "Hi."

"This is a surprise, Dex?"

"Everyone can use a little magic in their life."

With an elbow nudge, I say, "You, sir, are a charmer."

"Thank you for coming on such short notice."

While he adjusts the mouse ears hat on my head, I reply, "How could I resist. I got a hat. I needed to show it off."

His laugh is contagious, or maybe it's because we're at the Happiest Place on Earth... or maybe it's because I'm happy to be here with him. He nods toward the entrance, and asks, "Wanna go for a ride?"

"Absolutely."

Taking my hand, he leads me through the winding railings that shape the line, miraculously empty, and I'm having a feeling this was also planned. We walk inside and are greeted by more happy cast members working the ride. Dex guides me onto the little pirate boat and we're off, through Wendy and her siblings' bedroom window, starting our own adventure.

It doesn't dawn on me until we're in the dark, immersed in the magic. Turning to Dex, I ask, "You brought me to Neverland?" Memories of our Neverland fantasies of the past squeeze my heart. It's a safe place for us, a place where our pasts don't matter and the rest of the world disappears just for a little while. A lump forms in my throat as I hold back the heavy emotions wanting to be heard while holding onto the safety bar in front of me. "I don't know what to say."

"It's not about what to say. Here in Neverland, I'm Peter and you're Wendy, remember? All that other stuff doesn't matter."

"I do remember," I say with a small smile. "In Neverland, no one can touch us."

"In Neverland, we work."

The pressures I feel when we're apart are gone, happiness taking over. Knowing we don't have much time in such a perfect place, I ask, "Why did you bring me to Neverland tonight?"

We cruise along in our flying pirate ship, past the ticking alligator before stopping over London. While staring out over the city below, he says, "How we left it at the beach that day... I make mistakes. A lot of fucking mistakes, bad decisions, and sometimes have poor judgment."

Tilting toward me, he adds, "But I'm getting better every day." He pauses and by his expression, I get worried, gripping the bar even tighter. "I used to wish you and Cory would break up. I had convinced myself that if you did, I would tell you how I felt about you. But you guys never did, and I'm glad. What used to be selfish wishes turned into something else. I liked you two together. You guys had the kind of relationship I wanted, one I envied. I need you to know that because of you and the boys, I would have traded places with him on that plane if I could. I loved him, Rochelle."

Looking down, I can't bear to hear him say that. "I know you loved him, but no, Dex, don't say that. He didn't have a choice and neither do we, so there's no point in thinking like that."

"It's the truth. Cory taught me to treat the ones we love with respect and to love them deeply." He shifts in the seat. "So even though I'm breaking our rule and bringing the past into Neverland, I need you to know that I understand how much you loved him. I'm not trying to replace him. I can't, but I want..." Dex looks away.

My voice is lower, just above a whisper when I ask, "What do you want?"

"I don't want to lose you."

Just as our ship begins to move again, I slide my hand across the hard plastic seat and find his. "You won't. I promise."

Our ship comes safely back into harbor and I hope our

relationship follows the same path. I'm about to say something, but the attendants are excited to see him. He thanks everyone, shaking their hands and posing for three photos before we walk out.

Bob is waiting for us when we step outside. He claps his hands together once and asks, "How was Peter Pan's Flight?"

Dex looks over at me and answers, "Perfect."

"Are we ready for the magic to continue?" Bob asks.

I nod, excited to see what else is in store for us.

Bob starts walking quickly. "Stay close and follow me back this way. To the castle we go." I love the adventure he takes us on. We find our way to a secret entrance on the side and go up an elevator. Dex is smiling and in this most unique and fun situation, I see the guy I met down on Sunset again. I've started to treasure these little moments that take us back to a time when life was so much easier.

When the elevator doors open, my breath is taken away. A fire is roaring in the fireplace and a table for two is set up in front of it with a bottle of champagne chilling on ice. Bob pulls out a chair for me and I sit just as Dex does.

"Cinderella and Prince Charming?" I say, "You're pulling out all the stops, Mr. Caggiano."

"Not all of them. I'm saving some for another day."

The champagne is poured and Bob disappears, leaving us inside the private suite of Cinderella's Castle.

I take a sip, then ask, "I thought this place existing was just a rumor."

"Nope, it's real."

"It's beautiful. Ornate and over the top. Exactly how it should be."

A waiter walks in with two pieces of chocolate cake and sets them in front of us. When he leaves, I lean on my elbow and smile. "I think I'm in Heaven."

"You deserve Heaven for the Hell you've been through."

I stare into his eyes astounded by his ability to say such perfect things at the right time. We clink our glasses, toasting to that. The first glass of champagne is gone and after eating my cake, I ask, "Dex, are you wooing me or trying to win me? Because either way, you're doing an excellent job."

"Good to know. But really, I'm just trying to make up for everything."

I sit up straight, and say, "You keep saying you make all of these bad decisions and screw up, but I don't see you that way. Maybe I should." I think of Firenza. "I really should after finding you..." I don't bother since I don't want to drag up the past right now and ruin the evening.

He's silent as he stands. Leaning his hand against the mantle, he stares into the fire below. "The madness of love is the greatest of heaven's blessings"

"The madness of love feels fitting."

"Plato has a way with words. I have that tattooed."

"Where?"

"It's the inscription inside the shield on my heart."

Slowly, I stand up and walk to him. Touching his shoulder, he turns. His fingers unbutton his grey shirt while keeping his eyes on mine. The shield of armor, his family crest is revealed. Dex takes my hand and presses it flat against his skin that's been heated by the fire, and whispers, "It's been too long since you've touched me."

The silence of the room exaggerates every swallow and breath I take. I drop my gaze from his eyes down to his chest and see the quote printed on the arched top of the tattoo. "Does this shield represent your family name or protect your heart?"

He cups my face, and says, "Both," then kisses me.

# 22

Going against everything I've said, Dex affects me like no other. He's gotten under my skin. Inside of Cinderella's Castle, I back up, pulling Dex with me toward one of the beds behind us. I take his shirt off and kiss the warm skin of his shoulder. When I look up, he kisses me as his hands slide up from my waist to my ribs, his thumbs running along the sides of my breasts. Slipping my arms around his neck, I pull myself against him. "Make love to me, Dex."

His breath covers my mouth as he pulls away. "No, it's not time."

"Time is irrelevant. We're living our own fairytale. I want to feel you again."

"I want more than just a physical connection to you, sweetheart. I want to own your soul the way you've taken possession of mine. It won't be quick and it won't be easy, but I'm gonna win you heart *and* soul, so much so that you'll be begging me to fuck you."

As much as his words hit that soft spot in my heart, they also make me want him even more. “I’m already begging.”

He chuckles. “Nope, you’re not quite there yet.” Backing away from me, he picks his shirt up off the ground. “And sadly, our time is up.” The grandfather clock in the other room chimes the hour as if on cue. “We have to go.” He buttons his shirt while I’m left dumbfounded, confused, and downright horny.

Disgruntled, I huff as I walk past him and head for the stairs, needing to burn off the rage I’m feeling over being abandoned in this state.

Bob is downstairs with the same big grin he’s been wearing all night. “Did you have a nice time?”

“I did, until the end,” I reply without thinking.

“Oh, my apologies. Was something not to your liking?” he asks while Dex laughs.

I quickly clarify, “No, no, no. You were all wonderful and the service was impeccable. My date on the other hand seems to think teasing a woman is the way to her heart.”

Bob nods, understanding without me having to go into the details. He clears his throat as he looks over at Dex. “Well, I’m glad Disney could be of service tonight. Mr. Caggiano, is there anything else we can do for you or Ms. Floros?”

“No, as Ms. Floros mentioned, it was perfect—”

“Perfect,” I scoff, still frustrated... sexually.

Bob smiles. “Wonderful. Follow me then and I’ll walk you out.”

We follow, side by side, but behind Bob. The stragglers from the park are making their way out as well. I feel Dex’s hand tap against me and then he loops his little finger with mine. I’m not really mad at him, but definitely confused, so I whisper, “What does tonight mean?”

“It means when the time is right, we’re gonna be together.”

"The timing isn't right?" I know it's a dumb question, but I guess I feel that maybe the timing *is* right, finally. *What am I missing?*

"We rushed into it the first time *and* the second time. This time, I'm not rushing, I'm changing so when we're together, I can savor and appreciate you."

"So you won't appreciate me if we get together now?"

"No. Because I still have to work on sorting my life out first. But I want you to know there's no one else for me. There never was."

His sweet words hit me like an arrow straight to the heart. His gentle side is so unexpected from the tough armor he wears for the public on a daily basis. "I don't know what to say to that."

"I don't need you to say anything. I just need you to know I may not ever be perfect, but once we're together, I'll always be true to you."

"And in the meantime?" I find myself chanting quietly, hoping he says what I want to hear. *Please say you won't date anyone. Please say you won't date anyone.*

He stops, pulling me to a bench, and sits. I do as well and I notice Bob stops up ahead, giving us a moment of privacy. Dex takes both my hands in his, then brings one to his lips and kisses the inside of my wrist. "I'm not gonna ask you to put your life on hold, Rochelle. I think you've done that for too many years already. But I will ask that you keep me in your heart."

My mouth drops open. "You're letting me go?"

"No, I'm letting expectations that are impossible for me to live up to go."

"So while you're sorting things out, you won't wait for me?"

"I'd love to make you a million promises, but right now I can't."

Disappointment settles in. "That's why you wouldn't be with me at the castle?"

He nods, releasing one of my hands. "It would have been so easy to make love to you and then tell you I need space." Dex presses his hand to my cheek and I find my eyes closing to the touch I missed so much, relishing it. He says, "I remember how it feels to be with you, to be inside you. But my life is a mess and I don't want to drag you and the boys into it."

I open my eyes, no tears to cry this time. My sentimental side touched by his thoughtfulness as my rational side agrees with his decision. "It's like we always knew, we can only be together in Neverland."

"It's learning how to make Neverland reality. One day I'll figure it out. You deserve it, Rochelle. You deserve magic and more."

"You say that I deserve so much, but so do you, so much more than you know."

Standing, he offers me a hand up. "Maybe one day I'll believe you. Until then," he says, signaling toward Bob who has stepped forward, unsubtly tapping his watch.

After taking a deep breath, I exhale long and slow. "Until then..." As soon as I say it, I start to worry how long 'Until then' will be and don't bother finishing.

Dex and my goodbye at the main gate of Disneyland doesn't last long enough, but it's sweet and when I lay my head on his chest, he embraces me with love.

I drive home replaying every part, every word, and every minute of our time together. Dex has grown, but he still has issues to deal with, addictions, and his family. He thinks he'll be whole, be better, be deserving if everything comes all tied up with a bow and wrapped up in a neat package. Life doesn't work that way. I know this firsthand.

But who needs tidy or pretty, bows, or happy ever afters? Romance is about the journey, the good, the bad, ugly and pretty, the highs, the lows. I don't need perfect and I don't want it. I want to be happy and enjoy this life I've been given. I want my kids happy and to be surrounded by love. I want that for Dex too and if that means he needs time to figure his life out, then I'll give that to him.

Strength and understanding guide my direction over the next week until finally, late one night, I realize how saying goodbye to Dex was like giving a piece of my heart away and hoping it finds its way home again.

# 23

The stars seem to sparkle tonight, so unlike most LA nights. Where are the clouds and the smog? I prefer when the weather suits my moods. My mood didn't seem to faze Mother Nature, which kind of bothered me.

I pull a handful of grass blades, hold it up in the air, and let them fall to the ground. There's no breeze to carry them, so they land on my stomach as does my youngest when he comes and flops down.

Grunting, I say, "Careful, buddy. You're getting big." CJ stands and I lift my legs, then bend at the knees. "Let's do airplane."

He moves quickly, always loving when we do this. I brace myself as he adjusts his belly onto my shins. When I lift, he squeals in happiness. "Look at me," he says.

"Look at you. You look like Superman."

His arms go wide and his legs straight out, and he says, "Superman needs to go potty."

"Eeps." I set him down and he runs inside.

Neil comes running from the swing set and stops next to me. "My turn. My turn."

"Yep, your turn." Neil rests on my legs and I lift. His smile is so sweet, so happy that I smile too. His arms automatically go out and his legs straighten.

Straightening my legs even more, I say, "Great Superman, Neil."

"My turn next." I turn to see Dex standing there.

My legs wobble when I hear his voice, but I steady them along with my heart. Glancing over at him, I smile, not able to hide my happiness.

"Dex!" Neil says, "Look at me."

"I'm looking, bud. Good job. How's the drumming?"

Neil shrugs, throwing himself off-balance, so I lower my legs quickly so he lands on his feet safely. With a smile meant just for me, Dex eyes me. "Hi."

"Hi," I reply. It's not hot out, but I feel hotter all of the sudden.

"Beth let me in. Hope it's okay." He licks his lips and it's hard to take my eyes off of his mouth, making me gulp.

Neil stands there, glancing between us.

Lifting up on my elbows, I say, "I'm free."

Dex questions, "Free?"

"You said it was your turn next." I signal to my legs.

Neil laughs. "Mom is strong, Dex. She never drops us."

"That's good to hear. I think I'd rather be base though." He comes and lies next to me in the grass. "Airplane?" he offers with a wry grin and slips his shoes off.

I nod as I get up. Positioning myself with his feet against my stomach, I reach down and our fingers entwine as our hands come together. The heat between us sparks fading embers back to life. He lifts up, surprising me, and we both laugh.

"Do Superman, Mom," CJ says, running outside, delighted by the sight.

"I'm Wonder Woman." I release Dex's hands and put my arms out and straighten my legs behind me. The boys start chasing each other, running around us in circles.

Beth calls the boys inside for homework. She gives me a knowing wink. "I'll just stay a little longer so you guys can talk."

"Thanks," I reply before turning back to him.

Dex stares into my eyes and says, "I never thanked you."

"Thanked me for what?" I ask, reaching down until our hands are connected once again.

"What you did for me that day. Coming to Barstow with Tommy and then... rehab."

Remembering what Johnny said to me years earlier, I say, "You don't have to thank me. The Resistance is a family. We take care of one another."

He nods a little before lowering me back to the ground. When he sits up, I sit down across from him. Lowering his gaze to the ground, he pauses. Just from his body language I brace myself. When his eyes meet mine again, I see the remorse in his entire expression. "I wanted to die."

Much like I was doing before he showed up, I grab a handful of grass, ripping it from its roots. This time from anxiety over the topic. "Why?"

"I couldn't see the big picture."

"You were blinded by the details."

"I was cursed by the memories."

I glance down needing a second, then say, "Memories of me?"

His fingers run over my knee, then his hand stills. "I hadn't done drugs since Cory's death, but I did them that night. I took everything I could find and then called friends who gave me more."

"They're not friends if they gave you drugs, Dex. They're enemies."

"Drugs are good about keeping your perspective skewed away from reality. Let's just say my perspective was skewed."

I don't mean to snap at him, but it slips out. "Where'd you meet those girls?"

He clears his throat. "I don't know." His tone then changes, lowers, just like his hand does as he replies, "I don't know how I got to Barstow either. I just remember that ride to rehab."

"That was a hard ride to take."

"God, that day sucked. But yeah, I never thanked you. I wouldn't be here if you hadn't been there for me."

"Tommy was there too."

"Tommy..." He shifts his weight and stands up. "...He's been a good friend to me." When he looks down, I see the words he's going to say in his expression. The embarrassment he feels coloring his words. "I was ashamed you saw me like that. But you should know that you were the only reason I walked out of that motel room."

"Dex," I say, feeling the pressure on my chest, making it harder to swallow. I take his hand and lead him to the tire swing.

"I wouldn't have left for Tommy. I know it. But then you were there... I hated myself for letting you see me like that. I hated myself in general. But I only got up because I couldn't do that to you. I couldn't put you through anymore pain with the pain you had already been through."

We sit opposite from each other and I cover his hand with mine on the chain. "You always say you're not a good guy, but a bad guy wouldn't have thought twice about my feelings in a time like that."

He doesn't blush but I see that the compliment embarrasses

him in a good way. "Do you remember that night at my party?" he asks.

"I could never forget."

He rubs his chin. "I shouldn't admit this, but I watched you down by the pool."

"How long were you up there?"

"Most of the party."

"Why?" I ask.

"I was sitting there in the middle of this party full of people there to celebrate my birthday and I realized I didn't like half of them. Most of the others I didn't even know. Then there was you." He spins us by kicking off from the ground.

I lean my head back toward the sky and smile watching the world spin out around us. Closing my eyes, I enjoy the cool breeze as he pushes off again. "What about me?" I laugh, loving the lightness of my body and the conversation.

"You're a tease, Rochelle."

I open my eyes and waggle my eyebrows at him. As he pushes off again, my body sways to the left and I go with it, letting my arms straighten. "I wasn't teasing that night. I felt lost, but when I think back, I wasn't." I lock eyes with him. "I was there for you."

"You were Eve in a garden of evil that night. An angel appearing out of nowhere." He plants his foot and we come to an abrupt stop. "You didn't come looking for me, but you found me all the same. Tell me it meant something."

"It meant everything to me." He releases his intense gaze on me and smiles. I hop off the swing and walk to him. Placing my hands on his shoulders, I touch him gently. "I'm not trying to inflate your ego. I'm just telling you the truth."

He playfully pokes me in the side. "Too late. My ego is already inflated."

Laughing, I surprise him and spin the tire, sending him spinning. "Well in that case, I'll have to try harder."

I walk away, leaving him whirling. To my surprise, I'm grabbed from behind just seconds later. His lips touch the shell of my ear, his arms holding me tight, and he says, "I like the sound of that."

My body is instantly covered in goosebumps as I take a staggered breath and lean my head into the nook of his neck.

One kiss. One sweet kiss to that most hidden place behind my ear. He makes me want to ravage him, his touch always filling me with temptation and desire. One day I'm going to torture him just as sweetly. When the heat of his body leaves mine, I realize today isn't that day. But soon.

Very soon.

# 24

The funny thing about revelations are that they hit you when you least expect it. I'd been sitting here the last week thinking Dex was choosing to work on his life, which means we get put on hold. What I hadn't thought about is how I play into his plans, his life, or his future. I also hadn't thought about what I want for my kids and myself. It was easy when we were together. Everything with him feels so right.

But when we're not together, I wonder if he falls apart like I do. I wonder if this is why he doubts himself. More importantly, am I in any position to help him? He hasn't committed some great sin that can't be forgiven. I think he's just caught in a cycle of destruction, one where he's more comfortable dealing with than the change ahead.

After texting him a few times and leaving a few messages for him after calling him and getting no answer, I did exactly the opposite of what I wanted to do and I backed away. *It was a hard month*. He stopped calling, the letters didn't continue, and unless I had business with him, I didn't hear from Dex at all. It made me wonder if he'd always be damaged enough to not see the good through the bad. For his sake, I hope not.

Sometime in early November something arrived at the house, a letter of a different sort. The letterhead was labeled The Roosevelt Hotel in Hollywood. I opened it and read:

***Rochelle,***

***I'm lost without you. I needed time, thinking it would get easier, but it hasn't. My life is worse. I've done things I regret and I don't know how to repent.***

***How do you save an unsalvageable soul that doesn't want to be saved? I want to drown in things that will make me lose my mind, so I can live in the numbness, even if only temporarily.***

***There's a void that music can't fill, that other women won't fix, that drugs won't blur, and that time won't relent.***

***My drug of choice these days is you…***

***Can you heal a damaged soul?***

***Love,***

***Dex***

He's gotten good at dropping these bombshells. But what he's written concerns me—Barstow coming to mind. The envelope is post-dated two days ago. Today is Friday and I have three hours before the kids get out of school. I grab my keys and head out, my mission—The Roosevelt.

Walking up to the front desk, I introduce myself. "Hi, I'm

Rochelle Floros, and I need to see if one of my business partners is still staying here."

The young man, mid-twenties, blonde, brown eyes, smiling. "Good afternoon. I'm Bruce. Hey, you're with The Resistance, right?"

"Yes."

"I'm sorry about Cory Dean. He was the most amazing guitar player."

I should be used to his name being spoken in conversation by others and hearing Cory spoken about in the past tense, but some days are easier for me than others. Today, I'm walking a fine line. "Thank you. I appreciate that. I know he would have too."

Bruce's smile tightens and he leans forward to whisper, "Are you here to see Dex Caggiano?"

"I am. Is he still here?"

"He hasn't left his room in four days."

I sigh. "I know it's against policy, but I need to see him, so is there any way you'll share his room number with me?"

"Actually, you're the only one he has on his guest list, so it's not a problem at all. He also left a key for you. Let me get it."

Trying to remain calm, like that's not a huge surprise is hard, but I manage to act as normal as possible. "Thank you."

After I get the key, I'm directed to the elevators. Though dread fills my stomach, feeling like an ulcer is forming, I don't hesitate when I exit onto his floor. I anxiously walk down the hall until I reach his suite. I'd knock, but something tells me he left a key for a reason, so I use it and walk inside.

Dex is lying on the couch, facing the window. The curtains are open with a perfect view of the Hollywood sign outside it. I set my purse and the key down on the table before sitting down in a chair next to him.

He asks, "Do you know what it's like to have your soul stolen?" His voice is rough, like he's been partying and smoking all night. I have a feeling he hasn't been out, but doing that holed up inside this room.

Keeping my gaze out the window like him, I reply, "Yes, I do." I know all too well.

Our eyes meet and he says, "Sometimes I say the stupidest shit. Ignore me."

"I don't want to ignore you. I want to hear everything you have to say."

"That could take days."

"I have a few to give if you want them."

He smiles. It's lazy and utterly charming. "I'd take them all if I could."

"How long have you been staying here?"

"A week. Maybe more. I've lost count."

"Why aren't you at home?"

He chuckles to himself. "That's a tricky question."

"I didn't mean it to be. Why's it so complicated?"

"It's strange when you're touring. You start getting used to living in hotels. At the same time, you can't wait to get home. But then you get home and it doesn't always feel like it once did. So I checked in here."

"To fill the space between?"

"To transition back."

I nod, going to my purse. I pull the envelope out and ask, "Do you want to talk to me about the letter?"

"Sure. Shoot."

I move to the couch, lifting his legs, sitting down, and then returning them to lie across my lap. Looking at him, he appears worn down. That makes all the wrong questions surface, but I feel I need to ask anyway. "Have you been doing drugs?"

Staring out the window again, he says, "No."

"Have you slept with any women?"

His eyes flash back to mine. "No, I've not had sex with anyone or slept with anyone."

"When's the last time you talked to your family, Dex?"

"A week. Maybe more."

"So they're the reason you're here?"

"No, I told you why I'm here."

"Then why the correlation in timing?" I ask, rubbing the top of his leg over his jeans.

"Everything I'm going through, you've been through with Cory. It's fucked up."

"Your feelings are your own. They're unique. I've been through more than I thought I could handle, but I'm here and I'm living my life the best I can. It doesn't mean that my heart doesn't ache when yours does or that I don't feel lonely or miss you. I do, all of the above."

"Cory was your soulmate."

"I used to be so sure," I say, pausing to gulp. "I'm not as positive these days."

"Don't discount his importance for me. I know I'll always be second best. It's a position my family trained me for. I think I'll be okay playing that role in your life."

"First of all, I would never discount Cory for anyone. Secondly, I'm starting to think that maybe..." I sigh, not sure if saying the words will make them real.

"Maybe some people are like stars in the sky. They burn so much brighter than everyone else that they—"

"Burn out sooner." I stop, resting my head on the back of the couch. Turning so I can see the blue sky outside, I add, "He'll always be better than the rest of us. It sucks he left us behind to fumble through the world making mistakes—"

"And bad decisions."

"Not knowing how to move on."

"Or if you even should."

Looking at him, I ask, "Have you ever thought about death?"

"All the time."

"But you go on. You always go on. That's the gift of a new day."

"It's not the day I live for."

"What do you live for?" I hold my breath waiting for the answer.

"You, Rochelle."

*Arrow right to my heart.* He wins with his swoony lines and broken rock star image. He's not too far gone though. I have faith in him to pull himself out of this cycle he's found himself in.

He lifts his legs and I stand up. Scooting over, he makes room and I slide onto the leather next to him. As I rest my cheek against his chest, I close my eyes. His arm comes over, holding me tight. His scent draws me in, making my insides twist in such an amorous way as well as calming my other senses, feeling much like home to me. I want to argue with my own logic, but he needs to know the harsh reality. Whispering, I say, "You can't live only for me, Dex."

"I'm leaving tomorrow."

Wrapping my arm around him, I ask, "Where are you going?" I know he can hear my fears, the loss of him already felt deep within.

"I'm going to my grandfather's house for a week. My mother called a meeting. My brother will be there."

"Would you like me to go with you?"

He kisses my forehead, then says, "I wouldn't wish that kind of trip on an enemy. Definitely never on someone I love."

*Love.* My head swims in the undertow of his words. "You say things like that so easily, like you think I won't notice."

That makes him laugh, which is something *I* love. He replies, "I'm tired of hiding my feelings, but that doesn't mean I'm gonna shout it from the rooftops just yet. I have a lot of shit to deal with that I don't think you should be dragged into."

"I think we're both tired of hiding. That's why I came over."

Maneuvering over me, with an eyebrow wiggle, he asks, "So you've finally fallen for my charms, huh?"

I smile. "Your charms have been working a lot longer than you know."

Hovering over me and with a cocky head nod, he says, "I knew I'd wear you down."

"Oh, Mr. Caggiano, you've worn me out... I mean down, several times."

Pressing his hips and his very apparent erection between my legs, he says, "And I look forward to doing it again."

"Who knew the wild, bad boy drummer of The Resistance had the willpower of a saint? Not me."

With a deep laugh, he says, "Me either. Just know when we're together again, it won't be just sex. It'll be an unwritten contract. A promise from my heart to yours."

My heart starts thudding in my chest and I pull him down, bringing his lips to mine and kiss him, making my own promise to him. When I fall back on the cushion, I open my eyes and smile when I see the happiness in his. "Go do what you need to do," I say, rubbing his back. "I'll be here waiting for you when you get back."

"I'm gonna hold you to that."

"I like when you hold me." Dex smirks and I return the favor before pushing up against him and adding, "Also, I want you to check out and go home. If it's not feeling like home these days, let me know, and I'll help you find what you're looking for."

"Bossy *and* sexy. You're turning me on. You should probably leave before I pillage your body for the remainder of the day."

"I like pillaging and plundering."

"Yep, plundering is good too."

Reluctantly, I stand and look at my watch. After taking LA traffic into account, I say, "As tempting as plundering sounds, I should go." He stands up as well and I can see his mood has changed for the better. "Walk me to the door."

I tug him by the end of his belt until my back is pressed against the door and he's pressed against me. He says, "Thank you for coming."

"Thank you for the letter."

His eyes steady on mine, our mouths just a few mere inches apart. Leaning in, he says, "You're my constant. My north. The only compass worth following."

Taking his face in my hands, the scruff is rough against my skin, his temperament gentle as I caress him. "I know you, the real you, Dex. You don't ever have to hide from me."

He leans his forehead against mine and closes his eyes. As soon as I close mine, he whispers, "I love you, Rochelle Floros." Then he backs away, releasing me and adds, "Go before this turns embarrassing and I start telling you everything else you make me feel."

Gah! This man. I just want him in so many ways... Smiling, I open the door and step over the threshold. But I stop, turn around and run into his arms, hugging him tightly. With my cheek against his chest, I say, "One day, I want to hear about them. Every side, every emotion, every thought you have." And like before at Disney, I leave him with, "Until then," but as I walk away, I add,

"You have my number if you need me. Use it sometime."

He nods, taking hold of the door before it swings shut. "Until then..."

# 25

## Antonio Dex Caggiano

I vowed never to come back to Diablo. At thirty, it finally seemed like the right time to sort my family life out once and for all. I sit in the Challenger for a good five minutes staring at the mansion before me and listening to Alice in Chains. "Rooster" somehow fitting right now.

I had so many good times and so many bad times here. It was where I learned my grandfather was not the overbearing monster my mom had sold him as, but later discovered he was worse.

My life seemed to develop and fall apart inside that stucco exterior. I was going one direction and then... and then everything changed. I sucked as a son and everything that my mother had wanted. I excelled at rebellion, so that's what I did to save my sanity. Now I'm back sixteen years later to face the demons that plague me.

Gage walks out, his head down as if he's already disappointed in me. Leaning his hand against the door of my car, I hear his wedding ring scrape against the metal, messing up my paint job. *No fucking respect at all.*

"Dexter. You're two hours late."

I pop the door open, hitting him, and step out. "I was given a day, not a time, so fuck off about some schedule you created in your head."

"Nice attitude," he says sarcastically. "And here I thought this week was about making amends."

Walking to my trunk, I open it and grab my leather duffle bag out. "So did I, so why are you out here busting my balls?"

Following a heavy sigh, he says, "There's an additional will that is to be read when the youngest Caggiano hits his thirties."

"I've been thirty for months."

My brother shrugs. "We've been busy."

Busy stealing I assume, but keep the thought to myself, figuring it's less confrontational that way. I walk past him and into the house. "Same room?"

Overtaking me, he goes to the bar. "Yep, same room you always had." I hear the ice dropping into the crystal glass. "Dinner's in twenty. Dress for it."

I stop on the stairs wanting to say something, wanting to give him a piece of my mind, but I keep my eyes forward and start back up. This week's gonna be hell.

I dump my bag on the bed and take a minute to look around. The room is exactly the same, like I never left. Being inside these four walls again makes me feel fourteen in the worst ways. I was abandoned here in the summer, feeling like I'd been forgotten. Anger builds inside.

Unzipping my bag, I choose a long sleeve, button up, but refuse to give in fully to their whims on decorum. Not wearing a tie is the only ammo they have on me when I have a luggage set of issues with them. After washing my face and brushing my teeth, I put on the clean shirt then head downstairs.

My mother is standing in front of the wrought iron doors that lead to the large lawn. Croquet is set up and I can only assume per my mom's request. She turns just as I enter the sitting room. With her token martini in hand, she smiles. It's small, rigid, but it's good to see she can form an emotion on her overly botoxed face. She was once a beauty queen. Sometimes I can see the girl who resides inside the bitterness of the woman. Sometimes I can't.

She stares at me. She always did say I was the spitting image of my father. I took it as a compliment to spite her inference. When she doesn't say anything, I tend to think she's lost in a memory of him. Finally, she relaxes and says, "Antonio, it's so good to see you."

I go to her and give her a hug because no matter what hurt she's caused me, I like to think her embraces are genuine. She hugs me back, careful not to spill her drink. "Hi, Mom." I take the spot next to her, looking out the window. "How are you?"

"You didn't wear a tie. Will you put one on?"

"No. Is dinner almost ready?"

"Always my non-conformist."

"Eh," I say, "It's working for me."

Her hand touches my cheek and I see a real smile form. "Don't ever change," she whispers, "You're perfect just how you are."

My eyes narrow, her unexpected compliment catching me off-guard. "What's going on?"

"So cynical, Son."

A loud clap disturbs us and Gage walks in bellowing. "Are they finally done with dinner? I'm starved."

At the sound, my mom's hand falls to her side and she sips her cocktail while turning back to look outside again. Bad timing on the interruption. It's been a long time since I've seen this side of my mother and I was enjoying it. A woman walks in and tells us dinner is ready in the main dining room.

"Good," Gage says as if he's been waiting all day for food. He rushes past us and takes the seat at the head of the table like he somehow earned it.

"You're an ass, Gage."

"I may be an ass, but I'm also rightfully head of the family as the oldest male."

My mother sits next to him quietly as if she doesn't hear the argument or she just doesn't care. Wine is poured and I thank the server. She's pretty, not flirty. Just tending to her job.

Dinner is tense with so many egos trapped in one room. I try to bring up the reason we're here several times, but nothing sticks. "Explain the situation with the additional will."

Gage uses all these hand gestures like he's lecturing a child in timeout. "The lawyer was held in strict confidence until your birthday or if you didn't live, your funeral." I glare at him. "What?" He shrugs. "I think we all know it was hit or miss with you."

"I'd call you an asshole, but I'm starting to think you like playing that part too much and you'll take it as a good thing."

My mom leans her elbows on the table, exasperated. "Boys, let's put all this animosity behind us and focus on the future."

Seeing her lose her manners in such an easy way makes me double take in her direction. Something's going on with her and I think Gage is too angry and too drunk to notice. The server comes in with our dessert plates. She serves Gage last. I'm thinking on purpose. He grabs her ass just as she sets his plate down.

"Excuse you!" she says, her face one of horror.

I stand abruptly. "I apologize for him. We'll not need anything else tonight."

She looks from him to me, her expression one of relief when our eyes meet. "Thank you."

When she leaves the room, I remain standing, tossing my napkin down. "I think we're finished here. I'm going to bed." I walk out, needing to clear my mind from the head trip laid on me tonight. The door is pushed open and I move quickly across the yard, stepping over a few wickets on the way. I go toward the shadows where I used to hide when I was a kid, but I break the pattern and pull my phone from my back pocket, dialing instead of drinking.

Rochelle answers right away and damn if I don't love that. "Hello?"

"Hi, it's me."

"It's good to hear from you," she says, "Everything okay?"

"Everything is complicated like always."

"Are you alright?"

I lie down in the grass and look up at the night sky. I can see a million or more stars out here, unlike in LA. "Go outside, Rochelle."

Without question, she goes. I hear her shuffling and the creak of a door. Then she says, "I'm outside."

"Can you see any stars?"

"Not as many as I'd like."

I smile. "I can see forever from here."

"Can you see to LA? I'm waving just for you."

"I can see you in my heart."

"I miss you, Dex."

"I miss you, too. It's good to hear your voice."

"You too, but you don't sound well."

"I'm okay. Tell me about your day."

"My day was boring," she says.

"Not to me."

I'm content listening to her talk, her voice soothing me. What she thinks is mundane, I find peaceful. It's a life I can only hope to have one day.

"...The boys still talk about you. They remember everything you taught them."

"Thank you for not making me the bad guy in their eyes."

"Dex, you're not a bad guy."

Taking a deep breath, I say, "They're reading another will of my grandfather's. You know how you found out I was from a wealthy family?"

"Yes."

"My grandfather was even wealthier. He was my idol once. He was a drummer."

"Ah."

"But when my mom was raped by my uncle, he blamed her."

I hear her sharp intake of air. It's a bombshell and no matter how it's dropped, it's gonna blow up, so there's no point in tiptoeing around the monsters in the family.

"Dex—"

"You don't have to say anything."

"You can talk to me."

I hear my mom calling for me, but I don't move. "I should go. It's getting late. I'm sure you need some rest and I need to escape."

"You're not in this alone. Call me anytime."

"Goodnight."

"Sweet dreams, Dex."

When I hang up, I start back for the house. Fortunately my mom is nowhere in sight. I've had enough of my family for one day and head to bed.

TR

My night is restless and I get up as the sun starts to rise. I don't bother with formalities. Boxers, jeans, and a T-shirt are good enough to go downstairs to get coffee. When I'm walking down the hall, the door to Gage's room opens and a familiar looking brunette is sneaking out—*the server from dinner*.

Her shoes in hand as she turns and then jumps, startled by me.

"Morning," I say.

"Good morning, Sir. I was just, uhhh, getting Mr. Caggiano his morning coffee." I wonder if lying makes her feel better and if she actually thinks I believe her? She continues, "I need to go."

She starts to dash off, but I say, "He's married with two small kids."

She doesn't look back again as she leaves the house. In the kitchen I find a Keurig with a variety of coffee pods to choose from. Popping one in, I wait as it brews. Gage walks in without a shirt and scratching under his arm. "Morn," he says, reaching for a mug from the hooks under the cabinet.

"What the fuck? You're married, Gage."

"I haven't even had my coffee yet. Can we hold this conversation until after we're caffeinated or better yet, never?"

"Britney loves you."

"And I love her, so what's the problem?"

I turn my back to him, leaning my hands against the marble countertops, trying to control the rage he brings out in me. As a teenager I used to smoke pot with my friends. We'd trespass and go up to Griffith observatory to escape. When the band became famous, we'd trespass onto the Hollywood Sign and do coke or X.

I thought the night Cory died would be the last night I ever did drugs. I think I did everything I could get my hands on that night in Paris and my body paid the price. But Cory saved me. Now I carry guilt for falling in love with his woman, or falling *more* in love, I mentally correct myself. I loved her since the day I met her. Then add dealing with my asshole of a brother on top of that guilt and all I want to do is go break some shit, smoke some weed, and escape.

I won't do it because of her and the kids. Good must be hereditary and those boys scored. It sure doesn't run in my family.

Grabbing the coffee before the last drop falls, I return to my room. Gage was smart not to continue talking to me. I stay in my room and work on a song I've been writing, the lyrics coming in waves as I write them down. The band returns to the studio in eight days to record and I want this song to be perfect before they hear it. I've never written one for them before so I know they'll be more critical.

A knock on the door causes me to look up. With a guitar in my arms, I say, "Come in."

My mom walks in with two drinks in hand. "I brought you an iced tea."

"Thank you."

"Can we talk or am I interrupting?"

"We can talk." I set the guitar down, then say, "I could use some fresh air. Would you like to go for a walk?"

TR

The sky is blue and there's a nice breeze outside as we follow the gravel path around the outside of the gardens. "I have cancer." I had the glass to my lips when she tells me. I bring it down and stop in my spot. She looks back and says, "I don't want to make a big deal of it. Let's keep walking."

"Cancer is a big deal."

"Yes," she says, "But we must die from something. Dying is a side effect of life."

"You're downplaying it. Death seems like a really bad fucking side effect."

She wraps her arm around my elbow and we start walking again. "It's inoperable and too far along to bother treating. I'm good with this."

My mind can't seem to grasp onto anything tangible, her words make no sense to me. Questions fill my brain as her justifications don't provide the answers I need. "I'm not good with it. What did Gage say?"

"He doesn't know yet. I wanted to tell you first."

"Why?"

She pulls me tighter to her, leaning her head on my shoulder. "Because you're a better man than I ever gave you credit for. And, I knew you'd be more rational with this kind of news."

I want to be anything but rational. Feeling aggravated to have this laid upon me like this makes me mad. I'm trying to hold that in because she seems to crave peace and after years of craving her attention, she's finally giving it to me. I don't want to blow it now. "Why are you not fighting?"

"Because the doctors said weeks. Not months or years. Weeks. And I don't want to spend my remaining time fighting a battle that clearly cannot be won." She lifts her head and releases my arm. "I know what they will say and I'm worried about Gage and his troubled situation."

"Troubled?"

"Britney has left him and taken the children. He's blown

through a lot of his inheritance and has asked for loans against future deposits." We come to a bench and she sits, her body sinking down only a bit as she does. Always a woman of pride and propriety, her posture is not reflective of her condition. I sit beside her, and she says, "Gage is not a Caggiano. He was conceived out of wedlock thus negating his claim to any of your grandfather's money or estates. The first will covered him. This second one will eliminate him from receiving anything more."

My head goes back in disbelief. "Holy shit."

"Please don't swear. Anyway, I know this is a lot to take in, but I need your help now. I'm not sure what to tell him. I think he'll be more upset about the loss of funds than finding out that he's the son of a poet passing through town. Or that I have cancer."

"He'll care. You two were always very close."

"We haven't been in a few years."

"Since the situation with me."

"Yes. I think it needs to be revisited. He needs to come to terms with the damage he did. You need to find it in your heart to forgive him, for me. You'll only have each other soon. As for me, please don't worry. I don't feel any pain. That's much different than I imagined when I was told. I'm just tired." She's calm, so calm as if she's come to peace with her past, present, and future all in one day. "I want to die at home if you don't mind forgoing the hospice the doctors will insist upon."

"Of course," I say, no hesitation to help her find that peace. "I'll get you whatever you need."

"Antonio, continue to shine like the star you are. I'm so proud of you and your accomplishments." She looks at me, and says, "I used to be a star, the belle of the ball."

Her confessions have me intrigued. Leaning forward, I rest my elbows on my knees and look at her. She speaks as if she's worlds away, maybe living in the memory she's recalling. "Your father, Joseph, was a wonderful man when I met him. I was sitting at a restaurant in downtown Diablo with Gage and he was having lunch next to me. He commented how I was a good mother to my baby, giving the baby all of my attention. One thing led to the next and he joined us for lunch."

"Was it love at first sight?"

"Most definitely." She sits back and raises her chin up while closing her eyes. "So handsome. So much like you," she says, glancing at me. "I don't think you have any of the Dexter features, except maybe my sparkling personality."

*And here I thought she didn't know me at all.*

"I've seen you on TV so many times. You're captivating and charming. I see why young women fall for you. But tell me, has anyone mattered? Is there anyone special? That woman you brought around to the country club perhaps?"

"Rochelle." I stop there, contemplating how much I want to share versus how much I should share. I decide there might not be another chance, so I say, "I fell in love with Rochelle the first time I ever laid eyes on her."

My mom smiles and asks, "When was that?"

"Eleven years ago. When I was nineteen."

Her eyes widen. "Well, that's a long time to be in love with someone. Why have you not been together?"

Sitting back, I sigh. "Life is complicated. Even when you think it falls at your feet, there's always something more, something just out of reach."

"Is Rochelle within reach?"

"Now she is." Smiling at her, I say, "She has two kids. Sons."

"Oh. And the father?"

"He's passed." I don't go into details. It still hurts me to think of

Cory and face the fact that he's gone forever.

"You were close?"

"He was one of my best friends. He was in the band." I should be offended that she seems so careless in regards to knowing about my life. But I didn't share with her either and it's not worth the argument now. "They're great kids too. I'm teaching them to play drums. The older one, Neil, he's good. Natural talent. The younger one is four. CJ can charm the socks off anyone with his smile."

"You love them." A statement.

I shift, then smile. "Yeah," I say, "I do. I love Rochelle too."

# 26

## Antonio Dex Caggiano

It's ten at night when I call Rochelle. I'm hoping to catch her in bed before she falls asleep so she can talk. She answered after the first ring. "Hi there."

"Hi there yourself."

With a chuckle, she asks, "How's Diablo?"

"Umm..." I scratch my head, then look at the TV, which was keeping me company before I called her. "I'm not sure."

"Interesting. Are you doing okay?"

"I'm not sure."

"Do I need to be worried because you're totally worrying me right now."

"I'm not sure."

"Stop saying that, Dex." Her voice gets pitchy. "You're freaking me out."

I close my eyes, draping my arm across my forehead. "I'm

kind of freaking out myself."

Her words are rushed and demanding. It feels good to know that she cares so much. "Tell me what's going on."

But scaring her was not my intention. I'm just unsure how to tell her everything or if I should. "I called because I need to ask a favor." She's patient and lets me speak. "Is there any way you can fly up here tomorrow and spend the night? I'll drive you home the next day."

"You want me to be there with you and your family?" Her tone is now light, unbelieving.

"You're my family." It sounds so matter of fact, but she's right. We're family. "Will you come?"

There's a long pause before I hear her, her voice wavering with emotion. "Dex…" She sucks in a shaky breath and I can tell she's trying to stop from crying. "If you need me, I'm there. Always." Tapping is heard. "I'm looking up flights now."

"I'll buy your ticket," I say.

"I can afford the ticket. No worries."

"I know you can, but I want to buy it."

"Okay," she relents. "There's a flight into Oakland that leaves at one I can make."

"I'll send the confirmation to you."

"Thank you."

I yawn, worn out. "You're welcome, but really I should be thanking you."

"You'd do it for me… You've done it for me. You were there when I needed you most." She yawns.

"I'll let you get some rest and I'll pick you up from the airport. I'll be in the Challenger outside of baggage claim."

"I'll see you tomorrow."

"Until then…"

"Until then..."

TR

As soon as I see Rochelle walking out of the terminal the following day, I pull to the curb, throw the car in park, and run around to greet her. She's beautiful as always, her long hair flowing over her shoulders. Her eyes bright and her smile big—just for me, so I kiss her, savoring the feel of her skin, her lips, the way her tongue caresses mine.

Leaving her breathless was my single motivation. I think it worked because she sighs, then whispers, "It's good to see you too."

After opening her door for her, I take her bag and put it in the trunk. I slide into the driver's seat and say, "Welcome to hell."

Fastening her seatbelt, she looks up and says, "And here I thought Diablo just meant devil."

It doesn't take long to get to the estate, less than an hour's drive with traffic. Rochelle's mouth opens when we pull up the long driveway. "This looks like what I imagine Hearst Castle looking like."

"My grandfather hated the Hearst Castle. I wish he was here just to hear the comparison."

"Do you want to talk about him?"

I park the car and look at her, the air vents blowing her hair wildly behind her. "I used to think he was this stuffy old man, then I found he was worse."

"What happened?"

"I found out he called my mom a liar and a whore after she was raped." I get out not wanting to see Rochelle's face or tears, her sympathies. I need to be strong and right now, I don't have enough strength for both of us. Grabbing her suitcase from the trunk, I set it down as she joins me. "Let's not talk about it. Okay?"

"Sure. Okay." She nods.

"Oh and ignore Gage. He'll offend you in some way, so it's just best not to pay any attention to him."

She takes a wavering breath and says, "I'm here for you, Dex. Only you."

Taking her hand in one and her case in the other, I lead her inside. At the top of the stairs, I say, "There's a guest room across the hall from mine..." I wait to see what she wants to do, hoping it's the same as what I want.

"I'm not staying with you?" If I'm not mistaken, her lashes flutter, reminding me of a butterfly.

My thoughts momentarily drift back to her mentioning her love of fireflies. "I want you to stay with me," I whisper, giving her hand a little squeeze.

A pink covers her cheeks, making me want to do so much to her right now. She says, "I'd like that."

Leading her into the bedroom, I set her bag down and she walks to the window, not giving the king size bed a second thought. "Your window overlooks a garden. It's beautiful."

"Nothing like your beauty."

She smiles at me, then turns back. "Roses are beautiful but dangerous. I've always been fascinated by them. What grows in the greenhouse?"

"I'm not sure. I haven't been back there since I've been here." Standing near the door, I ask, "Would you like to freshen up or for me to give you a tour of the house?"

Turning, she jumps onto the bed and falls back. "You're so formal here. It reminds me of when I lived in Boston."

"There were very strict rules when I visited here. Old habits die hard."

With her arm outstretched, she summons me to her. Pausing, I stare down at her, the image of Eve and all her mortal sins corrupting me to my core. But like Adam, I can't resist the temptation. Crawling onto the bed, I move on top of her. My weight balanced above her until her hands travel from my neck down to my waist. I drop down lightly, balancing just above. "What are you doing to me?"

Her eyes look into mine, our connection always present. Pushing me gently up, she giggles and says, "You're right. I'll take the tour."

She squirms her way to the side, but I grab her by the waist before she escapes and say, "We'll pick up where we left off later."

Her eyes give her desires away. She's not playing hard with such a sexually mischievous look in her soulful browns. "I look forward to it."

Following her out the door, we head back downstairs to the sitting room where I saw my mom last. Gage is near the door at the bar when we enter. He stops and eyes Rochelle blatantly, top to bottom and back up, and I want to punch him in the fucking face for it. Instead, I possessively take her hand and lead her to the couch across from the chair where my mother sits. She smiles at me and then to Rochelle before speaking. "It's so good to see you again, Rochelle."

"You too, Mrs. Caggiano."

My mom looks down and smiles while toiling with the throw on her lap. "We only had nine years together, but those years seem to have shaped my entire life."

Rochelle looks to me for further explanation when it's clear my mom is not going to give one. I lean back, getting comfortable. "My father and mother were married for nine years before he died."

My mom looks at Rochelle, new blood in the mix to share her stories to. But this time, I don't mind. This time, I make the time to listen. "He was the most handsome man I had ever see—"

"Nine years?" Gage asks, staring at us from across the room. "That's not right, Mother. You're forgetting in your old age."

"Shut-up," I say to him before turning back.

"What? You need to show off for you girlfriend here? Like she'll find a 'shut-up' impressive. I'll show her impress—"

I stand and cut him off. "Shut the fuck up, Gage, or I'll shut you up."

Gage cackles and swallows more of his drink. Looks like Scotch. "There's the fighter we all love to hate. Doesn't take much to provoke the lower class."

"You don't even know what you're talking about, man. Just stop, Gage. Okay?"

"Speaking of lower class, how's that band thing working out for you ever since that guy died?"

Rochelle stiffens beside me, her breath stopping altogether.

My mother says, "Gage, find something useful to do, like finding a job."

"After this meeting, I won't need a job." He walks into the other room, slamming his glass down on the cherry wood of the sideboard before exiting.

"I'm sorry." Both Rochelle and I look at my mother as she apologizes. "I'm sorry for your loss."

"Thank you," Rochelle says with a nod and a taut smile in place.

Squeezing her knee, I ask, "Are you okay?"

"I am. Your brother's an asshole though."

"Yep." I laugh. "He majored in it at Brown." I stand up and help my mom up. "We need to go or we'll be late."

In the garden, I hadn't noticed how frail my mom has become. Out there she fooled me by the way she held my arm. The change in her is more obvious now just a few short hours later.

"Would you like to come, Rochelle?" she asks.

Rochelle's eyes target me, asking the question again, silently between us this time. "I think you should stay. I'm not sure how long this will take. You can rest up for tonight."

"What's tonight?"

"I have big plans in store for us."

"In that case, I'll take a nap, so I can enjoy these *big* plans."

My mother clears her throat as she passes us. "Save that kind of talk to when your mother is out of the room." She laughs, but stops and turns toward me. "Follow your heart..." Her eyes land on Rochelle, and she says, "I'm very glad to have seen you again."

Rochelle smiles. "It was really nice to see you again as well."

TR

"My apologies, Mr. Caggiano," the lawyer speaks directly to Gage. "I can't proceed with you in the room since the will is confidential and only allowed to be read to the beneficiaries."

Gage's mouth is hanging open. The shock of being told our father was not his makes his face go red with anger.

I reach over toward him, but he stands up. "What the fuck?" Staring at my mom, he says, "You were a whore and I'm the bastard who has to suffer for it."

I stand abruptly, at the ready if I need to kick his ass. One more comment like that and he's going down.

"Gage," my mom starts.

He pulls the door open. "I don't want to hear it." The wall takes the brunt of the impact when the door hits it.

The time seemed to pass in an orderly reading of a list, one item at a time. When it was all said and done, the car ride was silent as my mother and I returned to the house. After settling my plans for later with a few phone calls and staff help, I awoke my sleeping beauty with a kiss. Her eyes slowly blinking open and happy to see me. "How did it go?"

"Well."

"That's good," she whispers.

"I want to take you somewhere."

She nods and then sits up, rubbing her eyes. "Are jeans okay or do I need to change?"

"Never change. You're gorgeous just how you are."

# 27

## Antonio Dexter Caggiano

We walk from the back of the house down the large steps to the crushed granite path. Rochelle smiles, which causes my own. I veer to the left, off the path, and through a grouping of pink flowers, taking her on a short cut. We're both careful not to crush any as we hop over the bushes. Her laughter draws me to look her way, her beauty captivating my heart entirely.

I'm nervous for some reason, but I keep guiding her. A few more steps and she'll see it. She stops, another smile gracing her stunning face. The greenhouse is ahead, trees and tall bushes making for a dramatic presentation. The front is covered in a vine of Purple flowers and the entrance is lit by the setting sun, making it more magical, even to me.

"Dex, it's even prettier in person than from the window upstairs."

"I'm glad you like it." I walk forward and open the door for her.

Following her inside, I let the door close on its own. Moving to the other side of the center row of plants, I copy her slow, but steady pace as she admires the flowers blooming all around. I don't bother with the flowers and admire her instead.

She says, "This is one of the most beautiful places I've ever seen."

"My grandfather let the gardener do whatever he wanted. This was the gardener's private sanctuary."

"It's where he kept the good stuff."

"Yeah, it's where he kept the good stuff."

I hear a small gasp and look over at her. She says, "Dex, did you do this?"

The table for two is draped in linens and set with the finest china and crystal. A vase of pink flowers is in the center. "I arranged it. Does that count?"

"Yes," she says, nodding. "That totally counts. It's beautiful. Are we having dinner out here?"

"I thought you might like it."

"I do. So much." She comes to me, wrapping her arms around my middle and resting her cheek on my chest as we both look at the display before us.

It wasn't meant to be a big deal, but somehow I realize at the same moment Rochelle does, this is a very big deal. And I'm not talking about the dinner or the little touches, or the surprises I still have in store for her. Being here with her, like this, is a big deal.

"Champagne?" I ask. I feel her nod against me and when she holds me a little tighter, I embrace her fully. "You okay?"

"More than okay. Thank you for doing this. I'm really touched."

"C'mon before you get me all sentimental too." I grab the champagne and pop the cork. After pouring her a glass, I set it on the table and pull her chair out, wanting to impress her. When I sit across from her, we toast, "To good times and even better company. Cheers."

Dinner is served in three courses. I want us satisfied but not stuffed. There's more planned for the evening ahead. After dessert, the table is cleared by the staff and the champagne bottle is replaced with a bottle of wine. With our glasses in hand, I escort her to the back part of the greenhouse where the heat sensitive and specialty plants are kept. I open the door and as we walk under the arbor, I spin her around, keeping her back to the surprise. "I wanted to thank you for coming here." Before she can say anything, I kiss her, then slide my tongue down her neck, stopping to suck just enough to taste, but not enough to leave a mark. "You taste edible."

A small moan escapes her before she whispers, "Are you wooing me, Mr. Caggiano?" I can tell she's succumbing as her hands glide roughly over my shirt and stomach. She has a thing for my abs I've discovered. I do extra sit-ups just for her.

"Trying my hardest."

"You don't have to try that hard. I'm already pretty smitten."

"I like you smitten," I whisper. "Turn around."

The queen size bed is on a platform angled in the corner. The sheets a pale green, the comforter white. Mosquito netting is draped around with flowers hanging down. Cynthia did a great job making this happen.

With a hand covering her mouth that's dropped open in awe, Rochelle quickly closes it and says, "Do we get to sleep out here tonight?"

"If you want."

"I definitely want to. It's like a fairytale come to life. Dex," she says, her excitement getting the best of her. "I can't believe you did this. You gave me Neverland, again." She takes my hand and does this little sway of her hips. "I'm liking this romancing business." Signaling toward the bed, she adds, "I'm feeling like going to bed early. Wanna join—Oh my God! Are those butterflies?" Rochelle chases an orange and black butterfly until it lands and a yellow one flutters by, grabbing her attention. "Dex! They're everywhere. Look around on the plants. Butterflies."

I smile, enjoying seeing her so happy, flirtatious, and excited. Running up to me, she grabs me hard, her arms tight around my neck. "You did this. You did all of this for me?"

"I did. It's all for you."

"I'm going to spend all night showing you how grateful I am to have you in my life." She kisses me and it's not gentle.

"Ms. Floros, I could get used to this kind of gratitude on a regular basis."

"You haven't seen anything yet."

"Neither have you," I say, holding her steady in my sights.

"You don't even know what you do to me." Another kiss lands on my lips as she holds me by my shirt to her. "Make love to me, Dex. I want you."

The darkness outside and the plants along the walls protect us from outside prying eyes. "Take your clothes off and show me how much you want me."

Her eyes are sultry, the challenge tempting her. Moving across the room, I turn the lights down, the glow of the candles adding to the mood. The shadowed butterflies still fly about and I lie on the bed, getting comfortable.

Keeping her eyes on me, she takes her shirt over her head and drops it on a chair nearby. Her fingers toy with her jeans like she's toying with me. My cock is hard and getting harder from watching her before she even takes her shoes off. She turns around and bends over, giving me a full view of her fantastic ass as she takes her jeans down. The lace thong is a tease just like her. My palm rubs over my dick and I decide to give myself some more room to grow by unfastening my jeans.

Her arms reach around her back and she undoes the clasp of her bra with ease, letting it hang while she takes one strap and then the other down her arms. She turns back around, not hiding, but smirking and confident. Lifting the netting, she joins me on the bed by crawling up my body and pushing my shirt up as she goes. "Take *your* clothes off, Dex. Show me how much you want *me*," she says, repeating my earlier demand.

Like her, I strip my clothes off, but without the production, then kneel down in front of her. Slowly, I run my hands up her soft skin. When my fingertips reach her panties, I start to descend, taking them with me. I press my lips to the inside of her thigh. This time sucking hard, wanting her marked as mine. Her fingers find the top of my head and she rubs them through my hair. Moving to her pussy, I mimic her by moving my tongue around her clit, her back arching as her body lowers, bringing her closer. I slide my hands under her ass, gripping her hips and licking, taunting, and fucking harder, eliciting the sexiest moans I've ever heard.

My hair is tugged and I inhale her while driving her mad with pleasure. She squirms and I hold on tighter until I hear her breathing stagger and her body starts to tighten. With her head tilted back, her mouth wide open, she comes with desperate moans as her body is overwhelmed and tremors.

"Dex!" Her back falls flat against the mattress and her breath returns, her thighs easing around my head. I place one more kiss on her pussy before I slide up next to her. Her lids are heavy and a smile resides on her face. "It's been a while," she says, as if I'm judging her.

"It's been a while for both of us." I roll over so I'm resting on her bare chest, our bodies aligned. She kisses me, then I whisper, "I haven't been with anyone except you in almost a year."

She kisses me again this time lingering on my lips. "I've not been with anyone else in the last three."

My heart starts racing as I take in her words, her confession, and her commitment. Hovering over her, I feel the need to release my own confession, but this time not running away from fear of rejection. I say, "I love you."

Her eyes stay locked on mine and she says, "I love you too."

Pushing inside, her eyes close as her warmth engulfs me. I close my eyes and begin moving. The soft skin of her hand finds the rough surface of my face and she caresses. "Open your eyes, Dex." Her words are uneven like our breathing.

When I lift my lids, I finally see the love I've waited for what feels like a lifetime. It lies in the depths of her amber eyes. A jolt of reality restarts my heart to make every beat count from this moment on. Her nails scrape lightly up my back setting every nerve on fire and I start thrusting, all my energy put into the act.

Rochelle squirms, taking all I give and giving all she has, her desire a turn on and her confidence sexy. "God, Dex. You feel so good."

"You feel better." My words are slurred from the haze I'm under. My body moves of its own accord, sensations and frustrations building deep inside. Her body drives me for more, making me want to steal her soul like she's stolen mine. "Fuck. I'm gonna come soon."

"Come with me. Harder. Faster." Her words just escaping breaths. Her mouth tantalizes me, flipping my world upside down, and making me want to fuck her into oblivion. I fuck. I fuck hard as her groans of pleasure instigate. My eyes shut tight as I overcome desires that turn into bonfires, my body burning in her ecstasy as we come. I pulse and she squeezes, our bodies working as one with no end and no beginning, just us together.

I collapse, exhausted with no will or inclination to move. Rochelle's fingers weave into my hair holding my head to hers. "I love you," she whispers in my ear, making me smile.

With my eyes closed, I say, "I really could get used to this."

"I hope you never tire of me."

Lifting up, I push her dark hair away from her face and kiss her chin, her cheek, then the side of her mouth. "I could never tire of you. I've loved you my whole life."

She smiles, soft and more beautiful than ever before. "You keep saying things like that and I might start believing you."

With a chuckle, I lean my head against her chest. "Deal." When I hear a soft sigh of contentment, I ask, "Are you tired?"

"I am." She moves to get up. "Is the nearest bathroom in the house?"

"Just through the office in the corner over there. Sorry, it's small."

"No worries. I'll be right back."

I lay there, my chest burning. Putting my arm across my forehead, I stare up past the netting and through the glass, the moon seeming bigger and brighter than usual. My mind drifts to the woman I just made love to, curious if we can move beyond this night. The door opens and I look over, watching her, wanting us to be more than tonight, wanting it more than I have ever wanted anything else.

When she returns, she crawls under the covers and I take my turn in the bathroom. I come back and start turning out the candles.

She takes one and looks at it. "It's battery-operated. That's cool."

"Can't have the greenhouse filling with smoke."

"Clever."

"Not my idea, but I'll let Cynthia know."

She laughs lightly, then says, "Let's go to bed."

After I turn off the last candle, we lay in the dark, letting our eyes adjust. Lying on our backs, we look up as moonlight fills the greenhouse. "We should have made love with just the moon above." Cuddling into my side, she closes her eyes.

Whispering, I say, "Keep your eyes open just a few minutes longer."

She readjusts and looks up. As if on command, the first one lights up on her side of the bed. Sitting up abruptly, she says, "Are those fireflies?"

"They are. Lay back with me."

Slowly, she lays back down and smiles. "It's magic. Butterflies and fireflies. You gave me magic, Dex. It's the most romantic thing I've ever seen."

"You deserve romance and more. I'll give you everything I can because you gave me a reason to live. You gave me life." Rolling onto my side, I run my hand over her arm. "I never thanked you properly for saving me."

"I didn't save you, Dex. I think you might have saved me though. You fill my heart where a hole used to exist. Expecting more would be greedy."

Caressing her cheek, I lean forward. "I like you greedy... and horny." I slide my hand between her legs and her eyes look up to meet mine as a small, devious expression appears.

"Let's be greedy and horny together."

Under the moon, in a house made of glass, we make love slow and gentle, taking our time, frivolous in the knowledge of having a forever together.

TR

When I wake up in the morning, I open my eyes, and see the love of my life asleep next to me. An orange, black, and white butterfly sits on her temple, slowly opening and closing its wings. Both of them true beauty personified. I take a mental picture since I know it will fly away if I move.

Cautiously, I put my finger to her temple and the butterfly moves onto my finger. When I lift it up, it flies around the enclosure of the mosquito netting before finally settling on the sheer fabric.

"A fairytale," she whispers and I look over before following her gaze up. The outside of the netting is covered in butterflies of all different sizes and colors. Rochelle kisses me on the cheek and says, "Enchanting."

I kiss her hand, letting my tongue taste her sweetness. "Like you, my love. Good morning."

"Good morning."

"We should go soon. We have a long drive back."

"Can't we stay forever?" Although I know it's rhetorical, the way she asks makes me want to make her dreams come true.

"I promise you, I'll fill your life with magic."

"I don't need magic, Dex. I just need you."

# 28

# Rochelle

Dex has been quiet for a large portion of the trip. "What's on your mind?" I risk breaking the silence just to hear his voice again.

He glances over while sliding his hand from my thigh to my knee and giving it a little squeeze. "Sorry." He smiles. It's small, but thoughtful. "I didn't mean to be so quiet. Just lost in my head. The will stuff and Gage. My mom."

"Do you want to talk about it?"

Dex has a way of confessing with such honesty. He's direct and sometimes it catches me by surprise. With his eyes back on the road, he says, "Gage isn't my brother by blood. My mom told me the night before the will was read. Gage found out during the reading and they made him leave the room."

Not sure what to say, I blurt, "I'm sorry." I have no idea if that's appropriate in this situation or not.

"He's an asshole for sure, but he's kind of always been my asshole of a brother. Know what I mean?"

I nod.

He continues, "I'm just not sure where this leaves us. He screwed me over before and now he's just lecherous since his wife left him. His life is unraveling and he's the one pulling the string. I'm not sure what to think about things."

"It's a lot to take in. You need time to process."

"Yeah maybe." He nods this time, then exhales heavily. "Thanks for being here."

"Thanks again for inviting me."

Changing the subject, he smiles and an excitement comes over him. "So there's this spot I want to take you to. It's a little off the beaten path, but we'll only lose a few minutes in drive time. Is it okay if we go?"

I can't deny him this happiness. "I'd like that."

We veer from the highway and travel about ten minutes, then down a secluded road near a house perched on the hillside. He stops the car and parks on the dirt shoulder just in case any traffic comes. He takes the top of the car down and I sit up on the edge of the door and look out at the ocean that stretches the entire expanse of the horizon before us. The sun is still high since it's before noon, but I imagine the sunsets here are incredible. "It's amazing here."

Moving around the car, Dex comes to my side and faces me. "You're more amazing."

"Charmer."

"I'm not charming you. I'm just telling the truth." He leans forward and kisses me.

I pull him closer, loving the freedom I feel here in the open to love him.

With an eager expression, he asks, "Wanna do it?"

I burst out laughing. "Sure. Let's do it," I say, teasing him while poking him in the ribs. When I see he's not joking, surprise takes over my face. "You're serious right now?"

"Dead."

"Don't say dead."

His expression softens. "Yes, I'm serious. I want you." He slides his hands up my thighs, stopping on my hips.

Looking around, expecting to find an audience, I say, "We can't. This is like someone's property or something. We could get busted and arrested. I can't be arrested, Dex."

"It's mine."

"What's yours?"

"It's my property. All the way from the main road down this private street, which is technically a drive." He points to the house. "I own that house too. And right down there," he says, pointing further down the drive. "I'm going to build a house with a wall of windows overlooking the ocean. Right there on the side of that cliff."

My mouth must be hanging open because he adds, "Nobody other than my lawyer knows I own this property, but I wanted you to know. I've imagined bringing you here many times, an escape from the rest of the world. The boys can hike the cliffs with me and explore the beach. I don't know, just seems kind of idyllic."

Moving my fingers through his hair, I kiss the side of his lips, lingering a moment before I say, "It is idyllic."

With a mischievous look in his eyes, he asks, "So we can do it then?"

Wrapping my arms around his neck, I whisper, "C'mon, handsome. No time like the present." I slip back into the seat and he hops the door and falls into the backseat.

His hands go behind his head and he smirks. "I want you on top."

"God, you're so demanding."

"Say that again."

I laugh as I'm climbing into the backseat. "You're so demanding."

"No, the other part."

Tilting my head, it's my turn to smirk. "God?"

His smile widens and he nods so arrogantly and so fucking sexily. "You're so bad."

"I think you should punish me over and over again by sitting right about... are you wearing underwear?"

Adjusting on top of him, I sit, looking down. "Yeeeesss, of course."

"I don't approve of that at all."

I roll my eyes. "I think you'll survive. After all, it is me wearing them, not you."

"I want them off." He lifts up and I stand the best I can, allowing him room. He undoes his pants and slides his jeans down... he has no worries of underwear since he's not wearing any.

Lifting my flowy skirt, I reach under and slip off my panties...

Dex is fast with the condom, but slow with his kisses and caresses. At one point, he sits up with me on his lap, our bodies joined together. His gentle rocks and thrusts are not hurried, but slow and languid, building my inner desire, twisting my insides until I come, squeezing him in the process.

With his lips pressed to my neck, he opens his mouth and his teeth scrape lightly while he holds me tight. A couple more thrusts and his body tenses as moans fill the open air around us—his and mine together.

When normally our bodies are allowed to go slack, relaxing in the aftermath of the euphoria, Dex holds me closer and kisses me with the passion most give before sex. I relish it, taking his passion and absorbing his heat. The moment is intense like he is and though our declarations have been spoken aloud, I feel his love filling my soul.

I pull back, wanting to see his eyes. When he opens them, he looks at me just as curiously as I look at him. "What?" he asks.

"You love me," I respond.

"Yes, I do, but you know that."

"No. I've heard you say it, but..." I know I must sound insane right now, but I say it anyway. "It's different. I feel it."

"Good." He smiles—gentle and satisfied. "Love is not for the ears, but for the heart."

I shouldn't cry. I really shouldn't, but I feel his love. I feel amazingly lucky and happy. The tears come from a place of joy and I don't bother to hide them. He readjusts back down and I come with him, resting on his chest. "I'm sorry," I whisper.

His hand slides under the back of my shirt and rubs, the touch is warming and comforting. "Why are you sorry?"

"Because I heard you say it and I've seen it in your eyes, but I never allowed myself to feel it until now."

With my ear pressed to his chest, I hear his breathing and heart beating just as he whispers, "I love you, Rochelle."

"I love you too."

TR

We get back to LA just after the kids arrive home from school. When we walk in, my boys run to me. It was only one night away, but I missed them just as much. In a three person hug huddle, I rest on my knees so I can fully embrace my sweet boys. But then I feel a nudging. Out of the corner of my eye, I spy CJ's arm around Dex's leg, including him in our group hug. I wrap my arm around his leg too until my hand holds my youngest as well. Dex takes all of us in when he spans his arms around our small family. And there we stay for a minute or two.

When we stand up, I give my boys more kisses, then meet Beth's eyes. She has a wide grin on her face and I realize she's a witness to the start of something new, the start of something that feels like it could become a constant, something permanent. "Welcome home," she says. "Did you have a nice time?"

"I did. Thank you for coming on such short notice."

Her eyes glance to Dex before coming back to me. "No problem. I love spending extra time with the boys. They were great. Right, guys?"

Neil laughs, obviously not telling the whole truth. "Yep, we were super good for Beth."

CJ's face is serious when he says, "I only got sent to time-out two times, Mama. Only two."

Trying to stifle my own laugh, I say, "Well done, buddy. Maybe next time, you won't go at all."

"I try harder."

"That's my boy."

Neil asks Dex, "I've been working on some new beats. Can I show you?"

Dex seems surprised. "Yeah, absolutely."

Neil takes his hand and drags him through the living room and down the hall to his room. CJ announces that he's hungry and disappears into the kitchen looking for a snack. Beth remains, smiling at me. That smile that says she knows that I not only had sex but that I'm obviously head over heels for Dex. I don't even have a chance to say anything before she says, "Wow, that must have been some night."

Sitting down on the couch, I play dumb. "What?" I shrug. "He needed a friend to talk to. I'm glad I could be there for him."

"You mean in the friends with benefit kind of way?"

"Not everything has to end in sex, you know."

She crosses her arms and looks at me incredulously. "Really? You're gonna pretend like nothing happened between you two?"

"Who says I'm pretending anything?"

Pointing at me, her finger swirls in the air. "Then explain that hickey that's forming on the right side of your neck?"

"Uh!" I gasp, jumping up to see in the mirror.

"You totally just gave yourself away. There's no hickey."

"You play dirty, Beth."

"Eh, it's a gift really." She walks to the kitchen door and says, "But I want you to stop trying to hide the obvious and accept whatever you've got going on with Dex. It's making you all sunshiny and shit and you look good happy."

I roll my eyes, but smile after. "Sunshiny and shit? Nice."

"I'm just telling you the truth."

"I'm really liking all the truths I've been getting lately."

With a loud laugh, she goes into the kitchen leaving me there with my own thoughts on the matter. A hand touches my shoulder making me jump a few moments later. Beth says, "I'm gonna go." She takes her purse and backpack from the floor near my feet and adds, "Call me if you need me."

"Thank you for being here. I know the boys love spending time with you." I stand and walk her to the door. "So tomorrow after school?"

"I'll be here," she replies walking down the steps and to the gate.

I close the door and lean my back on it, wondering how long Dex and I can really hide our relationship from the outside world when apparently everything about me is oozing it. But just thinking about the word 'oozing' makes the smile disappear and makes me want to take a shower.

CJ walks out with a PB & J and we join Neil and Dex in his room. Sitting on the floor, CJ makes himself at home on my lap and I wrap my arms around him, holding him close. Neil and Dex have an interesting dynamic. There's a mutual respect for each other that is heard through the way they talk to each other and their patience. Maybe I'm witnessing the beginning of a friendship, the start of a bond that can last. I hope so.

Dex shows Neil one more beat that he's been working on then says, "I'll send you a demo of it. I want you to practice it until you've nailed it. Then you're gonna play it for me on my drums. Okay?"

Neil excitedly agrees.

CJ gets up when he's done eating and says, "I want to learn too."

Dex, who's on his knees bends down until he's eye-level with him and smiles. "You still have the sticks I gave you?"

"Yep."

"Then how about I get you a drum pad too? Would you like that, CJ?"

CJ turns to me and says, "I gonna be like Dex and Neil, Mama."

I nod, but in that moment, the walls waver around me. Using the wall to help steady myself, I feel my way up and hurry out. I tug the back door open abruptly and run outside. My lungs feel lighter the second I inhale the fresh air. Closing my eyes, I raise my chin to the sky and breathe slowly.

"I know how hard it is to ask for help," Dex says, his voice quieter than normal, controlled. Turning to look over my shoulder, I see him standing in the doorway. He continues, "I think you need to talk to someone, Rochelle. Someone who can help with these attacks."

"I just wanted fresh air. That's all." I shrug, but I can tell he doesn't believe me.

"You're in denial."

Turning my whole body around now, I feel my defenses growing. "About what?" I ask, crossing my arms.

"That back there with your sons, with Cory's sons." He steps closer and his voice gets even quieter. I assume so the boys don't hear. "I'm not gonna replace him."

"They want to be drummers."

"They aren't him."

I raise my voice though I don't mean to yell. "They'd be playing guitar if he was here."

Despite my emotions, his voice is soothing. "They still can because you're here to teach them."

A lump forms in my throat making it hard to swallow.

I'm face to face with him now, his hands holding my arms gently as they slide down until my hands are taken by his. He says, "Every time I see the excitement for music in Neil's eyes, I see Cory again. When I look at CJ's face, I see Cory. And they both have this kindness about them that they get from you. You both made them who they are, shaped them in features and personality. I won't let them forget who their father was, but if I can help them, I want to, if you'll let me."

Looking down between us, I sniffle. When I look into his caring eyes, I say, "You're a good man, Dex Caggiano. Not many men would want to take on two crazy kids and their even crazier mom."

"You're not crazy, Rochelle, but I do think you've never allowed yourself to grieve the way you should. Let your friends and family be here for *you* now."

I hug him and when his arms wrap around me, I close my eyes and take in his scent. Just like always with him, I feel my body calming.

"Hello." We move apart quickly when we hear Janice.

Pushing the hair out of my face, I say, "Hi, how are you?" I'm too rushed, feeling guilty. "I wasn't expecting you."

"Hi Dex," she says, her smile not quite tight, but not welcoming either. She holds out a casserole dish. "I brought homemade spinach lasagna. I made an extra for you and the boys."

Walking over, I take it from her. "Thank you. We'll have this tonight."

She follows me into the kitchen and says, "I hope I wasn't interrupting anything."

I see Dex over her shoulder. "Um, it's fine. Are you staying to eat with us?"

"No, just stopping by. Where are Neil and CJ?"

"In Neil's room practicing a beat Dex just showed him."

She comes to me and says, "Are you alright? You look a little pale."

"I'm dating Dex." *Oops*. There goes our secret.

She looks stunned by my confessional outburst and like a faucet, I can't seem to stop the words from coming. "I don't care if you think it's a bad idea or you think he's bad for me and the boys. He's not. He's a good man and despite all that he's gone through, even though a lot of it he caused, he's in a good place and he loves us. He loves me, Janice. And you know what? I love him. I may have to hide this from the public, the paparazzi, and the band for a while, but I'm willing to do that. For him, I'm willing to keep this private until everyone else can learn to deal with it. But here, in my house, I will not. If you plan to be around us you will have to accept my relationship with him."

I peek over at Dex. His smile is not cocky or showy, but shows how proud he is of me. I step around her and go to him, hugging him tight.

When I look back at Janice, she doesn't seem upset or even disappointed. A small smile graces her features and with a slight nod, she says, "Okay."

"Just like that?"

"No. I've given it tremendous thought over the last few months. I've also Googled Dex a few times." There's a sparkle in her eyes when she looks up at him. "Seems maybe he has changed and considering the scum that's out there, I'm going to trust my gut and say okay."

As he rubs my back, Dex speaks before I do. "Thank you, Janice. I appreciate that."

"Just don't go breaking my trust or Rochelle's heart. I can be a bitch when I need to be."

"Janice," I say on the verge of a gasp. "You never swear."

"Well, I'm loosening up in my old age."

"You're not that old," I add.

"Well, it's time I lived a little."

I go to hug her and I can feel the sincerity of her words in her arms. "Thank you."

"You're welcome. Nothing would make me happier than seeing you and the boys living a happy life."

"Thank you."

She turns and says to Dex, "Take care of my family and yourself." Walking past him she stops. "I'm gonna go kiss my grandkids. Dex, you might like the lasagna. You should stay. I'll see myself out."

He sits down at the table and replies, "I think I will stay if it's alright with you, Rochelle."

"I wouldn't have it any other way."

# 29

We decided our relationship was best kept a secret—our secret for now, an intimacy that bonded us even more. Our bubble felt protected from outside opinions and judgment. But maybe it was the darkness that allowed us to believe in the illusion. The reality is, we knew we couldn't hide for long, but neither of us wanted to talk about it either.

So we continued over the course of a month, sneaking around in dives to grab a late night drink or sticking to the security of each other's house.

"How's your mother doing?" I ask, lying in bed with him. Glancing at the clock it's 5:30 in the morning.

When he turns to me, his brow is furrowed. "Really? We're talking about my mother right now? What happened to lying here recovering after sex?"

"Recovering? Do you really want to recover from sex with me?"

Rolling over, he rests on top of me. "You wear me out, woman!"

"With all of my sex demands?" I tease.

"Yes," he says, a short chuckle following. "You're a very demanding lover."

"Lover sounds so naughty and sexual."

He gets off of me, sits up, and turns on the lamp. "Aren't all lovers sexual? Like doesn't the word itself say sexual?"

I blush, my eyelids growing heavy. "I'm tired. I can't think straight at this hour."

He starts to stand, but I take his hand and hold him. "Don't leave."

Settling back down next to me, he tucks his arm under my neck and holds me to him. "The boys will be up soon."

Whispering, I say, "I know."

He reaches for the lamp to turn it off and I smile knowing today is the day, we become real, real to the world, facing the world together. When he stops, I look over at him and see him holding the small framed photo of me and Cory. My heart clenches. I quickly reach for him, not wanting to lose everything we worked so hard for. But he stands suddenly and the frame is abandoned in the spot he found it. The playfulness is gone as he walks to the bench at the end of the bed where he left his clothes. He starts getting dressed, so I ask, "You're going?"

"I should. I have some stuff to take care of."

When he sits on the edge of the bed to put his shoes on, I sense the change in his mood. I sit up and rub his arm. "Hey, what's going on?"

"Nothing," he replies too quick and a little snappy. Lying back, I watch him silently. His gaze is focused down and I watch the man I fell in love with disappear before my eyes. He looks back when the silence reaches him, our gazes connecting. He rubs my leg over the blanket. "I'm sorry."

Needing him to fill me in on what he's thinking, I ask, "For what?" My voice is meek and quieter than intended, but I can't handle my heart being broken again. And by the thickened tension, I'm feeling like that's close to happening.

His eyes leave mine before his hand does. "There's so much shit, so much to think about."

"What about the last month?"

He turns, slow and hesitant, his face one of regret. When he looks at me, I know what's coming before he even says it. I close my eyes to hide the tears I know will appear. "Rochelle," he starts, then pauses with a heavy sigh before continuing. "I need to sort through everything. I have legal appointments tomorrow..." He glances at his watch. "...later today technically. I'm seeing my mother for dinner. It's a miracle she's still here. And I still have to talk to Gage." When he stands, he keeps his back to me. He walks to the door and stops with his hand on the knob. Keeping his eyes focused on anything but me, he says, "I'll call you later." Then he leaves.

Our 'Until then...' isn't said. That's the moment I know we're over.

I roll to my side and pull the covers over my head. I thought I would cry, but the conflicting emotions I have surfacing are too confusing. Disappointment trumps anger, love, and the sadness I'm feeling. Dex is running. He's running from me, from everything despite how he's convinced himself he's not.

He's not used to being accountable to anyone, although I know he wishes he could be to me and the boys. He's just not there yet. Maybe the pressures of the new will and his mother's illness has stolen something from him that keeps him from being here for me. Maybe we were only as permanent as his surroundings are. Maybe our secret kept him only invested as much as he had to. What we thought was a way to protect something that was strong and growing has revealed the cracks instead. Like a side effect, the secrecy kept us fragile, something more delicate than we thought.

I look over at the frame that I know I should have put away long before now. Cory and I were only twenty-one and thought we had a lifetime to look forward to. I start to reach for the photo, thinking I can actually pack it away inside the drawer below. But I stop.

Dex leaving isn't because of a photo.

Dex will crumble with his family and unlike the last time, I can't save him. This would have happened if I had that photo out or not. I pull the blankets tighter around me and remember when I visited him the last time he was at rehab...

*One of the nurses told me I could find him out back near the cliffs, so I walk through the open doors that lead to a large patio and expansive view of the ocean. In any other setting, this would take my breath away. But I remember where I'm at, so I avert my eyes to the surroundings—other patients reading, chatting, and or staring at me. I keep walking down a small curved set of stairs and over some gravel before I reach the grass and see Dex sitting and another patient on a bench across the lawn.*

*The woman laughs and I hear Dex return with his own laughter. It's good to hear. It's been too long. I just wish it had been under different circumstances. When I approach, I suddenly hesitate, suddenly questioning if I'm interrupting. She sees me first, then nods to him to give him a heads up regarding my presence. When Dex turns, I see the lightness in his eyes, a happiness he shows me before his expression changes and a look of betrayal crosses his face.*

*"Hi," I say, hoping he doesn't hate me.*

*The woman stands, her hand rubbing across the top of his. "I'll see you inside."*

*He nods and she leaves. When we're alone, he rests forward, his elbows on his knees and scrubs his unshaven face a few times with his hands. Our eyes meet again and he asks, "What are you doing here?"*

*"Can I sit?" His hand swings out over the bench as an invitation. I sit down and look ahead at the ocean, seeing white caps in the distance. I feel his gaze on me, but when I turn, he looks away. His jaw is tense, so I ask, "Am I interrupting?"*

*"Jealousy isn't flattering on you, Rochelle."*

*I laugh, though I don't find his tone or words funny at all. "Jealousy? You think I'm jealous. Of what? Your friend there?"*

*"Why are you here?"*

*"I wanted to see you, to check on you."*

*He stands and walks ahead a few feet away. "I'm here," he says, turning around.*

*"How are you feeling?"*

*"How do you think I'm feeling? I want a hit of anything and I can't have it. But I stay because I want to stay in the band and if doing two weeks time in here will keep me doing the only thing I care about, then I'll stay."*

*"Why are you so angry with me? Because I brought you here?"*

*His eyes meet mine and he replies, "This shit is expected from Tommy, from Johnny. Hell, everyone, but you. I needed you, Rochelle."*

*"You had me. You have me now. I've always been here for you when you needed me."*

*"You sided with them against me. I could have worked through this at home. I had time before the tour. Instead you stabbed me in the back."*

*"You had seizures, Dex, just like you did in Paris. How many*

*times are you willing to put your life on the line for a 'hit of anything'?"*

*"Fuck this. I don't need your lecture. You know shit about what I've been going through." He starts to walk away.*

*I stand and shout, "You're right! I know shit because I've been dealing with my own shit, like Cory dying and raising kids—"*

*"Don't drag him into this."*

*"Drag? I didn't drag him into this. Some days I can't even breathe to save myself much less you. I've been dragged into something that's bigger than you needing to get high to escape a life of privilege."*

*I see the change in him before the hate is heard in his words. "Yes, Rochelle, my life of privilege has solved all my problems," he says sarcastically. "Doesn't money buy you happiness?" I can tell he wants to leave, but holds himself in place. "What we had... what we did, one day you'll see, it was everything to me."*

*"I don't know what to believe anymore when it comes to you. You're not the man I expected to see today."*

*He huffs and kicks the grass beneath his feet. When he looks back up, he says, "You're seeing the real me for once. Oh, and yes, you were interrupting, so excuse me I have an appointment in her room in five." Dex walks back not in any hurry, but walking away from me holding his head down and his shoulders tight.*

The car door slams behind me, causing me to jump. Neil and CJ run ahead as if they're at the park. They know exactly where to go since we've been here so many times before.

Thirty minutes later, Holli jogs to keep up, taking the boys by the hands and walking back to the car. Johnny stays silent, but I feel his heavy heart, like mine, weighing down the air around us. I move forward stepping directly on top of the grass. My heels dig in and I let them sink a bit into the ground. It doesn't matter. Not really. It gets mowed and tidied, cleaned up regularly. My shoes don't affect the dead.

But for some reason I step out of them. Maybe it's the grass I need to feel. The cool blades against my skin. Or maybe it puts me just a little closer to what used to be Cory. I don't know. I've lost my ability to reason in these types of situations. Nothing makes sense, so I don't bother trying.

I sit down and my skirt goes out around me. Cory never wanted to be buried. I did it for Janice, giving her a 'place' to visit. I get it now. I realize how important this is not just for me, but for my kids. And for the fans. The anniversary of his death always brings more flowers and memorabilia, tokens of appreciation of what he gave the world surrounds the tombstone. They sneak in to pay homage and respect to the man that has become a legend before his time. But maybe that's how legends are made.

The cemetery is private and has security, but they get in somehow without notice and leave their gifts to be found by... I'm not sure who collects all the stuff actually. One day I should ask, wondering what happens to everything they find here.

I slide guitar picks, photos, flowers, and other odds and ends to the side, and lay my head on the base of the tombstone. I close my eyes and in the serenity I hear his voice, his laugh, the last melody I ever heard him play for me.

"They're memories, Rochelle," Johnny says, his voice sounding as heavy as his heart. "You'll always have them, but live in the present."

"I want to be strong, but I'm struggling."

"We all struggle. That's life. But what's the fun in easy?"

"I wouldn't know."

"Yeah, neither would I." He sits down.

Lifting up, I sit up next to him as he rests his back against the tombstone. Flicking blades of grass, he says, "I miss him every day. Some days, I wake up and I've forgotten he's died. I pick up my phone to call him..."

I relax back too and lean my head on his shoulder. "I used to cry every night, but never in the daylight."

"That sounds like a song that needs to be written."

"Maybe we're all just lyrics waiting to happen."

He looks over at me and one side of his mouth goes up. "Maybe."

"I don't want to be sad anymore." I close my eyes.

"I don't want you to be sad anymore either." He sighs. "Tell me. Who are you when no one is watching?"

His question makes my heart ache for him. I straighten up again, wanting him to tell me so much more, to share with me the thoughts he's not. "What do you mean?"

"If you could be anyone without judgment who would you be?"

Reaching my hand down I grab a handful of grass. "I don't want to be someone else. I just want to be happy again."

"When was the last time that happened?"

"My kids make me happy. It might sound strange but I'm still amazed I have them. I'm so fortunate."

"Your kids are amazing, like their parents." In another bout of quiet between us, there's no reprieve from the obvious elephant. "Have you talked to Dex?"

"No."

"Do you want to?"

"Our situation is in his hands, not mine. I tried to be there and he pushed me out."

"What would you say if you had the chance?" he asks.

"I'm not sure. Why do you ask?"

The wind picks up, my hair covering my eyes.

"Look over there," Johnny says.

I tuck my hair back and follow in the direction where Johnny points to the car.

Dex is hugging the boys and then one quick one to Holli before Tommy brings him in for a squeeze. Dex looks over at us and down, says something, then starts coming our way.

Johnny gets up. "I think I'll go help Holliday with Neil and CJ."

"You don't have to go."

"Yeah, but something tells me Dex is here to see you, so I should."

I silently agree, thinking he's probably right. Watching as he walks away, they greet each other and talk. They both look at me, then away again. Something else is said and Dex nods. One more handshake and a hug, then Dex heads my way.

He stops a few feet away from me and squats. "Hi."

"Hi."

After a quick glance over his shoulder, he looks at me again and says, "Is I'm sorry even going to work anymore?"

I keep my head down, but can't resist peeking up at him. "I don't know. Try it."

"I'm sorry, Rochelle. I'm so damn sorry."

"Why? Why are you sorry?"

"Because I pushed the good in my life away again."

"It's a bad pattern, Dex"

Sitting down, he stretches his legs out and taps my shoes with his. "Has it really been four years?"

I take in a deep breath and slowly exhale. "It has." Looking into his eyes to see if I still know the man before me, I ask, "Why are you here?"

"Because I miss him and I needed to make things right with him before I tried to make them right with you."

"Looks like you get two for one today."

"I'm sorry."

"I'm tired of apologies. I'm just tired, Dex. You know nothing goes as planned when it comes to emotions. We can't control our feelings. We can only try to control our reactions. So as much as I want to open my arms and kiss you again," I say, "I can't right now."

He pulls something from his shirt pocket. When he turns it over, he shows me. It's the photo from his bedroom and the one I packed in his duffle before shipping it to him. "You've seen the photo, but I should explain."

"Is now the time?"

"I took it from Cory's stuff years ago. I shouldn't have. I always felt bad for stealing it, for betraying our friendship like that, for being in love with his woman. I didn't care when it came down to it. I couldn't give it back. I even helped him search the hotel room for it."

"Dex—" His name comes with a warning. He's getting too close to territory I can't have him enter or I'll lose it entirely.

"I came here to return it to him. I was a shitty friend to him and he never gave up on me. You never gave up on me either, so I can at least return the damn picture."

"The picture doesn't matter. Your honesty does. He'd understand."

He laughs. "He'd understand that his friend and the drummer in his band is in love with the same woman as him?"

"No," I say with a laugh. "Maybe not, but none of that matters now. Just say your peace and don't worry about the rest."

"Maybe one day I'll forgive myself and you'll find a way to forgive me again, to see the man I was when we were together."

"Maybe," I say, not to be cruel, but to let him know I can see he's not ready yet. I stand up next to him, dusting off my skirt. When I'm done, I remain there without looking at him, my arm touching his. "It all starts with seeing the errors of your way. Stop punishing yourself over the petty stuff that doesn't matter. There's a lot of pain that comes with life. Focus on the good you've been given." With my fingers grazing over his shoulders, I walk back to the car.

"Rochelle," he calls.

I turn around and stop, wanting to hear what he says... and maybe steal one last glance at him before leaving. "Yeah?"

"Do you think you can forgive me?"

"Try me sometime."

With a gentle smile and a nod, he says, "Until then..."

"Until then..."

# 30

Standing there in front of the mail basket, I didn't know what to make of the invitation in my hand. I'd read it three times already, but decided I need to read it again hoping it would clarify things for me.

***Dear Ms. Floros,***
***You are cordially invited to the home of***
***Katherine Dexter Caggiano***
***High Tea***
***Friday at 3:30 p.m.***

Nope, it makes no more sense to why Dex's mother is inviting me over than it did the first three times I read it. I pull up the planner on my phone and clear it. If she's asking me over, I feel I should go despite the absence of her son in my life.

*I start to wonder if Dex will be there or does he even know I've been invited?*

I miss him so much.

TR

Lara stops by with lunch.

"I missed you. Stop traveling so much," I joke. "I kid, kind of. Okay, I mean it. I've missed you."

"I've missed you too. I brought us sushi."

"Excellent. I'm starved. Let's eat outside." We walk to the back patio and sit down at the table I've set. White wine is poured and we dig into the food and fall back into all the latest gossip. "How was New York?"

"It's New York. It never changes, yet, it's always changing. That makes no sense, but I'm just not a New Yorker. I need sunshine and the ocean to inspire me and my designs."

"I'm glad you're back. I've needed someone to take my mind off things."

"So Dex hasn't called?"

"No." I drag my salmon roll through the wasabi, then say, "I've seen so much tragedy come to those who got too much in life too soon. But slowly we're all working through it, sometimes together, sometimes apart. Dex seems to be caught in a mixture of emotions. He's happy when he's with me. I can tell he's at peace. But something inside of him wants to destroy us, to destroy that peace as if he's undeserving of it. He's gonna have to figure this out or we'll never be together."

"So you're willing to wait and see?"

"I am for him, but he doesn't know that yet."

"You're a wonderful person. Better than most." Lara holds her glass up and we toast. Though I'm not sure what we're toasting to.

TR

I'm prompt, as everyone should be when invited to afternoon tea. I've never had high tea, but I understand there are rules and etiquette that accompany it. Being on time is probably one of them.

The door is opened by Charles. I remember him from the first time we stopped by. "Right this way," he directs.

I'm quickly intercepted by Judith and her wide smile. "It's so good to see you again, Ms. Floros."

"You too, Judith. Please call me Rochelle."

She nods, and says, "Right this way, Rochelle. Mrs. Caggiano is waiting for you."

With my hand, I stop her when I touch her forearm. "Should I be worried?"

Her smile eases into reassurance. Her hand covers mine, and she replies, "No, Mrs. Caggiano likes you. I've heard only good things from your visit to Diablo. But I will warn you that she's weak, weaker than she lets on."

"Thank you."

I walk into the conservatory. Dex's mother is seated in the far corner in a plush, floral fabric covered chair as she stares through the glass outside.

"Ms. Floros," Charles announces.

Mrs. Caggiano turns and smiles when her eyes land on me. "Come in," she says, starting to stand.

I rush over. "No, don't get up for me." Standing before her, she sits back down and reaches a hand out. I take it, and say,

"Thank you for having me here for tea today."

"I'm glad you could join me. Please. Sit," she says, signaling to a chair next to hers that also faces out toward the gardens.

"I must admit, the invitation was unexpected."

"Yes, but I'm glad you accepted. We didn't have enough time to chat in Diablo."

"Was there something in particular you wanted to chat about?" I ask.

"My youngest son."

"I should tell you that I care about Dex, but we currently aren't seeing each other."

She leans back in her chair and an understanding grin appears. "I know. I don't mean to pry. I've been hands off with him for many years, too many. I've failed him in so many ways. I've tried to reconcile that with him, but some scars are too deep to heal overnight." The tea and tray of finger foods arrive on a large silver tray, interrupting her. She waits until everything is set up on the table before us, then continues when we're alone again. "Antonio and I may not be able to heal all of our old wounds, but I hope he can carry on with less pain weighing on his heart."

"He's a good man."

"You love him though he's left you... in a way."

"In a way?" I question, curious to what exactly she knows about our situation.

"He loves you. He's being a silly man and hoping to spare you his burdens to bear. What he doesn't understand is that women are built to share our partners' troubles. Wouldn't you say?" She leans forward and pours the tea. "Please eat something."

"I would help him if I knew how, Mrs. Caggiano." I drink my tea straight and take a bite of a small chicken salad sandwich.

His mother says, "I've jumped ahead of myself and forgotten my manners. Please call me Katherine."

Setting the sandwich down, I dab the side of my mouth with the white cloth napkin. "Thank you."

After sipping her tea, she says, "I'll be gone soon. My expiration date, according to the doctors, has come and gone. Yet, I'm not really feeling inspired. I worry. Antonio has been left with a huge responsibility not only with my father's estate, but his company as well since I won't be around. I did the best I could to get things in order. I left an internal board to run things for years. I never had a knack for those types of dealings."

I touch her wrist that is resting on the arm of the chair. "I'm sorry."

"Thank you. Cancer is not how I expected to go… I wonder about my sons and if they'll make up. They disagree about," she says, with a light laugh, looking at the floral pattern of the chair, her finger tracing a violet peony. "Pretty much everything. Gage is troubled a lot like my father was. Anto… Dex is like his father. Troubled in other ways." She looks up. "I need to ask you a favor, Rochelle."

I want to readily agree, but my heart begins to race and without warrant I start to hold my breath in anticipation of what's coming next.

She smiles. "Take care of my son when he finds his way back to you."

A slow exhale is followed by me asking, "How do you know he will?"

"You're the love of his life. He didn't have to tell me that, though he did. I could tell the first time I ever saw you with him. Diablo confirmed my suspicions."

"What if he never comes back?"

"Then he'll miss out on his own love story."

I smile. "In Diablo, you told us to follow our hearts."

"Follow your heart. It will lead you home."

TR

On the drive home, I ponder her words and my thoughts drift to Dex and the mess he must feel his life is. It makes me want to call him, but I don't. Even Tommy told me to give him time.

So I do. I also wonder about my future and what role am I willing to let Dex play in my life and in the boys' lives. As much as I love starting this new chapter with Dex, hoping he follow his heart back to me, the reality is, I need to close other chapters, fully opening my heart to him.

The kids go through our nightly routine until I crawl into bed. My entries haven't been as regular recently, so I pull my journal out of my nightstand and write:

***Dear Cory,***

***I've been working on the tour that starts in five months and closed two deals for Kaz and Derrick. Johnny seems content with the music—writing and recording in his home studio to care about marketing. Tommy's been working with the tour designers and stadiums. We all seem to be caught up in our own thing, but Dex is lost to us all.***

***I'm worried.***

***He sends the boys videos, so they can keep learning. They miss him, but understand that***

***sometimes grownups are busy. They seem satisfied for now with the videos and packages he's sent them though they ask about him a lot.***

***I shouldn't bore you with this stuff. I'm sure you see right through me. You always could. So I'm just going to get this off my chest now.***

***I still hold onto the notion that time will heal all wounds. My heart wants to believe what my head logically knows is an impossibility. You will never be replaced in my heart. But maybe, just maybe, there's a little room inside for someone else too.***

***I know you wouldn't want me to spend my life alone. Nor I you, but it's easier said than done, like most things. I've been closed off for so many years that I've come to realize that I will be alone forever if I continue to live like this. You, my love, will always be a part of me. But now I'm asking you to loosen the reigns around my heart and let me live in love again.***

My tears drop down onto the paper, smearing the ink a bit, but I continue writing.

***Please don't hate me, Cory.***

***I don't want to lie to you or hide my feelings any longer. Hoping you find contentment in me finding happiness again would be amazing and freeing in so many ways. I'm not sure if that will ever happen, but like Holli always says, Dare to Dream.***

***So I'm not sure where this leaves us—you and me, Mr. Journal. But I think this might be my last entry. Before I go, I must say this one more time—I Love You, Cory.***

***Goodbye.***

***XO***

# 31

This is not how I planned for us to see each other. I didn't have any real plans, but this was never a thought until now. I see the gravesite up ahead and the gathering of people circled around. Despite my deep-seeded desire to run away, I walk forward. I go because Dex needs me.

I don't quite make it to the grave when I spot him off on the other side of a tree sitting down. His sunglasses are on and I'm thinking they might be hiding more than his eyes. He sees me walking across the groomed lawn when I veer toward him, breaking away from the crowd. He doesn't say anything when I reach him, so I sit down despite that I'm wearing a dress. I decide not to say anything for the moment, not sure that anything I say is wanted. But I do lean my head on his shoulder, selfishly wanting to be close. Dex doesn't move or say anything until Gage spots us, sending a glare our way. "I'm now the head of an empire I never wanted."

I lift my head and look at him, seeing behind the dark lenses to the eyes that have cried over the death of his mother and maybe more today. "You only have to be what you want to be."

He looks my way. "How'd you hear?"

"Tommy. Why didn't *you* call me?"

Turning back to watch the last of the cars unload and the mourners joining the funeral, he says, "When we left Diablo, I thought we finally had our chance. I didn't count on the impact my mom's illness and the new will, Gage, all of it would put on me."

"I was there for you."

"I know you were." The left side of his mouth goes up quickly before disappearing again. "But I was being buried alive with responsibilities I never asked for. The company is generations old and I own it. All. What do I know about manufacturing?"

"You have a strong team of lawyers and other managers to help you figure this out. It doesn't have to be the same week your mom passed away."

I catch his eyes on me again and he doesn't turn away this time. "I missed you. Do you know that?"

I exhale, my heart starting to beat faster, then say, "I missed you so much."

"You know, Rochelle, we've been through a lot. You've been through more. I didn't want to put you through anything else."

"That's why you left?" I ask.

He nods. "One of the reasons."

"You can put on this big show for everyone else, but I know who you really are, Dex, and you're not gonna scare me that easily. I didn't stop caring about you because you stopped calling."

I see the corners of his mouth go up. "I didn't stop caring either." He wraps his arm around my shoulders and says, "You're pretty damn strong, sweetheart."

"I'm here to share the burden. Just let me in."

Dex stands and helps me to my feet. "C'mon. The sooner we do this the sooner we can leave."

Just as he turns to join the others, I stop him by taking hold of his arm. "Hey Dex?"

"Yeah?"

"Don't rush through the funeral. I understand the desire to get through this and to be anywhere but here, but this is important, not just for others, but for you. Stay present in the moment, for your mother."

I see the emotion he's held back start to show as he looks down, lifting his sunglasses to wipe at his eyes, then lets them fall back into place. "I don't want to sit in those chairs. That makes it real."

His denial is familiar. I remember thinking the same thing years ago, but I didn't want to upset Cory's family by not sitting next to them. "You don't have to. Stand where you want. I'll stand by you."

Shifting, he swallows hard. "I didn't do the same for you at Cory's."

"You didn't have to. I understood. All that mattered is that you were there."

"I didn't know you saw me," he says, reaching for my hand.

When our fingers entwine, I reply, "You were leaning against a tree. You wore a black shirt and sunglasses. You were holding something shiny. I remembered it catching my eye as it reflected in the sun."

He releases my hand and pulls out his wallet. Digging inside, he produces an oval coin. I recognize it before he says anything, my heart beginning to throb out of my chest. "Cory gave this to me in Paris. It's St. Christopher." My breaths shorten as he continues. "He said he's the patron saint of travelers."

"I know." I take it from him, holding it in the palm of my hand. A tear joins it. "I gave this to him the first time he left to tour without me. He didn't want to go alone." I look up at Dex. His sunglasses in his hand, his tear-filled eyes on me. "I told him he was never alone. He had you, Johnny, and Tommy. And you guys would always be there for him when I couldn't." I fold my fingers around it.

"He told me this coin would help me find my way home." His hand wraps around my fisted one. "It was the last thing he said to me before he left Paris."

The sob I was trying to hide from him breaks free. I sniffle, then ask, "Did you?"

"It led me to you, Rochelle." He puts his sunglasses over his eyes again and releases my hand. His voice shakes when he says, "I just wish it didn't come at the expense of him."

Adjusting my sunglasses down over my eyes, I say, "We didn't come at the expense of Cory. The universe doesn't work in such cruel ways. This is how it was always meant to be."

Taking my hand again, he asks, "Were we always meant to be?"

"We may have taken the scenic route to get here, but we're here now, baggage and a few cute kids along for the ride."

"Dex," Gage calls from behind us.

Dex turns to look. When he turns back, he says, "Guess we should go over there, but before we do, I want you to know that having you share the journey has made the road less traveled worth the risk."

"Dex!" Gage yells, ending the conversation.

Dex turns and with me by his side, we stand behind the chairs, two people mixed in with the large crowd and watch as his mother is put into her final resting place.

TR

I stand back in a corner of his mother's living room with Johnny and Holli, Tommy, Kaz, and Derrick. None of us are talking much. I'm not surprised. Funerals suck.

Holli nudges me. "Maybe you should go hang out with him."

"I don't want to add to his obligations today. Everyone wants a piece of him to help them find peace with his mother's death."

She touches my arm. "I understand, but you being there isn't a burden to him."

"Everyone knows about us, don't they?"

Nodding, she says with a reassuring smile, "And supports you. He's a good man. It just took a while to get to know the man underneath the façade. You're good for him."

"He's good for me."

Johnny takes Holly's hand and moves closer. "Holliday's right. I remember Dex being pretty cool back in the day. He just lost himself along the way. Fame does that to some people... to most. You reminded him of who he really is. I think he might have done the same for you, you know, reminding you of who you always were." He steps forward. "We're gonna go talk to him and take off unless you want us to stay, Rochelle."

"No," I reply, "it's fine. You can go. I might help him escape soon anyway."

Johnny and Holli leave after a hug and Derrick and Kaz follow closely behind, leaving me and Tommy there. When I lean against the wall next to Tommy, he says, "You know that time we went to Barstow?"

"How can I forget it?"

He rubs his chin in a thoughtful manner. "When Dex called me. He told me two things. One was the motel's name. The other thing... he said and I quote, "If I die, tell Rochelle I'm sorry."

I look at him in shock. "Sorry for what?"

"He didn't say, but something inside me thinks he really was close to death that day. Something made him want to apologize to you and I'm guessing he wanted to go with a clear conscience."

"I'm guessing it was the drugs," I remark dryly.

Tommy pushes off the wall, and says, "I'm gonna go. We should talk about the tour soon. Call me next week."

"I will," I say, nodding.

I watch as he goes over to Dex and Gage, shaking their hands. Dex's eyes meet mine across the crowded room before he looks back at Tommy. Once Tommy leaves, a few other mourners talk to them as I make my way over, weaving between small groups of people. I veer to the back door and nod toward it when Dex looks at me. He smiles though I can tell he feels guilty for the small act of happiness when he's supposed to be sad. I remember battling the same contrasting emotions.

Outside, he finds me smelling the roses. While I'm bent down, his hand slides over the curve of my hip. I turn to him and smile. "Frisky?"

"I couldn't resist."

"You've been resisting for a while now. What gives?"

"The company is in the capable hands of my cousin and Gage has reconciled with his wife."

"What about you?"

"I have a tour to prepare for, the album releases soon, and there's this girl I've been meaning to talk to you about. Is now a good time?"

My heart drops to the pit of my stomach. But I'm not surprised.

It's Dex—handsome, funny, so sexy, and famous. He has his pick of women and I guess over the last month or so, he decided not to pick me. I raise my chin a bit, hoping I'm come off as strong, something he said he always admired about me. "Sure," I say while looking away from his brown eyes that hold me captive every time I look into them. *Stay strong.*

His fingers grace my cheek. "Rochelle, look at me."

When I finally look up, daring to meet his intense gaze, he says, "I'm in love with you. I always have been. But, I'm no good for you right now."

"I don't understand. Why are you the judge and jury when it comes to me?"

"Because you have responsibilities that I can screw up. I've got to get my life together. But I'll make you a promise right here. I won't be with anyone else. I don't want to be. I only want you. I'm just hoping you can hang on a little longer and wait for me as well."

"How long, Dex? My heart can't take this back and forth."

"I want to give you answers. I do, but all I can say is that we'll know when it's right. I need to deal with my family first... Gage will always be my brother whether we share the same blood or not. He's the only family I have left."

"You've got me and the band, the boys, and Tommy. Dex, you have so much goodness. Don't lose it to the troubles of today."

"I have to get my mom's estate settled. I've had a lot of time to think. It's been good for me. I don't know the last time I really blocked out the noise of my life, but I liked it. I also thought a lot about us. About you. Nothing new there, but I just want you to know that I love you. I keep saying it hoping you'll believe me."

I touch him, my fingers around his hand. "I believe you. I just want to be with you. I shouldn't. Not with how you've left me in the past, but I love you too much to let this fade away as if it never happened."

"You're so damn beautiful." He laughs and looks around. "The old me would take you upstairs in the middle of this depressing party and fuck you."

He makes me smile with his confession and I ask, "And the new you?"

"The new me wants to take you upstairs and make love to you."

Laughing, I squeeze his hand. "You know, you don't have to change on my account. I like all your sides."

"You're the best reason for all the changes in my life. I don't do drugs anymore. I don't have seizures anymore. I wake up with a clear head though sometimes my heart is cloudy."

"Sounds like a song."

With a grin, he says, "It is. I want to play it for you soon."

"Dex?" Gage calls from the back door. He doesn't see us and Dex doesn't make a move to respond either.

He finally says, "I should get back. You were right."

"About what?"

"Being here. You once told me that you never had a chance to be weak because you were so busy being strong for everyone else." He signals over his shoulder toward the house. "That's what this is. It's about helping everyone else through the loss they're experiencing."

"What about you?"

He smirks. "I could ask you the same."

"I've mourned. It may have taken me a long time to do, but I've done it. I'm choosing to live my life now."

Leaning down, really close to my ear, he whispers, "You're incredibly sexy. Go home. I'm gonna kick everyone out shortly. I'll give you a call."

"I hope you do. Oh, and why are you sorry?"

"Sorry?"

"Back in Barstow. You told Tommy to tell me you were sorry. Sorry about what?"

"Dex?" his brother yells outside again.

Dex says, "That's my cue. We'll talk soon."

# 32

I watch the drapes blow in the breeze slipping in through the cracked open French doors. Rolling onto my side, I grab the other pillow, cuddling it to me. I know it won't satisfy, though I'm hoping it does, like it can somehow fill the void that Dex has left. I wish we could go back to those times where it was just the two of us, happy. I wish I could take away his pain and heal him. Thinking about the last four years and the roller coaster of our relationship, I smile. Ridiculous I know, but Dex makes me smile... still.

Maybe I can heal him, slowly. Maybe I'm what he needs. Pushing down my doubts, I pick up my phone wanting to get past all the hurt and I text him: ***You make me so mad sometimes.***

A minute later, my phone pings with a message from *Dex:* ***When you're mad, you have this fire that burns on the inside and sparkles in your eyes.***

*Awwww.* That's so sexy of him to say. I don't let him win

though. I need to get this out. My fingers begin flying over the letters as I type: ***When you push me away, it hurts my feelings***.

I stare at the phone for a minute before the next message pops up: ***I envy your ability to stay strong when everyone else is weak.***

*Me:* ***Your long hair used to annoy me.***

*Dex:* ***Good thing I cut it off then. You can do better than that, Lovely Rochelle.***

*Me:* ***You use sunglasses on stage like a shield to protect your heart.***

*Dex:* ***I never wear them around you.***

*Me:* ***Your arrogance is not as charming as you think.***

*Dex:* ***So you admit it is charming though…***

*Me:* ***I admit nothing.***

*Dex:* ***You're stubbornness is sexy.***

*Me:* ***You're always horny.***

*Dex:* ***Only for you.***

*Me:* ***I'm sorry for any pain I've caused you.***

*Dex:* ***Rochelle, you only bring me happiness.***

*Me:* ***I'm sorry for dropping you off at rehab like I did.***

*Dex:* ***It was worth it in the end. I'm sorry for hurting you when you visited. You were the only one who visited btw.***

*Me:* ***I visited two other times, but never got out of the car.***

*Dex:* ***I know. I saw you.***

*Me:* ***I missed you.***

I gulp and go for it, putting my heart on the line again for this sweet, vulnerable, mess of a man. I type: ***I miss you now.***

There's a pause and my heart starts to beat a little faster from waiting. When my phone dings again, it reads: ***I miss you between every sunrise.***

I take in his words like a word problem, then it dawns on me and I reply: ***You miss me every day?***

*Dex:* ***Every day, all night long.***

I stop, holding my breath as I read his message over and over again. I finally press the key I should have pushed long before now. When he answers, I say, "Come over."

"If I come over, this is it for us. There's no more late night or early morning goodbyes—"

"Only good mornings and goodnights."

"So we're on the same page?" he asks.

"We're on the same everything, Dex. Come over."

"I'm on my way."

The phone goes silent and I finally understand that giving into him doesn't mean giving up on other things. He makes my life more vibrant and brings a steady rhythm to my days. Dex makes me feel and crave, reach and strive for more. More that I didn't know was possible before.

He gave that to me. So when he shows up just after midnight, I let him not only into my house, but into my life. Open arms. Open heart. Wholeheartedly. "Come in."

With a soft smirk playing on his lips, he says, "I love you, Rochelle. And I want you to know that I've waited a lifetime for this day, for you. I would have waited another if I had to."

"This was all about my life too, right? Me not mourning how I should have?"

"Yes. You weren't ready before. I know you think you were, but you weren't."

"So, I had to lose it all again to see what I missed?"

"Did you mean what you texted me? Did you miss me?"

"So much." I step forward and lift up. Just before my lips press against his, I say, "I love you, Dex."

# Dex

She pulls me by the belt into the bedroom and shuts the door. After locking it and with a fucking sexy smile on her face, she asks, "Why are you wearing so many clothes?"

With a chuckle, I reply, "You stole my line. You seem to have a knack for stealing things of mine." She knows what I mean without me having to say it. I slide my hands under her old Nirvana t-shirt. "Sleeping with the competition I see."

"They were never competition," she says and takes the shirt off abruptly.

Her hair covers her, so I push it behind her shoulders and look her over. Her tits are perfection—pert and begging to be touched, fucked. Reaching up, I take them in hand and squeeze, watching as her eyes struggle to stay open. "Make love to me, Dex." Her voice is raspy, exposed, and completely sexy.

She unbuttons my shirt, then pulls it down over my shoulders and arms until it falls to the floor. Her lips are wet when they press against the skin of my chest as her hands undo my belt and pants. She moves around, her hands caressing my shoulders as she kisses my back. I feel her fingertips outlining the tattoo she's never seen before. I say, "The Phoenix rising."

She doesn't question, just responds, "I like it. It suits you."

Even more turned on by her approval, I help her along by

flipping off my shoes, spinning her around, and moving her toward the bed. Her legs hit the mattress and she falls back. My pants drop. I take off my socks as she removes her underwear. Both of us naked brings back all the good that we've always been together. Like a predator, I hunger for her, to taste her, to feel her all over again.

Her hands go from my neck up into my hair, her body leaning until I'm on my back and she sits atop of me. Moving until I'm positioned, she looks up at me.

"You're stunning," I say, her body taking me in and causing my eyes to close briefly.

Seated with me fully inside her, Rochelle whispers, "You once told me your soul is damaged. We're all damaged inside. It's how we carry on that changes the outcome."

Grabbing a hold of her hips, I want to move, the sensation of her tightness around me makes me want to fuck, but her words feel like a remedy to my burned heart. "Do you think it's too late for me to change?"

She begins to rock, resting her palms on my chest for leverage. "I think you have perfect timing. It's everything we've lived through that brought us here together."

Hesitant to ask, to ruin how damn fucking good this feels, I do it anyway because I need to know. "Do you have any regrets?"

Stopping, she leans down and kisses me, then whispers, "Only one."

"What is it?"

With a wicked sexy smile, she replies confidently, "Not being with you sooner."

Looking into her gorgeous brown eyes, I see all the possibilities of a life worth living. "You were the new start I always wanted. You're my second chance." I kiss her like I've never kissed, giving in and giving her everything I can as I flip her under me and make love to her, making up for wasting so much time.

My hips thrust causing her to moan, her chest pushing against me. “More,” she calls to me.

I move faster, not able to continue the steady pace, our making love morphing, scorching and carefree. Enjoying this too much, I take her body over and over again until she quietly calls out my name and I call out hers like a profanity slipping out.

Later, we’re lying in bed together and I have my arm wrapped around her, holding her to me. The silence that surrounds us isn’t tension filled or filled with questions. It’s light, airy and filled with a future we’re finally both sure we want, making me feel sentimental in my attachment to her. “I’m sorry for letting you walk out of my life the first night we were together.”

She lays there, still and quiet, then whispers, “I’m sorry for walking out.”

“Don’t be. Please know that it was never just about sex with you. You hurt my ego, but *you* were hurting more and I failed to notice. I’m sorry.”

“It wasn’t your job to save me, Dex,” she says, looking down. Dropping her forehead against my cheek, she wraps her arms around me and pulls me closer, making me smile. Sitting up suddenly, she looks at me with a big smile of her own on her face. “You always knew we’d be together, didn’t you?”

“We were written in the stars long before now. I love you.”

“I love you more,” she says.

“Not possible,” I tease, “you just don’t understand the depth of my love.”

“What I am going to do with you, Dex?”

“You’re gonna marry me.” I watch her face, not sure what to expect in reaction. But she just smiles.

"You're a romantic, Antonio Dexter Caggiano."

"Only when it comes to you."

"You know how to make a girl swoon." She looks up at me. "And maybe on the days it gets rough," she says, snuggling closer, "we can escape to Neverland again, even if just for a few hours."

"I don't need Neverland," I say. "Reality with you is better than any make believe world ever could be."

I rub her back, living in this moment, and she asks me, "You're here for good, right?"

Leaning down to kiss her, I say, "I'm here for good. Our destinies were always bound together."

She sits up and says, "I'm giving you my heart, Dex."

Sliding my hands up her arms and over her shoulders, I stop when I slip my fingers into her hair. Bringing her down until we're so close, I can almost taste her, I whisper, "You've had mine since the moment I laid eyes on you."

# Epilogue

***One year later...***

I open my eyes and exhale slowly. I can do this. It's just like at home. No different. I readjust on the stool just as Johnny takes to microphone. The spotlight hits him and the crowd starts screaming so loud that it's hard to hear him at first.

I feel Dex's hand on my lower back. "Play from the heart," he says, positioned on a stool next to mine with his guitar in his hands.

"What if I screw up?"

"You won't. Only us, sweetheart. Just like at home. Block out the noise."

"...most talented guitarists out there. She taught the great Cory Dean how to play and has written many of our best songs. It's time for her to show the world what she can do. Give it up for Rochelle Floros." I hear Johnny just as he looks back, his eyes locking with mine, a huge smile on his face as his hand swings out in our direction and the spotlight follows.

When the bright light hits us, I freeze, my mind going completely blank. I miss my cue altogether, but then I hear Dex, his soothing voice, full of enough confidence for both of us. "Only us. Play with me."

We were two people following our own melodies who discovered the music we create together is the sweetest song of all. My fingers start moving, knowing the notes without the mental reminder. I close my eyes and keep playing. I lean forward and the words come just like we practiced, just like they were supposed to.

Songs that had been written apart became a song together that we sit on stage singing for the world to hear today. Every note gets easier and easier and when I hear Dex join in, hitting his own cue, I open my eyes and smile, looking over at him. I'm given a smile in return as he sings into the shared mic.

We lean back, strumming to a song we wrote together. The violins sound out behind us as does a slow and steady drum beat, Kaz filling in for Dex. Johnny walks back to a microphone setup in the shadows across the stage just as his part kicks in. I continue singing and when the chorus starts, Dex leans in again, our cheeks almost touching and sings.

Three minutes of our love put out there for the world to hear. Just as the song ends, Dex moves from his chair and gives me a standing ovation. Exhilarated that I just played in front of eighteen thousand people, when I stand, I laugh, then take a bow. The stage goes dark, but the crowd is still cheering.

Dex says, "You nailed it." He kisses me, our guitars clanging between us. When we part, he adds, "It's time the world sees you for the star you are. It's your turn to shine."

He wraps his arm around my shoulders as we walk to exit the

stage. I wrap mine around his back. "Thank you for believing in me."

"Believing in you has always come easy, but you were there when I needed you most. I owe you my life more than a few times over." His guitar is taken by a roadie and he takes his sticks, shoving them into his back pocket.

"Two minutes. Get to your kit, Dex," Tommy yells from behind us.

I start to step off to the side, but Dex grabs my hand. "Hey," he says, gently moving my guitar to my back, the strap keeping it safe back there.

Surprised by how relaxed he is while everyone else is rushing around us. "You conquered your fears, Rochelle. You're still the strongest person I know."

"You are too, Dex. Don't ever believe otherwise." I touch his cheek. "You gotta go, your fans are waiting."

"I've got time."

Slowly, he moves forward as if he has all the time in the world. His hand slides into my hair and he lowers down to kiss me. I lift up, our lips meeting in the middle. His other hand caresses the side of my face. As soon as he moves it, I realize the spotlight is on us. I gasp as the realization that we are on display hits me. All of that is forgotten entirely when Dex drops to one knee in front of me. He reaches into his back pocket and pulls one of the sticks out, handing it to me. Wrapped around the middle of the wood, a diamond and platinum ring sparkles under the intense lights.

I gasp again, at a loss for any other rational response.

"Rochelle, I was everything you never wanted or expected. But you saw who I always wanted to be, you saw the potential when I thought I was a lost cause. You gave my soul the pulse I've spent my life looking for and in return, I'll give you a life filled with the beauty you deserve. You took a chance on me and trusted me with your heart. Now, I'm here before you asking you to take the biggest chance of all. Will you marry me?"

From behind me, I hear CJ when he says, "Marry Dex, Mama."

Tears fall when I spot my sweet boys behind me, Lara holding each of their hands off stage with tears of her own in her eyes. She nods and smiles. When I turn back, I reply, "I believe we were written in the stars long before now. We're a chance I'm willing to take, so the answer is yes, Dex. I want to spend the rest of my life with you."

I'm grabbed as he stands, his arms encompassing me, and our lips meet in a fit of passion. In that kiss, I don't hear the crowd, or the crew and the applause around us. The band waits patiently for us to have our moment together. But none of it matters. What matters most are the little arms that encircle our legs. When our lips part, I look at him, the man who stole my heart when I least expected to find love again. And I realize that sometimes we find love in the most unlikely of places... and sometimes it was there all along.

*The End*

# A Personal Note

Wow, what a crazy amazing journey. I'm so blessed and touched to have you all sharing it with me. Thank you from the bottom of my heart.

This book was an emotional book for me to write because of the journey my characters had to take to have their stories told the way I feel gave them justice. I fell in love with them like Rochelle describes her love—*Love finds most of us fast and unexpectedly, but when it came to me and these characters, it was slow and calculated as if it knew to hold on and wait.* I got lost in the magic. I hope you do as well.

Extra special thanks to my family. Their patience and support allows me to follow my dreams and I will be forever grateful to have such love in my life.

To the Dream Team who are not only amazing people to work with, but are incredible people and great friends: Cara, Danielle, Flavia, Heather, Irene, Lisa, Meire – You make this fun and exciting, challenging and so rewarding. Thank you for everything you do, not only for me, but for the characters and making their stories sparkle.

I'm so fortunate to be surrounded by amazing people who not only support me as an author, but as a friend. I want to thank a few for being there for me, making me laugh, and for being awesome: Amy, Jessie, Julie, Kerri, Kirsten, Margaret, Mary, Michelle L., Liv, R. K., Rachel, Ruth, Vilma, Yennifer.

Love you ❤

# About the Author

Always interested in the arts, S. L. Scott grew up painting, writing poetry and short stories, and wiling her days away lost in a good book and the movies.

With a degree in Journalism, she continued her love of the written word by reading American authors like Salinger and Fitzgerald. She was intrigued by their flawed characters living in picture perfect worlds, but could still debate that the worlds those characters lived in were actually the flawed ones. This dynamic of leaving the reader invested in the words, inspired Scott to start writing with emotion while interjecting an underlying passion into her own stories.

Living in the capital of Texas with her family, Scott loves traveling and avocados, beaches, and cooking with her kids. She's obsessed with epic romances and loves a good plot twist. She dreams of seeing one of her own books made into a movie one day as well as returning to Europe. Her favorite color is blue, but she likens it more toward the sky than the emotion. Her home is filled with the welcoming symbol of the pineapple and finds surfing a challenge though she likes to think she's a pro.

Scott welcomes your notes to sl@slscottauthor.com

87098118R00214

Made in the USA
Columbia, SC
20 January 2018